7/00

COLD COMPANY

BOOKS BY SUE HENRY

Murder on the Iditarod Trail

Termination Dust

Sleeping Lady

Death Takes Passage

Deadfall

Murder on the Yukon Quest

Beneath the Ashes

Dead North

Cold Company

COLD COMPANY

AN ALASKA MYSTERY

SUE HENRY

wm
William Morrow
An Imprint of HarperCollins*Publishers*

HarperCollins books may be purchased for educational, business, or sales promotional use. For information please write: Special Markets Department, HarperCollins Publishers Inc., 10 East 53rd Street, New York, NY 10022.

FIRST EDITION

Designed by Kate Nichols

Map illustration by Eric Henry, Art Forge Unlimited

Printed on acid-free paper

Library of Congress Cataloging-in-Publication Data
Henry, Sue, 1940–
    Cold company : an Alaska mystery / Sue Henry—1st ed.
      p. cm.
    ISBN 0-380-97882-2 (hc.)
    1. Arnold, Jessie (Fictitious character)—Fiction. 2. Women dog owners—Fiction 3. Serial murders—Fiction. 4. Women mushers—Fiction. 5. Alaska—Fiction. I. Title.
PS3558.E534 C66 2002
813'.54—dc21   2001044860

02   03   04   05   06   JTC/QW   10   9   8   7   6   5   4   3   2   1

In memory of my mother,

Lois Hutchison Hall,

whose most enduring gift to me has been

the love of words, books, and mysteries

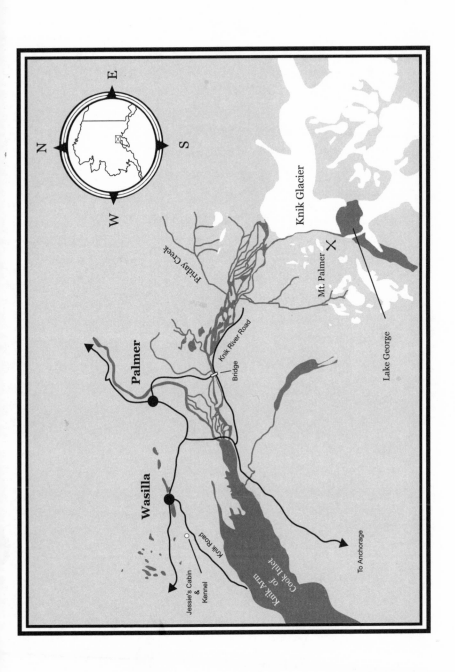

COLD COMPANY

Chapter 1

Spring was making itself heard in the Chugach Mountains south of the Matanuska Valley in Alaska. Among the bright new leaves of birch and the dark branches of spruce that shared the flats below the Knik Glacier, the songs of resident and migrating birds resounded. Swallows, thrushes, siskins, and warblers flitted through the trees, and joyful chirps of celebration filled the newly warm air of the season. Kingfishers and crows punctuated the chorus in raucous lower tones. Infrequently, from its perch on a tall spruce, a raven dropped an unusual bell-like tone or injected a grumpy complaint into the chorus, resentful of the invaders that now intruded on a territory it had claimed all winter.

Adding to the cacophony, melt from snow that had slowly receded to the rocky slopes of the high peaks above the tree line on both sides of the valley provided sustained background music in dozens of streams and waterfalls. Runoff poured down steep hillsides, tumbling pebbles with gleeful burbles and cleaning out last year's hoard of fallen leaves in its rush to join other rivulets in carving larger, deeper furrows into lower ground. Cutting through the gravel and sand of long-departed ice fields, ribbons of water twisted their way into the upper reaches of the Knik River, raising its flow to cover bars and banks the cold months had left dry and bare.

High above the river flats, beyond the steep flank of Mount Palmer, the Knik Glacier rose at five thousand feet in a giant ever-retreating river of ice that scoured a path, grinding away at the mountains through which it ran, moving inexorably if imperceptibly, sculpting out a channel between the ridges. Each winter's cold slowed its motion, and snow added to its bulk. Still it moved forward into the river valley at an angle that brought its foot into solid contact with the slope of Mount Palmer, forming a dam of ice that closed off part of its own melt and that of several smaller glaciers that surrounded Lake George immediately to the west.

In the spring, when the snow and ice began to melt again, this dam contained the resulting water, which backed up and gradually filled the lake until it extended far beyond its winter boundaries. As summer set in and the weather grew warmer, the glacial dam would become unstable and periodically calve away in great towers of dense ice hundreds of feet tall, which would fall crashing into the lake with a roar that reverberated between the peaks.

Where glacier and mountain met to form the dam, water was already gradually finding its way into a narrow crack between

the two. Just a few drops followed each other through the opening first, melting ice as they ran, widening the passage until their
drip became a trickle. Soon it would be a stream. Then, finally,
with a huge grinding rumble, the weight of thousands of gallons
of water would become too much for the weakening dam and
break it apart. Carrying chunks of the ice that had contained it,
floodwater would pour into the valley below with a force that
had been known to tear out the bridges and roads of early settlers. In March of 1964, the strongest earthquake ever recorded
in North America severely shook South Central Alaska and al-
tered the Knik River Valley terrain enough to moderate the
yearly flood and lessen its force. The water still broke through
with a roar that shook the ground and filled the river from bank
to bank with rolling turbulence, but the destruction it had visited
upon the works of man was reduced.

Even before this flood, however, the river rose dramatically
with the spring melt and spread powerful icy waters over shallows and sandbars that had lain untouched and freeze-dried
through the silent winter. Released from its ice-locked prison,
the water scrabbled and clutched at stone-strewn flats with icy
fingers, relearning old channels and inscribing new ones. Seiz-
ing fallen branches and logs to convey downstream, it carried
some into tangles among the roots of trees that now waded in
the shallows, hammered at bridge pilings with others, and finally
deposited its vast collection of floating debris miles away in the
salty waters of Cook Inlet.

The restless river explored the gravel of new paths with
avaricious fingers, learning what was possible to steal and what
lay too heavily or was too embedded for its grasping waters to

pilfer. Large boulders might groan and shudder, but most lay patiently, waiting for the river to give up and fall back below their level of dignified solidity.

Other things, however, it was possible for greedy waters to loosen and, in time, sweep away. The desiccated skin and bones of a fox fell with the collapse of an undercut bank and drifted off in a swirl of sticks and leaves. Little by little, sand was scoured from around three half-buried beer cans, tossed aside by a pair of hunters the preceding October, and one by one they bobbed away, slowly filling with water until they rolled beneath the surface to bounce unseen along the riverbed. A dead tree that had hung for several seasons over the water's edge lost its tenuous hold on the earth and, with hardly a splash, fell into the current. There it revolved slowly as it was coaxed farther from shore and finally borne seaward on the flood.

Far upstream the rising river tugged at a bit of fabric on a now-submerged sandbar, uncovered as the sand and silt above it was swept away like smoke in the water. At first it was only a square inch or two of dirty cloth, but inquisitive liquid fingers soon persuaded most of a stained blue shirt from its resting place. Gradually, through the long afternoon, sand and gravel were washed away until a shape foreign to the natural surroundings was exposed. A sandal floated from a bare foot and was snatched by the current. A tangled mass of long light hair swayed like some strange water plant, the scarf that had once bound it gone to follow the sandal.

When afternoon turned into evening, the length of a slender arm and hand were last to be revealed. A bracelet of purple bruised the wrist and two nails of the delicate hand were broken off short. The braided Celtic pattern of a silver ring circled the shrunken flesh of the index finger. As the water's flow gently moved the hand, the ring slipped off and, caught by the swirl of an eddy, was washed into the sand of the bank and half buried.

The river continued to wash over the still figure, cleansing some of the remaining soil from the blue shirt to expose rusty brown stains, pulling at it until, at last, the body rolled over and lay face up, staring with cold sightless eyes toward fading light reflected from the surface.

The chorus of birds had fallen into silence as they vanished to roosts in the surrounding forest. Only the late-spring thaw continued its relentless murmur in the gathering darkness, joined once by the haunting call of an owl, then by the howl of a wolf somewhere high on the mountain.

Except for a pale three-quarter moon and one faint star caught in a veil of cloud, it was full dark when the persistent river finally lifted the human form from its shallow resting place and tumbled it gently down into secret water.

Chapter 2

Late on a mild but cloudy evening of the second week of June, Jessie Arnold stood looking with satisfaction into a deep rectangular excavation in the yard of her property on Knik Road. In the bottom of what would soon become a basement for the new cabin she was helping to build stood Hank Peterson's Bobcat, waiting where he had left it to finish the digging on his return the next day. Two piles of wooden forms lay nearby, ready to be assembled in the hole before the pouring of a concrete foundation to support the log walls that would soon rise above it.

A light breeze had been whispering through the trees throughout the afternoon. Now it had all but died, leaving stillness in its wake, and from somewhere in the surrounding woods Jessie could hear the distant protest of a chain saw that one of her neighbors was using, taking advantage of the extended June light to catch up on his chores. A pesky mosquito whined in her ear and she swiped casually at it with one hand, used to the omnipresent annoyance warm weather encouraged.

Summer solstice was little more than a week away, a significant date for Alaskans. Many who live in lower latitudes all but ignore the hinges of the year, but people who make their home in the far north are extremely aware of them. June may be the welcome beginning of summer, but always in the minds of northerners is the knowledge that each day succeeding the solstice will be several minutes shorter. By mid-December, South Central Alaska's nineteen hours of mid-June daylight will have shrunk to five and a half, and the majority of each day will be spent in darkness, the country locked once more in frozen silence.

Jessie and winter had no quarrel with each other, for they were well acquainted and she was always ready to enjoy Alaska's compelling wilderness with her sled dog teams. But with each spring's return, she found her energy level rising as the days lengthened and the arc of the sun's increasingly northern path brought it higher in the sky. This particular summer would be filled with the construction of her new house. Impatient to get on with it, she was pleased with the pit she was examining. Before log walls could go up, the basement must go down. It was a significant and much anticipated beginning.

A late and rainy spring had kept the ground too wet and muddy for earlier digging. The soil was still damp, but contractor Vic Prentice had finally declared it acceptable, unwilling to wait longer. "If we don't get going now there'll be snow on our heads before we get it buttoned up." So all day the roar of the Bobcat had filled the clearing.

It had been gray and cloudy, threatening more rain that thankfully had not fallen to halt the work. But now, as the sun began to set, it sank below the overcast into a clear band of sky in the west, and sudden concentrated rays of golden light were cast across Jessie's cabin site like a benediction. A few midges, dust motes, and a mosquito or two floated lazily in the gilded brightness. The tall birch of the surrounding grove split the light with protracted fingers of deep blue shadow that contrasted with the richness of the sunshine. Against the shadows and threatening clouds the new yellow-green birch leaves caught the light so intensely that each one seemed to have an inner glow of its own, and they shimmered as one last breath of the dying breeze set them briefly astir.

The persistent mosquito, or one of her voracious sisters, returned to interrupt Jessie's appreciation with a high-pitched whine of complaint. Time to put on more repellent or go indoors, she told herself. But once again she waved the insect away and continued her inspection of the hole in her yard, reluctant to relinquish the pleasurable reassurance that a new cabin was about to rise like a phoenix from the ashes of the old. She could almost see what it would look like when it was finished, clean and new, fitting in companionably with the old-growth timber of the surrounding woods. Then, struck with amusement that a thing as mundane as a hole could be so inspiring, she smiled at her own enthusiasm.

Stepping forward to the very edge of the pit, back to the sun, she shaded her eyes with both gloved hands to take one last look, for the light of the setting sun had cast the depths into such dark shadow it was difficult to make out the earthen walls Peterson had carved so skillfully. As the movement brought into her line of sight a narrow section of the far wall that had been hidden by the Bobcat, an object suddenly stood out from the darkness of the vertical wall and caught her attention. From what she could make out, it was somewhat rounded in shape and pale enough in color to stand out against the rich brown of the dirt around it. A rock, she assumed. There had been several light-colored rounded stones dug up during the afternoon's excavation. What she was seeing was probably another. She decided to go down and remove it before quitting for the day.

Walking around the hole, Jessie went down the ramp Peterson had scraped out as access for his Bobcat. As she moved out of the sunlight into shadow, the scent of the recently disturbed earth rose up sweetly to meet her, and she was reminded of her plans to use some of this rich soil on her vegetable garden. She crossed the flat bottom of the pit, some of the damp loam sticking to her boots, and stopped to examine the object that had caught her eye.

It lay a little less than halfway down the wall, perhaps four feet from the upper edge and six from the bottom of the pit. The small amount of what was exposed seemed smoother and of a different texture than the stone she anticipated. She frowned and started to reach up for it but then hesitated, a hint of puzzled recognition slowly dawning.

Carefully, with one gloved hand, she was brushing at the dirt that clung to the object when, without warning, a large clod suddenly came loose from one side and fell to the ground at her feet. Jessie reacted with a gasp, clenched her fingers into a fist, and pulled them back hard against her chest as she took a step away and gaped in disbelief at what hung still half buried in the wall before her. The falling soil had revealed that the complete shape was not symmetrically curved as expected. Half turned in her direction, a round dirt-packed eye socket seemed to stare blindly over her head at the now-fading light of the setting sun, and a jawbone full of teeth appeared to grin in ironic if silent approval of its unexpected liberation. It was an old skull, nothing left but bone, pale and long abandoned by its owner, but unmistakably—alarmingly—human.

For a long minute, Jessie stood unmoving, scarcely breathing, her mind a blank confusion. Then another breath of the dying breeze rustled the birch leaves and one of her dogs yelped sharply from the kennel yard above her on the other side of the clearing. With a shiver, she blinked and looked away from her unwelcome discovery. "Someone walking on your grave," her grandmother had called such a shudder. *Not this time,* she reassured herself; this burial place belonged to someone else.

The bright golden rays of sunlight had disappeared and the world around her was once again a dreary gray. Her image of a new cabin had faded with the light and the depression in which she stood was just a hole in the ground, a hole that unexpectedly contained what had once been a person. Who? How had this body wound up in her yard? Like it or not, there were things she must do about what she had unearthed. There were people she must call, who would come with questions she could not answer, and delays she would be forced to tolerate.

With one last glance at the grimace in the wall, she straightened her shoulders and marched up Peterson's ramp.

Across the yard, a Winnebago motor home belonging to Vic Prentice was parked for the summer building season. During the day, she shared part of it with him as project office, but the rest of the time, at his suggestion, she was living there. It contained the telephone she now needed in order to call the state troopers, who would know what was legally required in such unusual and disquieting circumstances.

Troubled, her anxiety mixed with a spark of anger, knowing that what she had discovered would result in another construction delay, Jessie went to make her call.

Chapter 3

 In the brilliance of a sunny morning, John Timmons, assistant coroner from the state crime lab in Anchorage, peered upward at the skull that gazed sightless out of the dirt wall of the basement excavation for Jessie Arnold's new log cabin. A frown beetled his heavy brows as he strained to examine it, gave up, and whirled his wheelchair around to face the two state troopers who had laid planks over the ramp and the muddy bottom of the pit, so he could wheel down to inspect the evidence.

"Dammit! Get something to raise me high enough to have a look at the thing," he demanded. "Those wooden forms in the yard will do, two or three of them."

Watching from above, Jessie smiled to herself at the sound of his gruff voice, remembering a past comparison to the sound of gravel shaken in a tin can, and at the frustration with which he was now scrubbing at his fuzzy hair.

The skiing accident that had paralyzed Timmons from the waist down had not affected the attitude with which he would hurl himself and those around him headlong at this problem, like everything else in his life. Every challenge was an all-or-nothing proposition.

The two troopers immediately headed for the access ramp, intending to lug down the forms as directed. But Hank Peterson, who had been leaning against one wheel of his Bobcat to watch the interesting goings-on below, tossed away a cigarette and hopped onto his machine. Deftly wheeling it to the pile of forms, he loaded four across the bucket and transported them easily into the excavation where Timmons was expressing impatience. Leaving the Bobcat rumbling in idle, and with assistance from the troopers, he stacked three forms into a platform on the ground below the skull in the wall and slanted the fourth against one side to make a ramp for the wheelchair.

"Good man," Timmons growled and, perched on this jury-rigged accommodation, returned to his inspection of Jessie's macabre discovery of the night before.

A phone call from Phil Becker had not alerted the assistant coroner until after dark, so he had instructed the trooper to close the area and to expect his arrival when he could examine the remains in daylight. He had wasted no time that morning, however, showing up in his van in time to have coffee with Jessie while they and the aide he had ferried along awaited the arrival of Becker and a second trooper from the Palmer office. Hank

Peterson had also turned up early, and was soon followed by Vic Prentice and the rest of the construction team, ready to resume work but fascinated by the cause of the delay. Vic put them to work sorting out the forms they would need to use later that day; then they stood around watching while the investigation proceeded.

"Jesus, Jessie. Doesn't anything ever go normally for you?" Hank had asked, with a crooked grin and a shake of his head.

He had then asked John Timmons a dozen questions about the work of the crime lab and how he was able to accomplish it on wheels. Timmons had enthused about the excitement of wheelchair racing, with which he had replaced skiing after his accident. Some mechanical genius—or madman—had built him a four-wheeled version of a dirt bike, and he now raced off-road as well as on, whenever he had the chance, though winter restricted his opportunities. Halting his animated recital in mid-sentence, Timmons had tossed Jessie the empty cup he was waving and wheeled off in determined fashion toward the basement excavation.

"About time, Phil. Let's get a look at what Jessie's got for us this time."

As the three civilian spectators—for Jessie and Hank were soon joined by Vic Prentice—watched from around the pile of wooden forms, Timmons peered at the enigma embedded in the dirt wall, which appeared to stare back at him from its empty eye sockets with a maniacal grin of its yellowed teeth. When he had examined all that was visible, including the teeth, he selected a tool from the contents of his field kit and carefully dug away the soil from around the top and sides of the skull, leaving it on a rough dirt shelf, released to further inspection. "Hmm," he muttered, digging away more soil beyond the jaw. "Ha!"

"What?" Becker asked.

Timmons, focused on his work, continued the slow disinterment process without speaking. Gradually, as he expanded the cavity, more bones were uncovered—the vertebrae of the neck and then the left clavicle. A bit more digging and the top of the flat scapula of the left shoulder could be seen, along with several short upper ribs.

A trickle of loose soil preceding a chunk the size of a baseball followed his next attempt with the digging tool. It came abruptly away from the wall and fell into his lap, scattering dirt over his pants as it broke up.

"Enough," Timmons declared, dropping a hand to brush at his bony knees and squinting as he intently inspected what he had unearthed so far. "The wall will collapse if we don't cut down from ground level to get the rest out. Man your shovels, boys."

Swinging the chair around to face his fascinated audience, he gave Becker a wicked grin.

"Here's your chance to actually *dig* for clues, Phil."

•   •   •

It took the rest of the morning; and Jessie had brewed several pots of coffee by the time the skeleton had been more or less unearthed.

Timmons halted the work when less than an inch of soil remained over the bones and once again descended into the basement excavation and onto the platform, where he worked for another hour, carefully removing the rest of the dirt a little at a time to expose the whole skeleton.

It lay on its right side, facing into the pit from a semifetal position, as if the person it had been had simply fallen asleep comfortably, knees bent in a 45-degree angle, arms pulled in close to the rib cage and crossed at the wrists. As the flesh had decomposed and melted away into the soil, some of the earth that covered it had fallen in to partially fill the cavity left behind. Without muscles and tendons to hold them together, the vertebrae of the spine had sagged into misalignment. A few scraps of fabric, now greasy and discolored, could be discerned as underwear shorts that clung and defined the pelvic girdle.

Timmons growled under his breath at what he had found but made no comments until, with help, he had wheeled back up out of the hole and stopped at the edge of the pit, where Jessie came to stand beside the chair.

"Old," he said, after a minute or two of collecting his thoughts. "Not ancient—not archaeological, I mean—but old. Historic remains don't wear boxer shorts."

Toward noon, when he had done everything he could for the time being, Timmons accepted a sandwich from Jessie and settled at the edge of the basement excavation, where he could keep an eye on the rest of the proceedings. Phil Becker and the second state trooper helped the young lab assistant carefully remove the skeleton to a waiting van for transportation to the Anchorage crime lab.

Jessie had smiled at his assessment of the underwear but was more concerned with what he might have learned from his examination. "Can you tell yet what killed him?" she asked.

Timmons glanced up sharply to peer at her from under his shaggy brows. "What killed him? No, not yet. It's an odd position to bury someone in. Most people lay bodies out straight and formal. I'll probably be able to figure out the cause of death, but I doubt very much if we'll ever know who did the burying on one this old, dammit. Probably long gone anyway. And what makes you think it's a *him?*"

Jessie, who had just taken a bite of her own sandwich, gave him a startled look and swallowed hard. "Isn't it?"

"Well . . . yes. I'd say it's male, but that's not official till I get the remains into the lab. Just wondered about your assumption."

Jessie had spent a restless night, unable to stop thinking about the silent witness keeping her company in the pit next door to the motor home. As she had tossed and turned, trying to shut off her thoughts and questions, it had occurred to her that for years she had been sleeping almost directly above the bones that lay buried less than a dozen feet below. If her cabin had not burned, and if she had not decided to replace it and include a basement, she would never have discovered the skull. It would have remained at rest, peaceful or not, four feet beneath the surface, perhaps another seven or eight below her bed.

It was a disconcerting concept, but it had never entered her mind that the buried remains were anything but male. Now she wondered why not. Women died and were buried too. Interesting—and gruesome. But the skeleton *was* wearing men's underwear.

She turned back to Timmons with another question from her restive night. "What will you do with the . . . remains? After you examine them, I mean."

"They'll be held at the lab while we try to identify them. If we can't, they'll be buried as a John Doe, unless someone claims the body."

As the troopers and the lab assistant finished loading the bones into the van, Timmons swung his wheelchair around to face her directly. "How long have you owned this place, Jessie?"

"Almost ten years."

"Tell me what you remember. Who did you buy it from? Were there any buildings here?"

Jessie closed her eyes, visualizing the area before a lot of hard work and the help of a few friends had built her first cabin there and turned the yard into a kennel for her sled dogs.

"The clearing was a lot smaller," she told him, opening her eyes and waving a hand toward the dog yard. "I cut at least a dozen trees to make room for my mutts. There was an old prospector's cabin—a one-room sort of thing in pretty bad shape. The sod roof was falling in. We tore it apart to make room to build my cabin and used some of the logs for a shed."

"So no one was living in it."

"No. There'd been an old man, I think, but he died. It must have been his son who sold me the place. I don't remember his name or where he was going, except that it was out of Alaska— someplace warmer. I only met him once, briefly. Mostly I talked to the loan and title people."

"Well, we can go through the records and find out who it was. Where was that old cabin exactly?"

Jessie frowned and surveyed the clearing in an attempt to re-call how it had appeared before all the changes she had made in a decade. The dog yard now took up the majority of the space, with individual boxes for her more than forty sled dogs and room for them to move outside them on their restraints. The footprint of the cabin that had burned down three months earlier overlapped the space on which the new one would rise, but had been situated a few feet to the north. As she remembered, the old prospector's cabin had stood almost exactly where they were building the new one.

"You could almost have set it in the hole for the basement," she told Timmons.

"So this body would not have been buried by digging up the floor."

"I don't remember it that way. It seems about a yard from where the south wall stood."

He nodded thoughtfully. "I thought so. And that grave was dug from the surface. The fill dirt was a slightly different color than what was around it. Some topsoil got mixed in as it was shoveled back. You can see some color and texture difference if you look closely. A hole that deep means the body was probably buried when the ground wasn't frozen."

He looked up and nodded to Phil Becker, who had come across the yard from the van and stood listening to the last of this recital. He scowled at the question the trooper asked next.

"Is this a natural death, John? You think there could be any others? Should we be digging up more of this yard?"

At the incredulous expression on Jessie's face, Timmons's frown turned to a chuckle. "Don't panic. We're not going to put your construction project on hold with more digging. I think it's probably a single burial. Could be that the son simply buried his father next to the cabin he lived in and didn't want to move the grave. Wouldn't be that unusual. I'll check the records and see if the old man was buried somewhere else. We'll have to date the bones, but it's probably the old guy."

She thought about that for a minute, not understanding how anyone could bury a parent and then sell him along with the property, leaving no marker and making no mention of the grave's location.

"If this was his father, isn't it weird that he didn't tell someone about it? And why would he bury him with no clothes on?"

Timmons considered her question thoughtfully. "I should have known you wouldn't miss that one. He might have thought mentioning it would put the sale in jeopardy. I don't know, Jessie. People react all kinds of ways to death. It might have had something to do with their relationship—if it wasn't a good one. It's a little unusual, but don't worry about it. You can be sure we'll be doing some background checks and I'll let you know what we find out. Don't dig any more basements until I let you know, though. Okay?"

She agreed and let it go, but the idea still nagged at her.

Ten minutes later, after the van and the patrol car had turned from her driveway onto Knik Road, she glanced around her yard, contemplating the unwelcome thought of other bodies beneath the ground. The idea gave her another shiver, so she determinedly thought about something else: getting her cabin building under way again.

"Hey, Jessie," Hank Peterson called from the hole, where he was about to start up his Bobcat to complete the excavation. "If you want, we can put a basement window in this space they dug out. Whaddaya think?"

"Forget it," she told him emphatically. "I don't want to look out a window and remember that I found a skeleton there. Fill it in."

Chapter 4

Following the departure of the forensics team, the construction crew was half a day behind schedule in forming up to pour the concrete that would be delivered by a subcontractor the next morning. Taking advantage of the extended June daylight, they worked until after seven, Jessie laboring along with Vic Prentice's crew of four, while Hank Peterson used his Bobcat to level the ground and move forms into position.

It was an interesting and experienced crew that went efficiently about their business, stringing chalk lines to establish the exact location of the basement footings in the excavation, then assembling the forms in the shallow trenches that would hold them. As she helped by carrying tools and lumber back and forth, Jessie learned their first names.

Vic's foreman, Bill, a stocky, moonfaced man in his forties, who rocked about on short, stumpy legs, spoke with a surprisingly soft voice. He was clearly respected by the men, however, for his few suggestions—impossible to call them orders from their tone—were followed to the letter.

Jason, whom they all called J.B., was the exact opposite in appearance, tall and thin. He had a voice like a foghorn that could almost always be heard pouring out good-humored if off-key scraps of song, as he warbled along with the tape player he had attached to his utility belt. To Jessie's amusement, he seemed to know the words to every show tune ever written for the Broadway stage.

The other two crew members were new this season and tended to be more seen than heard. Dell was neatly bearded and wore his hair long, tied back in a low ponytail. He had the build of a football quarterback, slim and agile, with muscled arms and shoulders that he liked to show off by tearing the sleeves out of the sweatshirts he wore. He spoke little but seemed aware of everything, moving instinctively to where he was needed.

Redheaded Stevie, in her twenties the youngest, also went competently—and more energetically—about her business, with little direction from Bill. She wore her hair short and tied colorful bandannas around her head as sweatbands. Stevie caught Jessie's attention now and then with an infectious grin or a humorous comment muttered almost under her breath as she passed.

When they finally quit for the day, all was ready for the pour next morning, and Jessie was tired, dirty, and hungry. Waving good-bye to Vic and Hank, last to drive away, she headed for the motor home and a shower before finding something easy, quick, and probably canned to heat for dinner.

Billy Steward, her kennel assistant, had showed up late in the afternoon to feed and water the dogs, so she had no canine chores waiting. But wanting some company that wouldn't shout directions over the roar of a Bobcat, she unhooked her lead dog, Tank, from his restraint and took him into the Winnebago with her for the evening.

As she stripped off her filthy jeans and sweatshirt, he sat patiently awaiting her attention. All day, he and the other dogs had watched the unusual activity from their places in the yard, some leaping up to lie on top of their boxes, which gave them a better view of the proceedings.

"Hey, buddy. This is all pretty strange for you guys, isn't it?" she asked, grabbing a towel with one hand and leaning down to give him a hug and rub his ears. "But I need a box to sleep in too."

He reached up to give her an affectionate sloppy lick from chin to ear, making her grin.

"Okay, I can take a hint. Shower time."

Getting clean felt so good she stayed in the compact shower space until she ran out of hot water, washing her hair along with the rest of her. Satisfied with a quick towel dry, she ran her fingers through her wavy honey-blond hair, pulled on a favorite old pair of sweats and an Arnold Kennels T-shirt, and headed for the galley. There, she considered a can of chili but opted instead for one of several serving-sized containers of stew from a batch she had made a week or so before and frozen for just such an undemanding meal. Dumping it from its plastic container into a saucepan, she added a little water and turned the stove burner on low to thaw and heat it slowly. Some French bread went into the oven, buttered and encased in aluminum foil. Five minutes later, she had slipped Loreena McKennitt's *The Book of Secrets* into the CD player and settled at the table with a shot of Jameson's Irish for sipping and a sigh of contentment.

What could be better after a hard day's work? she thought, glad to have the place by herself for the time being and nothing but the music to replace the sound of construction outside.

With the music playing, she didn't hear tires on her driveway or the crunch of footsteps approaching her door. The fist that hammered on it startled her into spilling a drop or two of whiskey from the glass she was just raising to her mouth.

"Hey!" someone shouted outside. "Anyone home?"

"Dammit," Jessie swore under her breath, as Tank sat up from where he was lying at her feet and turned to face the door. "Who the hell?"

Setting down the snifter, she unwillingly got up, wiped the whiskey from her hand with a towel, and, frowning, went to answer the summons, as whoever it was pounded again—loudly.

"Jessie! Jessie Arnold! Are you in there?"

She did not recognize the voice or the face that confronted her when she opened the door to look out. But she had no trouble identifying the television van that was parked between her dog yard and the excavation for her new basement.

"Hey! Understand you found a body out here last night. What's the story?"

A camera crew had already climbed down into the excavation and was making tracks in and around the ready-for-concrete forms the construction gang had worked so hard on that afternoon. As Jessie watched, speechless, a tall gangly young man with a heavy camera on his shoulder tripped over a stake at one corner, knocking it out of the ground and loosening the form. Not bothering to replace it, he moved on, continuing a concerted visual search of the dirt walls and floor of the pit.

Jamming her feet into the muddy boots she had left on a piece of newspaper near the door, Jessie didn't bother to answer the question she had been asked but jumped from the motor home, slammed the door, and hurried to the edge of the excavation.

"Get out of there!" she angrily told the two men and a woman, who were in the process of examining the hole for evidence of the location of the body they had heard about. "You're wrecking the foundation forms. Out! Right now!"

"Aw, come on, Jessie. We just want the story. Where was the corpse? The report said you found it. What's it like to find a body? Any idea who it might be?"

The door-pounder had followed along to bombard her with questions. One of the three in the hole glanced up, but in their attempt to find something to video they all ignored her demand.

"Hey, Jim," the door-pounder called. "Come up here with the camera and interview Jessie. You can get shots of the site after she shows us where to look. Where'd you find it, Jessie? I need a story for the *Daily News*."

So it was both print and video news people. Though it usually took a lot to make Jessie lose her temper, fatigue and the interruption of her relaxation with such a blatant, inconsiderate intrusion was suddenly more than she could take. Whirling to face her questioner and taking a long look at his eager, almost voracious expression and the microphone he was shoving in her face, she was inspired to tell him off, had opened her mouth to loose the indignant, angry words that flooded her mind— including several of the four-letter variety—when she thought better of it.

Experience with print and television reporters is a large part of the sled dog racing game, and Jessie had long ago learned the hard way to think before she spoke; to assume that anything and everything she uttered would be grist for the media mill; that it would appear, often misquoted, to fit the slant of whatever story the reporter dreamed up. For a long moment, she stared at him resentfully, then turned once again to the crew in the pit.

"If you don't come up out of there immediately, I'm calling the police. You're trespassing on private property, and I am telling you all to leave. I have nothing to say and I'm going in- side now—to the phone."

She swung around, walked swiftly past the avid reporter as if he didn't exist, climbed back into the motor home, and closed and locked the door. Turning up the music until it drowned out the sound of the discussion that ensued outside, and ignoring the repeated knocking that had started again on her door, she gave the stew a stir, sat back down at the table, and sipped at the Jameson's until it and they were gone.

·　·　·

DEAD BODY DISCOVERED IN LOCAL MUSHER'S BASEMENT the headline screamed from the front page of next morning's newspaper, carried in from the box at the road by Hank Peterson, arriving for work. Though not the lead, Jessie found she had hit the front page in an article that followed the headline, which had been placed above the fold, where it would attract the attention of anyone who saw the paper. She was immediately torn between outrage and regret that she had not given the reporter the information he was seeking, for her refusal had clearly not only sparked his anger, but speculation in print about her connection to the bones Timmons had disinterred. Without actual accusation, the article and its headline were cleverly slanted in a manner to throw suspicion and allegation in her direction.

Jessie Arnold, local Iditarod musher, angrily refused comment yesterday on the remains of an unidentified body discovered on her Knik Road property during excavation of a basement for a new cabin. Unreasonably upset, Arnold, who was involved in a series of murders and arsons that included her own residence earlier this spring, locked herself inside her motor home and refused to answer questions concerning the remains unearthed earlier in the day by state troopers and investigators from the crime lab.

Leaning against the side of the Winnebago, Jessie sighed in frustration. "Damned if I do—damned if I don't," she said, shaking her head. "They were tramping around, knocking down forms and demanding information I thought they should get somewhere else. I told them to get out. They've made this sound like—"

"You don't have to explain to me," Peterson interrupted with a grin. "I was here yesterday, remember? Ignore them, Jessie. What can they do, take away your birthday? They'll sell a few papers, and it'll blow over in a couple of days."

She knew he was probably right but was offended anyway. Laying the paper aside, she went to meet Vic Prentice, who was arriving just ahead of the concrete truck, with its large spinning barrel. As they got to work, directing the flow of concrete into the footing forms, leveling and working it to ensure that there were no air bubbles trapped in the mix, she found herself taking deep breaths and trying to ease the tension in her back and shoulders and let go of her frustration. Hank's advice was good. The only thing to do was forget it, but she found that difficult.

There was more than just the current situation involving her emotions. It had been a crazy spring, full of confusion and anxiety, sometimes terror, with people dying one way or another. In February, during the Yukon Quest race from Whitehorse to Fairbanks, there had been a murder and the kidnapping of a rookie racer. Then an old acquaintance had unexpectedly appeared, along with murder and arson, including the destruction of Jessie's beloved cabin that the newspaper article had mentioned. A trip for Vic Prentice, to ferry the Winnebago from Idaho to its current location in her yard, had involved her in more killings, when she had longed for it to be a vacation from the stress of the spring. Now, with the discovery of the body in the basement, she had begun to feel claustrophobic, as if death were dogging her heels with an hourglass and scythe.

To complicate everything further, a relationship in which she had felt confident had ended, suddenly and without real warning, leaving her emotionally drained, wondering if her decisions had been the right ones and suddenly unsure of herself and others. Now she found another death and its mysterious overtones depressing. Hesitating, halfway across the yard to her storage shed to retrieve a pair of gloves she had unconsciously put down and forgotten, she looked around at the jumble of construction as if it belonged to someone else.

What the hell am I doing? she asked herself. Am I just trying to replace the past?

The idea of rebuilding the cabin she had lost in the fire had given her focus and pleasure. Now she wondered if it was an exercise in bad judgment. Was she making another mistake?

As she focused on her indecision, the construction sounds faded to a dull sort of background music. She didn't notice the roar of the truck, now empty of concrete and turning to leave the yard, as it lumbered toward her and the driver hammered the horn to attract her attention. Startled, she leaped out of its way, yanked back to the reality of what was going on around her.

Prentice came trotting across the yard to lay a hand on her arm. "Hey, Jessie. You okay?"

His concerned expression and the slight southern drawl that softened his words suddenly made her want to cry, but she caught herself just in time to turn to him with a smile, which, though forced, erased the concern from his face.

"I'm fine, Vic. Just woolgathering."

What a year! she thought, and went to work, grateful to have something to take her mind away from her problems and determined to maintain a positive attitude. Of course rebuilding the cabin was a good idea. Moving into a new cabin would be wonderful and give her back an important part of her precious independence. For now, she would bury herself in the construction process and keep busy. The body she had found this time had nothing to do with her, did it?

Chapter 5

 At sixty-one degrees fifteen minutes latitude north, Anchorage near summer solstice had over nineteen hours of daylight, and the sun did not set until ten-thirty. When it rose again at half past three, the four-plus hours between were more a darker and extended twilight than an actual night.

The deep evening blue of midnight made street and traffic lights glow like jewels and enriched the garish colors of neon advertisements on taverns and bars along Fourth Avenue. What darkness there was settled in deep shadows between the downtown buildings of Alaska's largest city, creating pockets of near invisibility for those who stumbled through them on their way from one drink to another. The hum of vehicle tires on pavement provided a background for the voices of the pedestrians passing along the sidewalks: an angry shout, a burst of inebriated laughter, a greeting called out to someone driving by.

Two city blocks—one a large parking structure, the other a vacant lot—separated the Bottoms Up bar from the rest of the watering holes scattered farther west along the street in the more crowded section of downtown Anchorage. The exterior of Bottoms, a nondescript concrete-block structure with a single sign in startling red neon, was architecturally insignificant, but its patrons, more interested in the topless gyrations of the exotic dancers on the runway inside, hardly noticed. At just after midnight, canned music of a bump-and-grind nature spilled into the street as the front door swung open and two men and a woman walked out and turned right into the shadows of the parking lot.

The three crossed the lot together and stopped beside a white car. While the owner unlocked the driver's door, the woman turned to entice the second man. Tossing her long blond hair and holding her shoulders back to exhibit large breasts barely contained by a tight yellow tank top, she made him an offer.

With a grin, he shook his head at the price she had named. "Naw. Too rich for me."

His companion made a quick counteroffer, but the woman, refusing to lower her price, swung away with a shrug and strolled off across the lot on her three-inch heels, swinging her hips suggestively in black skintight pants. The men watched her progress with amused appreciation until she teetered out of sight around the corner of the building; then they climbed into the car and pulled out of the lot. What they did not see was the expression of resigned frustration on her face. Knowing she had a pimp and rent to pay, she was already regretting that she had not lowered her price a little. It had not been a good week. A nagging cough, left over from a bad cold, had plagued her all evening in the smoke-filled bar, and she knew she looked less than her best, with dark circles under her eyes, residue of three days sick in bed.

Stopping in the doorway of Bottoms, she lit a cigarette, which brought on another fit of coughing, so she did not look up when the driver of the car honked as they passed on the street. She ignored them, her interest caught by a dark brown pickup that swung in toward the curb and stopped in front of her. Reaching up with both hands to lean against the cab in a position that would give the driver a good look at her cleavage through the open window, she licked her dry lips, summoned enough energy to look perkily in his direction, and asked her usual question.

"Wanna party, darlin'?"

In the half dark, she could see almost nothing of his face. He was mostly a silhouette against the street's lighting.

"Sure. I'll give you three hundred if you'll come to my place and let me take a couple of pictures."

Automatically starting to shake her head, she hesitated. It was an unwritten rule: Never leave the area with a customer. Still, three hundred was a significant temptation—more than she would make in a couple of nights at the rate she was going. It meant she could go home and climb in bed afterward and get the rest she needed to be back on her feet tomorrow night.

"Come on," he wheedled. She saw his teeth in the reflected light as he grinned. "I'm harmless—just don't like doing it in the truck. I'll bring you right back here when we're done. Even give you the three hundred now. Okay?"

He shifted to tug his wallet out of a right hip pocket, took out three hundred-dollar bills, and held them in her direction.

"Here. Get in."

The sight of the money was enough to silence her concerns. Opening the door of the pickup, she climbed in and took the bills, stuffing them into a pocket of her tight pants as he pulled away from the curb and headed east on Fourth.

"Where're we going?"

"Not far. You'll like it. I got a good place. What's your name?"

"Teri. Yours?"

"John."

"Sure."

He drove in silence for a couple of blocks, then turned south on Gamble, headed for the New Seward Highway. Before they reached it, he pulled off into the almost empty parking lot of an all-night liquor store and stopped at the end farthest from the door, with the truck facing the street.

"What kind of booze do you like, Teri?"

"Ah—oh, I don't care. Whatever you want."

"Bourbon?"

"Sure."

"Be right back. Don't go anywhere without me, now." He grinned at her playfully, shut off the engine, and took the key with him across the short space to the store. He was a big man, but had a nice smile and friendly eyes behind a pair of dark-rimmed glasses. She felt better, having had a good look at him, and relaxed a bit while she waited. At least he had a sense of humor.

In just a few minutes he was climbing back in with a bottle in a brown paper bag in his right hand, the left reaching to slam shut the door behind him.

"Here. You hold the booze."

As she reached to take the bottle, his left hand came up toward her. In it was a handgun, dark, threatening, the metal gleaming in the half-light of the cab. He had it pointed at the middle of her body.

"Hey—"

"Shut it, bitch. Don't scream, just sit still, or I can make you very, very sorry." His voice was rough, but the words came slow and quiet, almost a drawl. The friendly grin was gone, replaced by a grimace that exposed his teeth, wolfish and predatory.

With the terror that flooded through her, she probably couldn't have moved anyway, wouldn't have tried to, but one hand went instinctively to the handle of the passenger door.

"Don't try it," he warned, switching the gun to his right hand and shaking a finger of the left at her as if she were a disobedient child.

She felt as if she were smothering, could scarcely breathe.

"What—do you want?"

"I want you to put that bottle on the seat and keep your hands in sight, both of them."

She laid the bottle down and watched her hands shake as she placed them on her knees, not wanting to look at him again or at the gun he was holding.

He reached under his side of the seat. There was a gleam of metal, and she could see he had a pair of handcuffs. He held them out to her.

"Put 'em on. Now!" he told her, satisfaction in his voice, and—when her wrists were securely fastened together—"Turn around and get down on your knees on the floor, facing the seat."

"Please," she begged him. "Please. Don't hurt me. I'll do anything you want. Anything, really. Please. I won't tell anyone." She could hear the high, thin quality of her pleading. Knowing how scared she was made it worse.

"Show me," he commanded. "Get down there—now. Maybe I *won't* hurt you, if you're a very good girl."

When she had knelt on the floor, as directed, head on her hands on the seat, he started the pickup and drove across Gamble to another one-way street heading in the opposite direction, back the way they had come. A few blocks farther, he turned right, away from downtown Anchorage, heading east on what would become the Glenn Highway that led to Eagle River and the MatSu Valley beyond. All she could see were the streetlights as they passed, casting light in through the passenger window, but she knew where they were so far.

Where was he taking her? she wondered, so frightened now that she could hardly think straight. There seemed to be nothing she could do that would not result in his using the handgun that lay in his lap as he drove. No one knew where she was or even that she had gone. She had left Bottoms Up after her topless dancing shift was over for the night, tired, craving her bed and a good night's sleep. Her overture to the two men in the parking lot had been a futile attempt to make a few extra dollars she needed badly. What had seemed an opportunity to make enough to solve her current cash-flow problem had turned, without warning, into a nightmare of unimaginable proportions. All she could do was wait and hope that he wouldn't hurt—wouldn't kill her. Maybe there would be one moment of opportunity, one chance to run, to escape, to hit him with something, to defend herself. She didn't see how, but—maybe, if she watched carefully and didn't lose it completely. She took a deep breath.

For the moment, all she could do was crouch in the vulnerable and uncomfortable position he had demanded and feel the tears that wouldn't stop running down her face onto her hands that were quickly going numb from the pressure of the cuffs she had fastened too tightly.

Oh, God, please, God. I promise I'll be good. If he doesn't . . . If . . .

Teri couldn't bear to think what *if* might be.

She could only go on breathing, praying, living—and hoping to still be doing all those things when this was over.

If . . .

Chapter 6

With the footings poured and curing, the cabin-building crew went to work the next morning to raise the forms necessary for pouring basement walls.

J.B. began the day with bits and pieces of old Mario Lanza hits.

"Give—me—some men—who are—stout—hearted—men," he sang, cheerfully off-key but enthusiastic and in time with the strokes of his hammer.

"Stouthearted but weak-brained, maybe," Stevie commented to Jessie, who replenished her supply of nails and grinned at the green bandanna that contrasted brightly with her carroty hair.

*   *   *

When they were finished, two days later, the truck once again arrived and backed up to dump concrete into the hopper of a pump that would force it through a long flexible hose, four inches in diameter, to wherever it was needed. A tall boom raised the hose high in the air and swung it into position across the thirty-foot width of the basement.

Jessie was impressed with how fast the pour progressed, though it took three truckloads of concrete to finish the job. When the forms were full, she carried around a bucket of long, heavy, five-eighths-inch anchor bolts and, one by one, handed them up to J.B., who carefully measured and sank them into the top of the wet concrete, leaving the threaded ends extending above it. When it had set, they would be firmly attached to hold the sill and first logs securely to the foundation.

When all the anchor bolts were correctly positioned, J.B. came down and stood on the edge of the excavation with Jessie, looking out across the finished work.

"Looks good," he commented. "Thanks for the help."

She let Tank off his tether in the kennel part of the yard, and J.B. knelt to pet him affectionately.

"Hey, buddy. You're a handsome devil."

Tank sat down next to Jessie, clearly knowing he was being admired, but accepted the tribute with his usual dignity.

"This dog special?" Jason asked.

"He's my leader," she told him. "Couldn't run races without him."

"Must be exciting—running those long races."

He looked up at her with a smile, and she suddenly realized he was more interested in the conversation with her than in admiring Tank.

"Mostly it's a lot of hard work," she told him, not completely comfortable with the attention. "Races are just the result of a lot of training and kennel care."

"But you like it?"

"Yeah. Wouldn't do it if I didn't."

With relief, she noticed Prentice on his way across the yard.

"Here comes Vic. I'd better see what he wants."

With Tank walking beside her, she moved away to meet the contractor and, while they talked for a few minutes about the next stages of building the basement, J.B. wandered off, whistling, to finish cleaning up for the day.

* * *

With five or six days before the concrete was hard enough to re-move the forms, the work temporarily came to a halt, giving Jessie a chance to spend some time working with her dogs. She got up early the next morning and soon was driving her four-wheeled ATV from the storage shed and attaching a gang line for a team to the front of it. With no snow on the ground, most mushers train their teams with ATVs during the warm months of the year, giving the dogs something to pull and the trainer something on which to ride.

The dogs knew the ATV meant some of them were going for a run and were all instantly on their feet, barking and leaping with excited anticipation and the hope that Jessie would choose them to harness and hook to that gang line. Tank, with his usual dignity, sat waiting at the end of his tether, straining slightly against its restraint but confident that, as leader, he would soon be moved to his place at the front of the team.

Carefully not making eye contact with the dogs she did not intend to take along and thereby raise their hopes, Jessie harnessed and moved ten dogs from their tethers to the gang line, one by one, Tank last, then walked back to start the ATV. After their long rest, the eager dogs were more than ready to run and pull. When she released the brake, they broke rules and took off without waiting for her signal, throwing themselves against their harnesses, yanking the gang line taut and the ATV forward with a jerk.

"Whoa!" Jessie shouted, setting the brake and dragging them to a halt. "Wait," she told them sternly. "Wait!" When most of them had stopped trying to move forward, she once again released the brake, with the same unruly result. It took two more enforced stops and a walk forward on her part to inform them in a firm voice that, without her permission, they were going nowhere, before they calmed down enough to wait for her direction. Then they waited, but unwillingly, and, as soon as she allowed, were once again pulling with all their strength, which made for a very fast start.

As they reached the Knik Road end of the driveway and turned off onto a trail that ran beside it in a wide ditch, she let them run, knowing there was plenty of room for a mile or two for them to work off some of their enthusiasm. They flew along at a lope, with the ATV in neutral, and Jessie let them go, only slowing them when they had to come up out of the ditch to cross a neighbor's driveway, where she looked both ways for traffic.

As the winter accumulation of snow melted and disappeared, many sled dog training trails had vanished into tangles of brush, soggy bogs, and untravelable routes, leaving few choices. Summer running had to be done on established trails, many of which lay beside local roads and were also used by the three- and four-wheeled ATVs of local residents. That meant keeping a close eye out for careless joyriders—who were going somewhere in a hurry and paying little attention to dog team traffic—as well as for vehicles turning onto or off of the paved road beside which the dogs were running. It was difficult at times for drivers to see teams that were often below the level of the road, and Jessie refused to assume that they would slow down and give her mutts the right of way. She had never had an incident with a car or truck, but knew mushers who had, to their and their dogs' detriment. Always she was glad when winter returned and she could take her teams back onto snow-covered wilderness trails, far from the danger and noise of motor vehicles. She looked forward to the first few training runs in the fall as the best of hundreds she made in a twelve-month cycle.

But sled dogs require dedication year round and must be run with or without snow. How quickly they forgot and grew lazy, lying around a kennel. Their inattention to her commands was witness to that, a red flag that it was time to get back to regular coaching. The summer would be full of building, but if she was to have teams ready when the winter racing season began, she could not let it interfere completely with this normal activity.

By the end of the afternoon, she had run three different teams for two hours each, in groups of young and older dogs, harnessing experienced dogs with rookies, and would run the rest tomorrow. Some dogs that had not been taken out on a run had been hooked up to the training wheel to exercise in circles, including some of last fall's puppies, who were not yet ready to join a team. She was weary and hoarse from yelling commands that had, at times, been ignored or misinterpreted. As she drove the last team of the day up her driveway toward her kennel and construction site, she was not sorry to have this be the final run. It was time to water and care for all her animals, before going to the motor home to care for her own tired and hungry self.

She was not unhappy, however, to see a state trooper's car parked near the Winnebago and Phil Becker leaning against it, western hat tipped back, one ankle crossed over the other in a relaxed stance, watching her approach.

"Whoa, guys . . . whoa now. Hey, Phil. Been waiting long?" she asked, braking the ATV and dog team to a halt in front of her storage shed.

"Nope. Passed you on the road headed this direction and figured you'd be back soon. Still looks silly to me to see dogs pulling one of those things with wheels."

"Well, it may look funny, but it's great for training, as long as you stay on a trail. But it's a heavy mother to haul out of the brush if the mutts make a wrong turn, as they did twice today." She glanced at the jeans, civilian jacket, and western hat he was wearing. "Let me take care of these guys, and then I'll find us a drink—if you're off duty."

"Give you a hand?"

"Sure. The whole crew's gotta be watered. You can start on that while I get these guys out of harness, if you don't mind."

He nodded, heading for the buckets standing by the outdoor tap.

Half an hour later, chores done, they headed for the motor home, passing the excavation full of forms and drying concrete on the way. Becker hesitated on the edge of the pit.

"You've got a ways to go. When do your logs show up?"

"Next week." Jessie grinned, brightening at the thought. "All cut, sized, numbered, and ready to raise."

As they walked on, she dug into a jeans pocket for the key but stopped before using it.

Sitting on the step of the motor home stood a small vase from some florist, contents wrapped in typical green waxed paper.

"Hey, somebody loves you," Becker said. "Your birthday or something?"

"No," Jessie said, with a puzzled wrinkling of her forehead. "My birthday's in October."

Picking the vase up, she opened the door and led the way inside, setting the offering on the table as she passed, headed for the galley, where she retrieved the bottle of Jameson's.

"This okay, Phil, or would you rather have a beer?"

"Beer, please." Becker removed the western hat and hung it up before sitting at the table.

Jessie handed him a cold bottle of Killian's from the refrigerator and, pouring herself a splash of the Irish whiskey, settled across the table from him. After raising her arms behind her head to stretch her back and shoulders, she leaned both elbows on the table, took a sip of the Jameson's and sighed.

"They ran me a merry chase. I've let their training go for a few days, and they were rested and full of the devil." Reaching, she took the small green bud vase and stripped off the paper to reveal a single red rosebud, standing tall and just beginning to open. "This is a nice surprise. Wonder who sent it?"

Seeing that there was no card attached to the flower or vase, she searched the green paper she had cast aside for some clue to the identity of the sender, but although there was an envelope bearing the florist's name stapled to one corner, it was empty.

"Card could've dropped off somewhere in the delivery truck," Becker suggested. "Or else you've got a secret admirer." His grin was full of mischief.

Jessie felt herself flush and glanced at her watch to hide her unexpected reaction to his teasing. Six-thirty: too late to call the florist. "Well, it's a treat, whoever sent it. I'll check in the morning and find out."

"Good idea." Becker took a long swallow of his beer, then reached to pull some folded pages from the pocket of the jacket he had tossed in a chair. As he smoothed them open on the table, Jessie pushed the rose and vase aside and leaned forward to look.

"The autopsy report?"

"Yes. Thought you'd like to know what John found. He tried to call but got no answer."

"I was out running today's rodeo with clowns for a team. What'd he find?"

"Well, it's the body of an old man, all right. I won't go into the justifications for that observation, but you know Timmons wouldn't make a mistake."

"Sure. What else? Does he know how long ago it was buried?"

"Not yet, but he's estimating sometime between twenty and twenty-five years. There's no sign of violence, no evidence of injury, no bullet or knife mark on any of the bones. No drugs or poisons showed up in the tests he ran. It looks like he just died naturally, but . . ." Becker frowned and hesitated.

"But what?" Jessie asked, watching his easygoing expression shift to one of concern mixed with uncertainty.

He glanced up, still frowning, and shuffled the papers on the table uneasily. "This is not for publication and it's not in the report, because there's no evidence. But you know how John gets hunches sometimes?"

She nodded.

"You mustn't tell anyone, but I'll tell you what he told me on the phone. The way the body was positioned, in a fetal curl, with the arms drawn into the chest and the knees pulled up, made him wonder if the old guy, whoever he is, might have frozen to death."

Jessie took a thoughtful sip of her whiskey, then shook her head. "He wasn't buried in the winter. John said the ground couldn't have been frozen when the grave was dug."

"That doesn't mean he died when he was buried. Might have died in the winter, and whoever buried him waited for the ground to thaw. It's possible. Many places in Alaska they don't bury people who die in the winter. They store the bodies where they'll stay frozen and bury them all at once in the spring."

"You're right." She sat up straighter, staring at him. "I'd forgotten that. One fall in Anchorage, they decided to dig a few graves before the ground froze, so they'd have them ready. But when it got cold, some homeless people moved in for shelter, even built fires to keep warm, so they went back to the cold storage idea."

"I remember." Shuffling papers again, Becker found one in particular and held it out to her. "There were two other things. This is one."

It was a fax copy of a photograph, but the item on some kind of dark background was clear and identifiable: a pendant in the shape of a butterfly set with several light-colored stones, hanging on a delicate chain. Gold or silver, it was impossible to tell in black and white.

"Gold," Becker said in answer to her question. "John found it in the chest cavity, mixed with dirt that fell in as the body decomposed. He thinks it was probably laid or tossed into the grave on top of the old man, before the soil was shoveled back."

Jessie stared at the necklace in the picture, mystified. "That's weird," she commented, looking up at Becker, who nodded agreement. "It doesn't look like something that would have anything to do with an old man, does it?"

"No."

"You said two things. What else?"

Becker gave her an oddly intense professional look and thought a moment before answering.

"You've absolutely got to keep this to yourself. There were two threads in a loop around the wrist bones. From the adhesive he found on them, John knows they came from a piece of duct tape and thinks the wrists had been taped together and the tape removed before the guy was buried. Whoever pulled off the tape didn't notice the threads."

"But that could mean that somebody . . ."

"Killed him? That's what it makes you think, all right. John wants to know who. He's taking this one slow and careful. It may be a while till we know much more."

She laid the photo of the necklace on the table and stared at him, thinking hard. "Did John find out who he is?"

"Not yet. Two Anchorage shooting victims and a guy somebody stabbed in Nome came into the lab all at once, day before yesterday, so he's been swamped. Said to tell you he'd get back to it soon. What he actually said was, 'The old guy's been in the ground so long he won't mind waiting awhile longer.' "

Jessie smiled, hearing Timmons gravelly voice in the second-hand words.

The conversation moved to other things—a girl Becker was dating, the construction under way in Jessie's yard. It was half an hour before Becker left, off duty and headed home.

She made herself some eggs, bacon, and hash browns. Becker had forgotten to take the picture of the butterfly necklace; it still lay on the table, and, fascinated, she examined it again as she ate, wondering how it had ever wound up in the lost grave of an old man who might have frozen to death, might have been murdered and buried sometime afterward, maybe around this same time of year.

Tired and knowing she had another strenuous day with the dogs ahead of her, Jessie readied herself for bed. Then, before propping herself on pillows to read until she grew sleepy, she turned off the lights, opened the door, and stood looking out into the clearing with its surrounding birch trees, their slender trunks so white they almost glowed in the late northern light. As she watched the gray evening shadows steal color from the new green of the birch leaves, she was reminded that in about a week, the summer solstice would swing the year on its hinges again and the days would begin to shorten toward winter.

From somewhere among the trees, a hint of wood smoke drifted in on a breath of breeze that whispered through the birch leaves—her neighbor taking comfort from the cool night air in the glow of a fire. The dog yard was quiet, all her mutts comfortably settled for the night.

She took a deep breath and leaned against the metal door frame, content with what her senses brought her, and was rewarded with the soft call of an owl from somewhere close in the dark under the trees, like someone blowing gently into an empty bottle. *Whoo.* A silence. Then, *whoo* again. Such a deadly fierceness of feathers for a small bird, she thought as she listened, a silent shadow, armed like a Scythian with scimitar beak and talons, hunting in the night for the unwary mouse or shrew.

"Good luck, owl."

Locking the door, she went quickly through the almost-dark toward bed, her wish to read overpowered by a sudden irresistible desire to lay her head on the pillow and curl up under her warm quilt. As she passed the dinette table, the dark silhouette of the rose in its slender vase was visible for a second against the fading light of the window. She wondered again who had sent it but was back to planning the next day's training before sleep gradually erased all puzzles from her mind. Two runs would assure that all her dogs had been exercised and would take until lunchtime. Then she intended to drive to Palmer, to satisfy a growing curiosity of her own.

Chapter 7

 At two o'clock the next afternoon, Jessie pulled her pickup into the parking lot of the Matanuska-Susitna Borough building in Palmer. Up a short flight of stairs, on the first floor, she located the assessor's office and waited at the tall counter for assistance.

"I want to find out everything I can about the background of the property I own on Knik Road," she told the tall man who stepped forward to help her. "I need to know everyone who's owned it."

"Which part of Knik Road are we talking about?"

"Approximately eight miles from Wasilla—just before Settlers Bay on the north side of the road."

"Do you know the number of the lot?"

Jessie explained that her records had burned with her cabin

in the spring and that she was still in the process of collecting duplicate copies of deeds, insurance records—everything. "I have the insurance papers at home. I can show you on a map, but do I have to prove I own it to see your records?"

"No," he said with a grin, as he reached below the counter for a map. "They're public records, but if you want to go all the way back to the original owner or homesteader, we don't have everything you need. Earlier papers are filed in the recorder's office next door—some may even be in Anchorage."

The map he unfolded and spread out in front of her covered the whole counter and then some. They located Knik Road and the lot that belonged to Jessie and then began the search for information.

Two hours later she was driving toward home, the seat beside her full of papers, copies of maps and records, and two paperbound books of the area's history, including Knik Road. She had learned a lot more than she had anticipated when she began her quest for information, even without a trip to Anchorage. She had visited three different offices and spoken to the assessor, an archaeologist in the Cultural Resources Office, and the recorder of deeds. Now she could hardly wait to reach home and study what she had collected, but first she had one more errand.

Pulling into a mall between Palmer and Wasilla, she parked and went into the florist she had identified from the small envelope on her single rose.

A short dark-haired woman wearing a rainbow-striped apron met her at the counter. "Can I help you with something?"

"I hope so," Jessie told her, and described the floral tribute she had received the day before. "The card must have fallen off, and I'd like to know who to thank."

Opening a drawer, the clerk took out a clipboard that held a list of the previous day's deliveries. Laying it on the counter, she asked for Jessie's name and address, then ran a finger down the delivery record. Partway down, she hesitated, then looked up with a half-embarrassed, half-delighted smile. "Oh, that one. A red rose in a bud vase, right? Sorry, there wasn't supposed to be a card with that one."

"Why not?"

"The person who ordered it didn't leave a name, just asked for it to be delivered without a message."

Jessie stared at her in dumbfounded silence for a long moment. Who in the world would send her flowers without a name? And why?

"Was it a man or a woman?" she asked.

"I can't say. This person specifically requested that it be delivered anonymously."

"Why?"

"Didn't give a reason, just the order."

"Was it somebody local?" Jessie asked. She had expected that identifying the sender of the rose would simply be a matter of contacting the florist. Now she found herself thumbing through her mental file of friends and acquaintances, confused and somehow irritated at not being able to accomplish that goal. The self-satisfied smile of the woman across the counter did not help to quell an uneasy feeling that had crept in along with exasperation.

"Look," she said, trying another tack, "I promise I'll never let this *person* know that you told me, but I really need to know who sent me the rose."

The woman shook her head, still maintaining her prim I've-got-a-secret smile, though it wavered a bit. "Sorry. A promise is a promise. You wouldn't like it if I spoiled a surprise *you* wanted to send someone, would you?"

"*I*"—Jessie leaned forward with both hands on the counter to take a deep breath, finally out of patience—"wouldn't send someone flowers without a card or a message. It's a little creepy, don't you think?"

"No," said the florist, her smile vanishing as she took a step back, tossed the delivery list back into the drawer, and shut it with a sharp report. "No, I *don't* think so. I think it's nice and you're just insecure." She walked away, leaving Jessie alone at the counter, staring after her in astonished resentment.

. . .

"*Insecure!* I'm *insecure?*" she muttered to herself, during the fifteen minutes it took her to drive back to the Cottonwood Mall south of Wasilla, where she stopped for groceries. "The smug bitch! Whoever *sent* the damned thing is insecure. Why not just include a name and have done with it?"

Still, the idea of an unidentified fan or well-wisher was not totally without appeal—someone who had gone to the trouble to send her a lovely thing they thought she would enjoy. It had to be a positive thing, didn't it? Negative feelings were unlikely to be expressed with flowers. But she remembered a bouquet of lilies sent to her at the hospital by a stalker, after he had tampered with her truck and caused a near-fatal accident. It didn't make her feel better.

By the time she had done her shopping, loaded three sacks of groceries into the pickup, and was headed out Knik Road, her sense of humor caught up with her and she couldn't suppress a chuckle, remembering the woman's stunned expression at hearing that Jessie considered the anonymous gift creepy. Guess I could have found a less shocking word, she decided. Odd, maybe, or unusual. Creepy may have been a bit over the top.

Throughout the evening, whenever she noticed the rose in its green glass bud vase, she had to grin. Knowing who had sent it really didn't matter much, and things had a way of eventually working out. She would probably find out in time and be able not only to thank the sender but to relate her experience with the unyielding florist as well. Giving up on her mental list of possible candidates, she turned her thoughts to more mundane matters.

Then, having cared for her dogs and in the process of pouring pasta into a kettle of boiling water, a single obvious name popped into her mind that she realized she had been suppressing: *Alex Jensen,* the state trooper whose move to Idaho had broken up their relationship four months earlier. Stirring the pasta so it wouldn't stick to the bottom of the kettle, she stared unseeing at the boiling water, her heart doing odd thumps in her chest.

It made perfect sense—was the sort of thing he might do. Though their split had been clean and she had suggested they not write or talk to each other, she really hadn't expected the silence between them to last long—had thought he would write anyway—or call. Twice, when she had answered the phone and heard nothing but open silence on the line before someone quietly hung up, she had suspected it might be Alex and not just a wrong number. When her cabin burned, she had half expected him to get in touch. She assumed that his friend and fellow trooper, Phil Becker, must be keeping him up to date on her, but, not willing to provide false hope through a third-party communication that might send an unintended message, she had never asked.

Laying aside the spoon and leaving the pasta to cook on its own, Jessie sat down at the table and pulled the rose across to rest in front of her. Fully opened now, it glowed deep red in a late-afternoon sunbeam that found its way in through the venetian blinds that covered the window. She frowned as she examined it thoughtfully. Even from Idaho, he could have sent it; there were telephones and credit cards. Or he could have had Phil do the legwork, she realized, remembering that a person had gone into the florist shop. She recalled his comment and mischievous grin, the day it had appeared: "Or else you've got a secret admirer." If Phil was involved, his suggestion could have been an attempt at misdirection and camouflage. But she couldn't find out without a direct approach and was determined not to question him.

With one finger, she gently touched a perfect, soft, velvety rose petal. Leaning forward, she took a deep breath, then frowned and sat back in disappointment. Why didn't roses have fragrance anymore? It seemed a comment on the lack of substance in much of the modern commercial world.

If the rose *was* from Alex, why send it now? What could he mean by such a subtle gesture? Well, she thought, shaking her head, two could play at waiting games. When the timer rang for the pasta, she had decided to say nothing—just wait and see what, if anything, transpired. It might not be Alex after all. Perhaps she only wished it were.

A soft knock on the door startled her, as she was tossing the drained pasta with a light sauce of fresh tomatoes, garlic, olive oil, and basil that she had set to marinate earlier. Wiping her hands on a kitchen towel, she went first to look out the window.

A man stood outside, looking at her dog yard with his back to the door, hands thrust into the pockets of a light jacket. Another reporter? Not recognizing him, Jessie hesitated, then reached for the handle, feeling a bit silly at her own paranoia. If it was anyone from the media, she would send him packing.

At the sound of the door opening, her visitor swung around to offer her a familiar and unexpected grin.

"Hey, Jess. I hoped you'd be here."

"Lynn Ehlers! You're a long way from home. What the hell are you doing back in Alaska?" Jessie shoved the door wide open and stepped back to give him room and a welcoming smile. "Come on in!"

As he accepted her invitation, he pulled off a billed cap with YUKON QUEST, 1,000 MILE SLED DOG RACE printed on the front and held it with both hands in front of him like a schoolboy.

The hug Jessie gave him was full of surprised pleasure and affection for the Minnesota musher, with whom she had shared good times and bad during the previous February's Yukon Quest distance race.

The hug was returned, with enthusiasm and warmth. "Hey, you're looking good."

"You too."

Stepping back, she made an appreciative assessment of Ehlers. He was a little older than herself but about the same height, and the lower part of his face was still covered with a neatly trimmed dark beard, enlivened with a sprinkling of gray. The creases around his mouth and eyes spoke of time spent squinting into the glare of sun on snow, though they fell attractively enough into a frame for his infectious smile.

"Sit, sit." She waved a hand toward the table. "Have you eaten? I was just about to. What can I get you, beer? A drink?"

Ehlers shed his jacket, tossed it aside with the cap, and sat, as instructed.

"Guess I could use a beer," he told her. "I was going to suggest we go out for dinner, but it looks like I'm too late."

Fishing a cold Killian's from the depths of the refrigerator, Jessie set it in front of him. "Glass?"

He shook his head. "Naw, I'm fine."

"Eat with me," she invited. "This is just about ready."

·   ·   ·

They had cleaned up the pasta, finished the new six-pack of Killian's. It had been late enough to be growing dark when Ehlers drove his pickup, its box of individual compartments for hauling sled dogs filling the bed as usual, away down Jessie's long driveway. Silhouetted in the light that fell through the open door of the motor home, she looked after him and waved as he turned onto Knik Road, heading toward town.

What a great surprise, she thought with a yawn, as she tossed the last empty bottle in the trash, turned off the light over the sinkful of dirty dishes, and headed for her bed in the back of the Winnebago.

They had talked for hours, catching each other up on what had filled the months since they ran the same race from White-horse to Fairbanks, with all its complications. Jessie told him about discovering the body in the excavation, the plans for her new cabin, and the construction she anticipated would fill the rest of the summer. Ehlers explained that he had moved to Alaska from Minnesota, at least temporarily, to train his teams in the area in which he intended to race them the following winter.

"Want to have another shot at the Quest and decided I didn't want to drive all the way up here next fall. Nothing to hold me in Minnesota, so I might as well train 'em here. Besides, there's a lot of territory I want to have a look at."

He was sharing a kennel with an Iditarod musher between Wasilla and Willow, a few miles to the northwest.

"We'll have to do some runs together between here and Skwentna," Jessie suggested. "As soon as there's enough snow, I take my guys out there for overnighters. We could go together. More fun for everybody."

Now, as she brushed her teeth, she was again pleased at the idea of having someone besides Billy, her handler, with whom to run dogs. Billy was a sweet kid. She liked him and appreci-ated his help with the work it took to keep a kennel going. But it would be nice to have an older, experienced racer with whom to share the trail—especially Lynn, who was good, easygoing company.

Warm and drowsy in her bed, half asleep, she suddenly remembered the question he had asked her during the February race: "You and that trooper . . . an item?"

He had not asked again tonight, for which she was grateful, knowing she didn't want to talk about that particular relationship and its painful ending just now. The afternoon's speculations on the origin of the rose had raised some old feelings she did not wish to examine, content with her decision to wait and see what, if anything, came of it.

She also wanted to know more about Ehlers's move to Alaska. People came north for many different reasons, some leaving problems rather than solving them. Perhaps the racing and training was all there was to it. If so, it was enough and had been for many sled dog racing aficionados. But she had a feeling there was more involved. There had been something reserved in his brief explanation of a decision that must have required serious consideration, for he did not impress her as a person who did things on the spur of the moment.

Thinking back, she recalled his saying something about a divorce during the Yukon Quest. Perhaps coming to Alaska was part of a move to start over in a place where he wouldn't constantly be confronted with a failed relationship. If that was the case, given her split with Jensen it was a situation she could understand. She wondered if she might not be projecting her own feelings of failure, on one hand, and relief on the other, in clinging to her chosen lifestyle and occupation.

Lynn Ehlers was a bit of a puzzle. There was something reticent and wary about the way he changed the subject once or twice during the evening, as if the conversation had touched on areas too close to a nerve for his liking—or his willingness to pursue. It was probably nothing but her imagination, Jessie decided, and would work itself out eventually. After all, they didn't really know each other *that* well, and everyone was cautious in new relationships, weren't they? She certainly was.

Rolling over and wrapping the quilt comfortably around her, Jessie drifted off. Her last conscious thought: There would be work tomorrow; Prentice and crew would be back to prepare to pour a floor in the basement.

Chapter 8

 The day was slightly overcast, with patches of blue between clots of cloud that were sweeping over the Pioneer Peak, when a green Durango SUV swung off Old Knik Road across from Bodenburg Creek just east of the bridge and parked. A short, stocky man got out and strolled across the lot to the edge of the bank to look down at the river below. The water was high, swollen with snowmelt from the surrounding heights and opaque with silt, ground into a fine powder by the extreme weight and motion of nearby glaciers and washed into the river's flow by countless streams and rivulets.

With a boyish grin, he turned and walked quickly back to the SUV, the spring in his step reminiscent of a kid playing hooky, as in a way he was. The note he had left on his desk in a Palmer office read, *Gone fishing! The Kings are in the river and my wife's out of town!* Though he knew that catching King, or any salmon for that matter, was illegal in the Knik River, the tempting idea of *accidentally* hooking into one of the few that found their way up it to spawn was irresistible. He would use tackle suitable to catching Dolly Varden, a cousin of the Arctic Char, with a medium to small spoon and some herring on 30-pound-test line, which was heavier than necessary for Dollies. If a King should take bait that was attractive to both fish—well, he could always let it go, couldn't he?

Putting on sunglasses and his battered fishing hat, he stepped into chest-high waders, adjusted the shoulder straps, collected his equipment, closed and locked his vehicle, and headed for the riverbank. A raven scolded him from the top of a nearby cottonwood, but he ignored the raucous reproach and was soon standing hip deep in water, casting a line into the current that he could feel tugging at his legs. Though the morning was warm, the water was icy enough to make him glad he had worn both long underwear and jeans beneath the waders.

Sunshine came and went as clouds continued to drift across the sky, making it difficult at times to see in the bright reflection of the river's surface. His second cast barely missed tangling with a deadhead log that came gliding along in the current and forced him to reel in quickly to avoid losing his lure.

Except for the whoosh and gurgle of the water, it was quiet and peaceful, pleasant to stand alone, outdoors and away from his cubbyhole of an office. Through the long winter he had felt like a nocturnal animal in the windowless space, arriving before it grew light in the morning and leaving after dark. He was not one of the Alaskans who suffered from SAD, Seasonal Affective Disorder, a winter depression caused by lack of sunlight, but he was always glad when the days grew longer and increasing hours of daylight gave him time to enjoy being outside without being cold. It was, after all, what had drawn him so far north in the first place, nine years earlier: unspoiled wilderness practically at his back door with plenty of opportunity for fishing.

For half an hour he caught nothing, though once something took the herring he had used as bait. Then he caught two Dollies in five minutes and had just swung his line back into the water when a shout of laughter drew his attention to the bridge on his left.

Two teenagers on bicycles were pedaling hard across it, the one behind calling to the other to slow down.

The fisherman watched, hoping they would continue along the main road that turned west at the end of the bridge. Instead, they turned left, in his direction, pulling into the parking lot with a crunch and rattle of gravel as they applied their brakes and slid to a dusty stop near the SUV. Dropping his bicycle, the taller of the two trotted over to the edge of the bank and looked down at the man in the water.

"Hey!" he hollered. "Catch anything?"

The other boy came to join him and immediately tossed a fist-sized rock into the current.

"Dammit!" the fisherman swore, turning to face the two with a scowl. "Cut that out."

"Well, sor-*ry!*" the kid returned, with a challenging curl of his lip.

"Look," the man begged, "I'm trying to fish here. Go somewhere else to throw rocks, okay?"

"It's a free country," the rock thrower snapped back. "We got as much right to be here as you."

He picked up another stone and hefted it speculatively, a sly grin revealing a chipped front tooth as he awaited a reaction from the man in the water.

With a sigh the fisherman turned his back, intending to ignore the two. With a *thook,* the stone hit the water near enough to splash his face and right arm.

"Goddammit," he growled, and swung around to make his way out of the river and clamber up the bank.

The two boys ran for their bicycles, shouting with glee. *"Nyah, nyah,"* the rock thrower yelled back over his shoulder, as they pedaled away in the direction they had come and vanished behind some trees.

The fisherman watched for them to come into view on the bridge, but evidently they had gone down the road beyond it, for they did not reappear. In a few minutes, however, he saw one of them sneak a look around the concrete pier at the near end that stood between land and water. Over the sound of the river, he could hear them hooting still and calling out challenges he was too far away to understand.

Rotten kids, he thought, wading back into the water and preparing to swing out his line. But he remembered being that awkward age—trying his best to swagger in manly fashion and confronting almost every new situation with defiance. As long as they left him alone, he would give them the benefit of a tolerance he knew they would resent if they realized it existed. At that age, you were either one up or one down, and none of them could stand to be one down. Individually, they were probably okay kids. It was measuring themselves against each other that made every encounter an irresistible dare. Aw, well. . . .

He had just cast out when another log came sweeping along, closer to the bank this time. Almost submerged, it drifted past as he stepped back and scrambled to reel in and yank the line from its path, barely succeeding. In the attempt to save his tackle he saw only a broken branch, which revolved with the log to disappear beneath the gray water, and a flash of some blue fabric that sank out of sight as it rolled and drifted away.

Settling back into his former stance, the fisherman cast again, then lifted his eyes to watch an eagle draw lazy circles in the air high over the river. It was looking for salmon, no doubt, for, exhausted with spawning, some of the big fish would have floated into eddies that washed them against the bank to die and become dinner for the eagle. In a few minutes the large bird landed in the top of a spruce behind the fisherman and perched there, keeping an eye on the water below, a silhouette against the snow that remained on the highest of the surrounding peaks. "Don't expect any of my catch," he told it with a grin.

A strong tug on his line reminded him of what he had come here to do. In seconds the fish seemed to realize that the bit of herring it had swallowed in a gulp was not free for the taking but came with a sharp price. Solidly hooked, it ran upriver to the extent of the line he had cast, so the fisherman played out more until it stopped and began to drift back toward where he stood. Then, reeling as fast as he could, he took up slack until, once again, he felt the fish resist, much closer this time. It broke water, and for an instant he saw not the familiar light bluish-olive of a

Dolly, with its bright orange spots, but dark spots on the silvery iridescence of a tail and body, slightly pink in spawning colors, that thrashed the water as it disappeared beneath the surface. A King! A medium-sized King, or Chinook, as it was also called.

Finally, a fish worth the catching! he thought, as he adjusted his stance, getting ready for the coming fight.

Three times the salmon ran and once it leaped clear of the water as it struck the limit of the line and all but danced on the surface. The fisherman heard a vehicle pass on the road behind him and prayed it was not a game warden about to apprehend him with an illegal fish on his line. But it continued on without slowing and left him to the battle joined.

Slowly the fish began to tire and its runs shortened. Closer and closer it came to where he stood. He had just calculated that in another run or two he would have it, when he heard the clatter of a bicycle falling onto the gravel in the parking lot behind him and running feet approaching fast.

Not now, he prayed. *Oh,* please, *not now.*

"Hey, mister," a tentative voice behind him called. "Mister? I'm sorry I threw those rocks. But you better come and see. There's a—there's somebody dead in the water under the bridge."

"Look, you little shit. I'm not interested in your games, so get out of here. Go play somewhere else." He tossed the words back over his shoulder at the kid, not taking his eyes from the river for a moment.

"Please, mister. It's not a game. There really *is* a dead woman. *Re-eally!* You better *come.*"

"Yeah, right. I'm supposed to believe—"

Something in the tone of the boy's voice stopped what he was saying and made him glance back.

The smaller of the two boys stood above on the bank, freckles standing out on his pale face, eyes wide, lips pinched tight to control their trembling. Nothing of the smart aleck remained. He was suddenly just a kid in trouble, looking for an adult to take charge of something beyond his ability to handle.

Startled, the fisherman went on reeling in his line, hands automatically continuing with their occupation, while he considered the situation.

"*Please*, mister."

A dead woman? Not likely. What the hell *had* they found?

The salmon did not leap again, but its dorsal fin appeared above the surface as it struggled weakly against the line.

With a sigh, the fisherman lowered his pole to horizontal above the water and gave it a sharp jerk. With a last twist from the tired salmon, the line parted, recoiling as it lost tension. The fish vanished into the depths of the river, taking his tackle and bait with it.

The fisherman raised a hand, pushed back the brim of his hat with his thumb, and gave his watery opponent a disappointed but respectful half salute with two fingers. Turning, he climbed from the water and went to see what could possibly have engendered such a shift in attitude in the boy who trotted along beside him toward the SUV.

"Thanks, mister," he said. "It's really gross. You know—*gross!* And scary," he whimpered to himself.

Chapter 9

Vic Prentice and one of his men had already been walking around in the basement space when Jessie stepped outside that morning. She had raised a gloved hand to wave and hiked to where he stood, assessing one of the forms with a grin of accomplishment on his face, while Dell used a hose to spray water over the concrete and forms.

"A couple more days and we can strip the forms off," he said. "In this warm weather, the mud's curing faster than I expected."

"Doesn't it have to be dry?" she asked, wondering about the water Dell was using.

"With concrete it's more a matter of a reaction between the cement and water," Vic informed her. "If you don't keep it wet, it won't cure correctly. Concrete can even harden under water, if it's the right mix. This is doing fine, but we've gotta keep it damp for a bit longer."

"Terrific. Then the basement floor, right?"

"Right. Remove the forms and the floor will cozy up to the walls to make sure they don't shift with the weight of the back-fill. I'm going to put you to work painting waterproof sealer on the outside before we add blue board insulation and have Peter-son shove back the dirt. Then we'll be able to walk up to the building when we start with the cabin floor and logs."

"What else can I do?"

"Well . . ." He thought for a minute. "Nothing, yet, but as soon as the forms come off, you can lay sill seal on top of the walls before we bolt down the plate and the first logs."

They were gone in an hour, leaving Jessie to spend the rest of the day with her dogs. She had not taken time to sort through the information she had collected in Palmer the day before, had a number of chores to do in the dog yard first, and planned to sit down with the paperwork later in the day. It was time to change the straw that made a bed for each animal inside its box, so she and Billy Steward were soon hard at work. Billy raked out the old straw, which Jessie replaced, spending a few minutes with each dog as she did so, checking its health and well-being carefully.

"Bliss, you old faker, come out of there."

The dog to which she referred lay soaking up the sun, half in and half out of her box, completely relaxed. She had opened one eye just wide enough to see Jessie coming, but, not wanting to move, had closed it again, feigning a snooze. Her head came up with a doggy grin as her owner dropped to her knees and gave the bitch's ears a friendly rub. With an affectionate lick to Jessie's bare wrist, she stood up, stretched, and leaned against the gifted hands that explored her belly.

"Pups on the way," Jessie commented, with a frown. "I didn't mean to breed her this year."

"Sorry," Billy told her. "I should have noticed that Tux was loose."

"Not your fault." She stood and shook her head. "If I hadn't forgotten to tighten the ring on his box, he'd never have pulled it out. Besides, Tux should sire good pups and I promised you one from the next litter, didn't I?"

Billy grinned and agreed, before using the rake to finish cleaning out Bliss's box.

They had completed their work in the yard and were repairing a sticky throttle on the four-wheeler when Jessie looked up to see the crime lab van once again travel the length of her drive and park beside the motor home. As she stripped off her gloves and moved to meet him, a lift lowered John Timmons to ground level in his wheelchair. Dressed casually in sweats with the sleeves cut out of the pullover, the muscles in his brawny arms were noticeably impressive as he maneuvered himself rapidly over the rough ground and halted near the basement excavation. Behind him, two lab assistants had climbed out and begun to unload shovels.

Timmons grimaced at the concerned expression on Jessie's face as she realized that more digging was about to commence.

"John—?"

Spinning himself around with gloved hands on the wheels of his chair, he faced her directly. "Sorry, Jessie. Hold on now till I explain. We're not going to dig up your project, I promise. But we've got to take another look."

"Why?" She stopped in front of him, hands on hips, demanding an answer. "You think there's somebody else buried here somewhere?"

"I don't know, but we've got to check. The necklace that was buried with the old man?"

"The butterfly Becker showed me."

"Yeah. Well, it turned out to be related to an old case, a particularly nasty one. You remember Hansen, the Anchorage baker who murdered all those prostitutes in the seventies and eighties—flew a lot of them out and buried them up the Knik River?"

She nodded, her attention now fully focused, as he briefly went over the case of the first and worst serial murderer in the state of Alaska.

In February of 1984, Robert Hansen, a churchgoing family man who was respected in the community, had gone on trial for assaulting, kidnapping, and murdering a number of prostitutes who had disappeared from the Anchorage tenderloin district over a twelve-year period. Three days after the trial started, confronted with a landslide of evidence collected by the Anchorage Police Department and the Alaska State Troopers, he changed his plea to guilty and, in two days, confessed to seventeen homicides. He was sentenced to 461 years plus life without parole for the four murders with which he was charged. The district attorney agreed not to charge him with the rest in exchange for his acknowledgment of their commission and his agreement to assist the state troopers in locating the bodies.

"Hansen confessed to only seventeen of the murders," Timmons continued. "He identified ten or twelve of the burial sites for the troopers—along the Knik River, a couple of other rivers and creeks, at Horseshoe and Figure Eight lakes—when they took him out on helicopter flights, but on a map they found in his house he had marked twenty-three different locations.

"In April when the ground had thawed they went back to the locations he had identified and dug up a few more of the women he had killed. Several other bodies were found in subsequent searches. One was found by accident by an off-duty police officer, but there were a number that were never located. He claimed that six of the marks did not indicate that a body was buried there at all and refused to talk about any more of the missing women. One, whom he claimed to have dropped off the Knik River railroad bridge, they hadn't a prayer of finding.

"A total of twelve women were identified and accounted for. The others—the ones he confessed to killing that they didn't find, and the ones he refused to take responsibility for—were not only lost but their identities were lost as well. Somewhere out there in the wilderness, there are still the remains of known or nameless working girls—Hansen's victims or victims of someone else."

Timmons paused, and Jessie waited, knowing there was more. Somehow the butterfly necklace tied the Hansen murders to the body of the old man she had found in the basement excavation. She also wondered about that last phrase: *victims of someone else?*

"The necklace," he went on at last, "was described back then, by an exotic dancer in Anchorage, as belonging to her roommate. The roommate vanished in 1979, while they were both working at a place called the Wild Cherry. We looked for it in a collection of the things Hansen took from the women he murdered—souvenirs found in his attic—but it wasn't there. Now, over twenty years later, it turns up here, with another body. I'm afraid the missing dancer may be here—buried like the old man. So you can understand why we've gotta have a look."

Jessie nodded. "Of course." But her heart sank, as much at the possibility of another body somewhere on her property as at another delay in building her cabin. "Nothing's going on here for the next couple of days till the concrete is dry. Will it take longer than that?"

"I certainly hope not. It shouldn't."

They began the careful process of going over the ground in Jessie's yard in search of any differences in soil color or texture that might reveal the presence of another burial, poking into it and digging it up in places. It was obviously a difficult task in a yard that had been heavily used as a kennel, especially considering the fire and the amount of earth that had already been moved from one place to another in digging the basement. They were still at it hours later when Becker's patrol car cruised up the drive.

Climbing out he crossed to Timmons, who was leaning from his chair to grab up a handful of dirt, which he rubbed between his fingers, frowning thoughtfully.

"Hey, John. Don't like to interrupt you, but I think you'd better load up and come with me. Couple of kids and a fisherman found a floater in the Knik. A woman."

Jessie, who, on her knees at a dog box, had been examining the condition of her pregnant bitch Bliss with careful, knowledgeable fingers, heard what he said, got up, and trotted over.

Timmons dropped the dirt he was examining and brushed his hands on his knees.

"The hell you say. When?"

"This morning—less than two hours ago. The lab said you were out here, so I thought I'd better round you up."

"Right. Shit, I hate floaters—almost as much as Jensen," Timmons growled, then stopped abruptly and glanced at Jessie, realizing the name he had dropped might not be welcome to her.

Becker lowered his head, refusing to meet her eyes, and scuffed at the ground with the toe of one boot.

Jessie couldn't help smiling at their chagrin. They looked like a pair of boys who had accidentally used a four-letter word in front of the preacher.

"It's okay, John. You *can* mention him, you know. We didn't split as enemies."

"Hurrumph." He nodded once, sharply, as he cleared his throat. "Yes—well. We'd better pack up and get on over there, Phil."

"Right."

As Timmons called his men from their search, Becker turned to Jessie with a request. "I've got a woman in the car who came out from Anchorage asking questions about the body we found here." He nodded toward the patrol car, and Jessie realized for the first time that there was someone in the passenger seat. "I brought her along to talk to John, but I can't take her out to this new scene and haven't time to go back to the office. Would you do me a favor and drive her back to her car in Palmer?"

"Sure," Jessie agreed. "I have to take Bliss to the vet anyway. Who is she?"

"Bonnie Russell, the sister of one of Hansen's victims—one we never found, Brenda Miller, Jo-Jo."

*　*　*

The woman who stepped from the patrol car was in her mid-forties, tall and slim. She stood very straight. As she walked across the yard with Becker, Jessie noticed that, though her hair was streaked with gray, she moved with the grace and posture of a dancer or a model. Her calm, dignified greeting was a nod, rather than a spoken hello, and her eyes narrowed slightly as, for a moment, she assessed the musher whom most of Alaska recognized, either by name or from newspaper or television pictures. When she finally spoke, her tone was low and strong.

"I saw you leave the starting gate in Anchorage the year you had such trouble on the Iditarod."

Jessie watched as the crime lab van followed Becker's car onto Knik Road and disappeared toward Wasilla. When she turned, she found Bonnie Russell looking not down the drive but into the basement excavation, strain drawing two deep vertical lines in her forehead above the bridge of her nose.

She glanced at Jessie and bit her lip. "You found a body in there?" she asked quietly.

"Yes. An old man. John Timmons thinks it was probably the original homesteader."

"But he thinks there might be other bodies, or they wouldn't be doing more digging here. Yes?"

"Maybe."

"Maybe my sister."

Jessie felt her stomach turn over and her heart rate increase, as a surge of tension swept through her. She did not want to talk to this woman—about her lost sister, Robert Hansen, or the body of the old man.

"Do you think—" Bonnie began.

Jessie broke in. "Look, I'm not ready yet. I don't want go to town in these clothes, smelling like a dog yard refugee. I've been working with my mutts all morning, and I need to wash and change. Why don't you come in and have some iced tea while I clean up? It won't take me long. We can hit the road in less than half an hour."

Hearing herself babbling defensively, she stopped abruptly and there was a brief silence, as they looked at each other, Bonnie with a half smile and a hint of understanding in her eyes.

"I make you uncomfortable," she said, turning toward the Winnebago. "It's all right. I make a lot of people uncomfortable. I'd like some tea, thanks. Go ahead and do what you need to do. I don't mind waiting."

"I'm sorry," Jessie stammered. "It's just . . ."

"It's okay," Bonnie told her, the smile tightening slightly. "I'm used to it."

When Jessie was ready and came back into the galley of the motor home, she found Bonnie still sitting at the table, staring out the window, her glass of iced tea only half gone. She looked up as Jessie paused in the doorway to button the sleeve of a plaid shirt.

"You lost somebody, didn't you?" she asked quietly.

Jessie's head snapped up in surprise. "How could you know that?"

"You get so you can tell. Recognizing another survivor isn't hard if you know the signals. Want to talk about it?"

"No," Jessie responded instantly, looking out the window into the branches of a nearby spruce that she didn't see. "I had a sister too. But it was a long time ago."

"Longer than twenty-three years, four months, and eighteen days?"

"Yes, but I don't—"

"That's all right. We all cope in different ways." Bonnie rose and laid a hand on Jessie's arm. "I left you my card." She nodded to a small white rectangle on the table. "If you ever want to talk—need a friend—call me. Anytime."

Jessie started to pick up the card and in the process brushed against a paper lying face down that Becker had left behind. It slid from the table to the floor and turned over, exposing the picture of the butterfly necklace Timmons had found within the chest cavity of the skeleton from the basement excavation. She leaned down quickly to retrieve it, but Bonnie Russell snatched the page from under her reaching fingers.

"Oh, God," Bonnie breathed. Jessie straightened to see that all the color had left her face. She collapsed onto the bench where she had been sitting, pale enough to faint, and stared at the photograph of the necklace. She had it clenched in a hand that shook so much the paper rattled against the edge of the table.

"Oh, my God," she whispered again. "Where did you get this? It's my sister's!" Bonnie added, more strongly. "I gave it to her, so I should know. Where did you get it? Tell me."

•   •   •

The drive to Palmer seemed long and silent. Jessie was not sorry to leave Bonnie Russell at her car and go back to the veterinarian, who examined Bliss while they discussed the impending birth of the puppies. She was glad to have something else to fill her mind—anything else.

Jessie soon had another subject for speculation, however, for she arrived home to find another floral offering on the front step of the motor home: exactly like the first, with no indication of the identity of the sender. It gave her such an odd feeling that she stood staring at it blankly for a moment, before picking it up to carry inside. It was identical to the rose that had been delivered two days earlier and was now in full bloom, had even dropped a petal onto the dinette table.

Who the hell was sending these things? she wondered, suddenly feeling a lump of uneasiness in her stomach. The flower reminded her of other items, less attractive but no less anonymous, that had arrived the previous year, terrifying gifts and communications from a stalker. Alex had been there then to investigate and finally identify the perpetrator. Now she was alone and probably more vulnerable, though she knew that law enforcement friends were as close as the telephone.

Determined not to let the floral tributes unsettle her further, or to think anymore about Bonnie Russell or the old feelings of loss she had unexpectedly raised in Jessie, she securely locked the doors and went about her usual evening activities. But she closed the blinds so no one could look in and made sure the Smith & Wesson .44 pistol that she usually carried on the trail with her dogs was loaded and close at hand.

Still, it took her a long time to go to sleep. Every small sound seemed magnified and unfamiliar. By defining the things she didn't want to consider she had given them significance, and each time she refused to recognize them they slipped back into her mind like a song she was sick and tired of hearing. It kept her awake and made her angry.

She couldn't help wondering: If the necklace had been found with one body on her property, could another—Bonnie Russell's sister—actually be buried somewhere nearby as well? I will *not* go there, she told herself, and made a new list of things to think about instead.

When she finally drifted off, she was mentally revisiting each and every community along the highway route from Coeur d'Alene, Idaho, to Anchorage, Alaska, in the order she had seen them on her trip in the Winnebago and declining to analyze the noises outside, recognizable or not.

There were a few that were not.

Chapter 10

 "This is a new body, not one of Hansen's," Timmons observed of the floater the boys had found under the bridge. The lab assistants had bagged the woman and were loading her into the back of the crime lab van. "Be lucky to find bones of his—like the ones in Jessie's basement. Whoever *this* is, she didn't drown. There won't be water in the lungs. She was shot in the back."

Becker, standing next to the wheelchair, nodded. "Must have washed out somewhere upstream. We'll have to get some people to see if they can discover where, but if the flow was high enough to wash her free, the site will still be under water."

"True. And if that's the case, she couldn't have been buried very deep, if at all. May have just been left on the surface. Either would mean she was left this spring—or possibly earlier. Looks like the body's been frozen, so it may have been last fall. Depends on where she came from upriver. I'll let you know, when I've had a look at it."

"You don't suppose . . ." Becker frowned, speculation making him uneasy.

"That someone's trying to lay one on Hansen?" Timmons shook his head and shrugged. "Don't think so, though whoever killed her may have thought that might be a confusing factor. Hansen's still locked up tight in Seward and will be—no parole. Besides, one body does not make a serial killer. That's old news, Phil, and just leaps to mind because she was in this particular area. Soon as we figure out who she is, we'll probably be able to guess who killed her. Husband, boyfriend—you know."

"Yeah. Well, sure."

Still, as a breeze came up and he settled his western hat more securely, the thought bothered Becker.

No one in law enforcement liked working the Knik River area. Having a new body found there brought horror back, for the women Hansen had murdered and dumped still troubled the men who had searched for them, some of whom were consumed with the knowledge that somewhere out there were several they had never been able to find.

It haunted the families of the missing as well. One or two kept coming back over the years to walk the accessible riverbanks and those beyond the end of the road, looking, always looking, trying to locate some trace of a body—something to give them closure—something to bury. One mother refused to believe that her daughter had been one of Hansen's victims at all, preferring to hope she was suffering from amnesia and would someday come home.

Bonnie Russell, the woman he had asked Jessie to drive back to Palmer, was not like that. She was certain Robert Hansen had killed her sister, Brenda, though he had not identified her picture or admitted remembering her name. If he *had* killed her, he seemed to have forgotten where he left her body or, for some sick reason, had refused to reveal it. After leading law enforcement officers on a helicopter search and gleefully showing them the burial places of a few of his victims—a process that excited him and sickened them—Hansen had refused to answer any more questions or reveal any more sites.

Anchorage police officers and Alaska State Troopers all knew Bonnie, for she had stayed in Anchorage and kept in touch, persistently and politely reminding them by her presence that her sister was still missing. Spring and fall, her car was familiar to people who lived along the old Knik River Road, parked at times in some pull-off when there was no snow cover and the water was low. A tall, solitary figure in a long dark coat, she would periodically be seen striding slowly across the flats, examining each possible burial site along a river drainage where sandbars shifted with the annual flood. To Becker, who had spotted her now and then, she seemed more haunting in her singular search than her sister, Brenda, who still lay hidden, her body abandoned and alone.

With a shudder, he returned to his car and headed across the bridge to his office in Palmer. Dark clouds were rolling over Pioneer Peak to the south, and it looked like rain.

· · ·

A wind came up in the night, howling through the trees with enough force to send tremors through the motor home and wake Jessie from an uneasy sleep that had been difficult to achieve. She could hear rain rattling on the roof like small thunder. Pulling an extra pillow over her head, she tried to shut out the sounds, failed, and finally sat up, listening to a spruce branch scrape against the wall outside.

An empty food pan rattled across the yard and hit the side of a dog box with a clang that drew a gruff woof or two from its occupant, barely audible in the roar of the wind. A dead branch fell from some tree and flew through the air to thump onto the roof of the Winnebago.

Jessie remembered waking to a thunderstorm in a Canadian campground the preceding month, when she had gone south to drive the rig up the Alaska Highway for Vic Prentice. The night had been full of crashes, vivid flashes of lightning that split the sky, rain that pounded on the roof and ground outside, and the smell of ozone. Such storms are rare to South Central Alaska, and though she had delighted in that one, this night's gusty cacophony was unwelcome. She had wanted the escape of sleep to stem the memories that crept insidiously into her mind. The wind and rain seemed a conspiracy of nature to thwart her.

Disgruntled and resentful, she swung her feet out of the warm bed onto the cool floor and padded into the galley, turning on the light over the stove as she passed. Switching on her CD and tape player, she searched her collection for something to drown out the voice of the wind, as well as the one in her head. Her hand, moving over the titles, hovered over an old James Taylor tape she had not played for a long time—hesitated, moved on, stopped, then returned to take the tape out of its plastic case and put it into the player. Turning up the sound, she put the kettle on for a cup of tea and sat down at the table to wait for it to boil.

It was a mistake, wasn't it? This particular music was always a minefield of anguish. Jessie knew and played it anyway— remembering that someone had once said that if you make a painful thing hurt as much as it can, get it over with, then you know you can stand anything. Believing that was true, she sat very still till the second cut on the album, "Song for You Far Away," began, took a deep breath, and closed her eyes.

As Taylor sang the haunting lyrics, the anticipated agony was immediate; the same shock of emotional identification she had felt the first time she heard it. She was twelve years old and it was all there again—the confusion and isolation, the pain, and the loss. Not just the loss of the sweet baby sister, who had disappeared without a trace, but the parents whose attention had been obsessively focused on finding her, leaving Jessie with the guilt of remaining and of being alive, when her sister wasn't.

"I had a sister . . . a long time ago," she remembered saying to Bonnie Russell that afternoon.

I had a sister.

The pain that swept through her chest and throat was physical and intense, born of tension that curled her body in on itself until she was huddled, arms hugging her body, hands over her mouth, eyes tight shut.

Stop it! she told herself. You can deal with this. You don't need anyone.

Another wave of grief and old familiar pain.

It wasn't my . . . it wasn't my . . . fault. I know they loved her best, but it wasn't . . .

The kettle screamed from the stove and the song ended.

Enough! I'm not going back there now.

Slowly, half blinded and emotionally drained, Jessie got up, switched off the gas under the kettle, and replaced James Taylor with Richard Wagner's "Ride of the Valkyries"—loud enough to drown most of the storm's turmoil, inside and out.

*　　*　　*

The wind had stopped, but rain still drizzled next morning when Jessie woke up late, still tired. Her throat felt thick and scratchy, and she ached all over. Probably catching a cold, she thought, and decided to take the morning off, glad there wasn't construction work waiting for her. Before the concrete foundations dried, maybe she could get rid of this infection by sleeping it off; at least she could rest and stay warm. She went out in boots and a raincoat to feed and water her dogs, then made herself a light breakfast and a cup of hot tea with honey and lemon. She was about to settle at the table with the pile of information from the city offices that she had collected two days before, when there was a light knock on the door.

Opening it, she found Bonnie Russell standing outside, her long, dark coat shiny with rain.

"I'm sorry to bother you again," Bonnie apologized. "I was hoping to find John Timmons here this morning. But I also thought maybe we could talk."

"About?"

"I tried to call Timmons, but he wasn't in, so I wanted to ask you if they've really searched your property for another burial," Bonnie told her. "I have to know if she's here somewhere."

"Your sister." Jessie wanted less than anything she could think of to confront this particular topic, but how could she discourage the woman without seeming emotionally callous and lacking in sympathy?

"Yes."

"They're looking. Something came up yesterday and they had to leave, but Timmons said they'd be back soon to finish. Shall I tell them to let you know?"

"Would you?" Bonnie's tense voice held a hint of pleading.

"Of course."

Wind whipping around the motor home blew rain into Jessie's face. She sneezed as she wiped it off. "Sorry. I'm catching a cold. John hasn't been here since yesterday."

Disappointment and resignation showed in Bonnie's eyes.

"Well, I can see it's not a good time. If he shows up, just tell him I was here."

"Sure," Jessie agreed. She felt pressured to invite the other woman in, but wavered, not wanting to repeat her emotional session in the night with James Taylor. "I'm just not up to conversation at the moment, okay?"

"Don't worry about it. I'm headed up the river anyway."

"Why?" Jessie asked, then belatedly chastised herself for the question, knowing that Bonnie's sister might be hidden there.

"Oh, I like to walk there sometimes." The answer came in a thin voice as Bonnie turned back toward the car she had parked in the drive. "Thanks."

As Jessie stood in the door, watching her move away, a sudden wave of compassion overcame her.

"Bonnie," she called impulsively.

The woman turned.

"Come on in, if you don't mind risking a few germs."

Bonnie came in. She hung her coat on a hook beside the door, accepted Jessie's offer of tea, and stood looking down at the pile of papers on the table.

"What are you doing?" Bonnie asked.

"Trying to find out who owned this property from the time it was homesteaded," Jessie told her. "I want to find out who the old man was—the body I found in the basement excavation."

Handing Bonnie a steaming cup, she sat down at the table and waved the other woman to the bench on the other side.

"Somebody loves you twice," Bonnie commented as she sat down, meaning the roses that had been pushed to the back of the table to accommodate the papers.

"Yeah, maybe. I'd like to know who."

"Where did you get all this information?"

"At the assessor's office in Palmer."

Spreading out two large maps, one labeled OCCUPANCY OF LAND OWNERSHIP, MATANUSKA VALLEY, ALASKA, JUNE 1955, and another from 1936 by the Alaska Rural Rehabilitation Corporation that showed the location of tracts and roads, Jessie explained how they compared to a copy of a much older map with only a few of the early homesteads in the area roughly sketched in.

"Here's Wasilla, see? It and old Knik—over here—were originally Tanaina Athabascan settlements. When the Klondike Gold Rush was going on, around 1898, over three thousand miners flocked into this area."

"That's a lot of people."

"Right, and some were already here. They all needed supplies and equipment, so west of here, at the end of what's now Knik Road—down there to the left, at the mouth of Cottonwood Creek—a village grew up to support them. The arm of Cook Inlet was deep enough so that ships could deliver passengers and freight."

"You know a lot of history," Bonnie commented.

"Well, you sort of pick it up when you live in the same place for a while."

"Did any of the miners get rich?"

"Not really. Most of them left in less than a year. But some of them settled in the valley and used money they made in the local mines to support their homesteads. They built cabins and barns and cleared some of the land. In 1915 they were allowed to record the homesteads, when the government decided to build a railroad through the valley. This map shows some of the original ones."

Jessie moved the oldest map to the top of the pile and pointed out a few homesteads blocked in along the Goose Bay Knik Road, as it had been called back then. The names of the home-steaders were written into the blocks: Moffet, Rising, Roescher, Donovan, Crocker.

"See this one? Anderson?" She laid a finger on one of the blocks on the north side of the road. "My place is part of his original homestead."

It was not the name of the man from whom she had pur-chased the property. Through the years, many of the original homesteads, some as large as 320 acres, had been sold more than once; almost all had been subdivided and were now com-pletely different in configuration and size.

"After he did the required clearing and building on his land, Anderson evidently sold to a miner named James O'Dell." She took a page from another pile that showed a record of the sale and listed a cabin and a shed as structures on the property.

"Is that the old man?"

"I don't know," Jessie told her, reaching for a tissue to blow her nose, which had started to run as she drank the hot peppermint tea. "It's not the name of the man who sold it to me, but it's familiar for some reason. I was just going to try and find out."

Frustrated now, she got up and went to the portable file box in which, as she replaced them, she was keeping all her important records. Somewhere in the mix, she half remembered, there was a note she had written to remind herself to check again on the duplicate deed she had still not received. Thumbing through the slim assortment of files, she found the note and was glad to see it included a phone number, which she used.

"When *will* it be mailed," she asked a woman on the other end of the line a few minutes later. "Next week for sure? Okay, I'll expect it. But can you do me a favor? I need the name of the person who sold me the property. Can you give me that much now at least?"

There was a long wait, during which Jessie stared out the window at the gray day and noticed that the rain had stopped for the moment. Would the weather slow the curing of the concrete—another delay? She hoped not.

"Yes, I'm still here. Daryl *O'Dell* Mitchell? O'Dell? You're sure it's O'Dell? Yes, thank you."

So there was a connection between Daryl O'Dell Mitchell, from whom she had purchased the property, and the miner James O'Dell, who had bought it from Anderson. The miner had to have been old enough in 1932 to own land, which would make him at least in his twenties. If Timmons was right and the old man's body they had found was buried twenty to twenty-five years ago—say, twenty—he would have been fifty. But John Timmons had said "old." Fifty wasn't what Jessie considered old. He must have been older when he bought the land. Adding twenty years to his age would make him forty when he bought it, seventy when he died and was buried. That made more sense. He could have been older—or slightly younger. His son could have been . . .

The computations and variables made her realize that her head ached. Perhaps the body wasn't that of O'Dell at all. If not, who was it?

She looked up to find Bonnie Russell watching her closely and waiting patiently for her to complete her thoughts.

"The man who sold this place to me was named Daryl O'Dell Mitchell," she told her. "So there's some kind of connection, I think. But I'm feeling too awful to figure it out today."

"You look like you could use a nap," Bonnie told her firmly, getting up to take her cup to the sink in the galley. "I'll get out of your way. Could I bring you anything—juice, cold medicine?"

Jessie smiled weakly up at her guest. Sharing her search for the old man's identity with Bonnie Russell had eliminated the awkwardness, and she realized she was feeling much more comfortable with her. Still, she was grateful that the question of the missing sister had not come up. The woman's reticence must have been learned through hard years of waiting that had taught her some difficult things about patience and time. Bonnie was likable. Why did that surprise her? She realized suddenly that what she was afraid of wasn't Bonnie but her own aversion to re-visit the appalling parts of her early life. But that aversion had been instrumental in creating her own strong sense of inde-pendence, hadn't it?

"No, thanks," she told her, returning to the question. "I think I have everything I need."

Donning her damp coat, Bonnie left, with the hope that Jessie would feel better soon.

Rubbing her eyes with the back of her hands, Jessie gave up and decided it *was* time for a nap. Washing down a couple of as-pirin with the last of her now-cold tea, she left the maps and pa-pers on the table and retreated to her bed in the back of the motor home. Soon she was snoozing more restfully than at any time the previous night, with no idea that sometime quite soon she would have another unexpected, unsettling, and unidenti-fied visitor.

Chapter 11

It was a warm day and Jessie left the door open, with the screen door shut to keep out the ever-present mosquitoes. A day off had banished most of her cold, and she had felt well enough this morning to take a team of her dogs for an early run. On her return, however, she decided to do some necessary yard work, rather than take out another. Halfway up a ladder, she was replacing the hinges on the door of her equipment shed, a job she had been putting off for too long, when she heard the telephone ring in the motor home.

Sprinting across the yard, she caught it on the fifth ring.

"Arnold Kennels."

She was pleased to recognize Lynn Ehlers's voice in her ear.

"Hey, Jessie. I was about to give up. How's it going?"

"Fine." She sat down, tossing her leather work gloves onto the table. "I was outside watching the concrete dry. But it's pretty boring, so I was balanced on a ladder, repairing my shed door."

"When will you start with the log part?"

"Logs coming late tomorrow," Jessie told him, reaching across absentmindedly to run her fingers up and down the smooth glass of the vase in which the second rose had arrived. "The crew's going to be here any minute to take the forms off. Then we'll paint sealer on. When it's dry—a couple of hours— they'll put on blue insulation and fill in the dirt around the walls. Tomorrow I'll help put sill seal on top of the walls and they'll lay the floor. The next morning we can start raising logs, starting with the half logs that hold the rest in place."

"I hear that satisfied grin on your face," Lynn told her. "How about taking time off for dinner with me tonight, after you're through? Nothing as fancy as the pasta you fed me the other night, but pizza, maybe—and a couple of games of pool?"

The invitation was tempting. It seemed to Jessie that lately she had spent all her time at home, either involved in construction or waiting for it or working with her dogs. An evening out would be a welcome break.

"I could be up for that," she said, her grin widening. "But it'd have to be seven or eight, I think."

"Terrific. Why don't you give me a call when you're done and I'll come pick you up."

"I could meet you in town."

"Naw. No sense in both of us driving."

He gave her his phone number and was gone.

She sat for a minute, looking at the two roses on the table; suddenly seeing them in relation to the phone call. Could Lynn be responsible for them? He was just as possible as anyone else she had considered, including Alex Jensen—probably more so. Ehlers had, after all, voiced an interest in her during the race in February and could be following up now. It seemed an odd idea, but she didn't know him well enough yet to judge.

Damned if I'll ask him, she told herself, and went back out to finish the hinges before Vic Prentice and his gang of four arrived.

·   ·   ·

They pulled in just as she was tightening the last screw. Carrying the ladder into the shed, she greeted them and went back into the motor home for a sweatshirt. As she stood pulling it on in the galley, J.B. stuck his head in the door.

"Hey, Jessie. Got a cup of coffee?"

"Sure. Come on in. Mugs're on the counter."

He poured himself a cup and waved the pot at her with a grin.

"No, thanks. Already had mine."

"Say," he said, sliding the pot back on the warmer. "Think you might like to get some dinner or see a movie tonight when we're through?"

Though she liked J.B. well enough as a working partner, Jessie had no interest in dating him. His offer made for a sticky situation, however, since he would be around for some time to come as part of the crew working on her cabin. Still, she didn't want to encourage him and have future invitations with which to contend.

For a moment she looked at him, thinking fast, before she answered with a smile. "Sorry, J.B. I've already got plans—with a guy I'm pretty fond of." It was true, if a little exaggerated.

"Good enough." He grinned and shrugged. "Can't fault a guy for asking."

"Not at all. Thanks anyway."

Gulping his coffee, he was out the door and gone, leaving her to hope he wouldn't be a problem later.

It never rains, but it pours, she said to herself, going out after him to join the crew.

• • •

Over twenty miles away, near the end of the Knik River Road, a car familiar to the scattered residents who lived along it was parked in a pull-off and locked. A local, turning his jeep into the curving quarter-mile driveway that led up to his house, noticed it, not for the first time, and frowned in concern as he continued uphill. Parking his Cherokee, he carried a sack of groceries into the kitchen through the back door.

"She's at it again," he told his wife, setting the sack on the counter next to the refrigerator.

"You see her?"

"Just the car. But she's down there, like she was last fall."

His wife turned and glanced in the direction of the river with a sympathetic expression.

"She'll never find that girl. It's been too long—twenty years. If there *was* anything, the police would have found it a long time ago."

Picking up a pair of binoculars from the windowsill, she went across the room to look down on the riverbank that was just visible through the trees far below.

"Well, you never know," he said, still frowning. "The river changes every year. This year it's washing out a new channel on this side. Hasn't done that in a while."

Still looking through the binoculars, his wife carefully examined what parts of the flats she could see, but they were empty. Just as she was about to give up and go back to the salad she had been making, a lone figure came into view, slowly walking upriver a few feet from the rushing torrent of water.

"You see her?" the husband asked.

"Yeah, she's there all right." Lowering the binoculars, the woman stared down at the figure she could barely make out without magnification and shook her head. "It's so sad. I don't know what I'd do, if it were me, but I don't think I'd still be searching down there. Gives me the creeps just watching her. What if she actually found something?"

*　　*　　*

It did not give Bonnie Russell the creeps. This walk was familiar and strangely comforting in a way, for there along the river, where she had been many times before, she felt closer to her missing sister. Though the river was high and would rise higher before the glacial dam above it broke and allowed the waters of Lake George to cascade in a flood down the valley, it was only water. The sound of its rushing burble was a calming, peaceful background music, accented with birdsongs and the soft wind through the birch and spruce that grew thickly upon the banks.

Bonnie had long ago come to the realization that she would

probably never know where her sister's body lay, never be able to bury her properly. But somehow this natural setting had come to feel more acceptable than a grave to her, though that was a different frame of mind from that with which she had started this quest. Here, next to the lively river, below the tall peaks of the Chugach Range, it was restful and lovely, a place in which she imagined Brenda could be at peace. Maybe it would be all right to leave her here, as she had left a memorial stone to mark an empty rectangle of ground in an Anchorage cemetery. Each year she took flowers to that stone, on Brenda's birthday and on the day she disappeared, not knowing the day she died.

Soon, she thought. Soon she should stop coming here to walk through an area she knew as well as she knew the way through that cemetery—each twist and turn recognizable, each bank and stream familiar, each change in the patterns noted and examined. It was almost time to move on. This obsession had destroyed her marriage, driven away a husband who did not understand and was unwilling to try. "You don't even know I'm here anymore," he had told her. "I might as well not be."

She smiled, remembering ruefully that she had stared at him with nothing to say that could matter.

A Steller's jay flew out of the woods ahead of her and perched on a leaning fence post that someone had abandoned years before. Cocking its black-crested head, the bird watched her unhurried approach. She stopped beside a heavy log that the river had carried along and deposited on the sandy bank sometime in the past. Sitting down on it, she watched as the bird with its bright sapphire feathers watched her.

"Shameless beggar," she named it, with a smile, "I have nothing you'd want to eat."

As if it understood, the jay flipped its blue tail and flew away across the widening water of the river. Bonnie watched it disappear into the trees on the far side. She had walked there too, in the early years, when she was still determined and angry. There was no road, but she had hiked up along the river as far as she could go to search, knowing that in the small plane he had flown, Hansen could have hidden a victim there as easily as on this side. She had thought it might be more likely but had found nothing.

"Where are you, Jo-Jo?" she said softly, using her sister's pet name. "Will you understand and forgive me if I give up? Little sister—baby sister—would you ever stop looking for me?"

A sudden movement farther up the bank caught her eye. Sitting very still, she watched a red fox trot confidently out of the trees onto the sand and gravel of a bar the river had left unclaimed. By a large rock, it paused to sniff at something on the ground behind the stone. Hesitantly, it reached out one paw to whatever it had found, raised and licked at the foot, then began to scratch the ground. Crouching, half hidden behind the rock, it seemed to be eating something. What had it found? A dead salmon, probably. But did foxes eat fish?

She stood up, curious, and at the motion, swift as a shadow, the fox was gone, melting into the closest grove of birch as if it had never been there at all, carrying something she couldn't see clearly in its mouth. The only sign of its passing would be a set of delicate footprints in the sand of the riverbank, if she cared to look. She was more interested in what the animal had found and began to walk toward the rock.

I'll look, she thought, one more time. Then I'll go home. And I don't think I'll be back here again anytime soon.

When Bonnie was halfway between the rock and the log on which she had been sitting, she could see the tracks of the fox: small indentations, coming to and going from whatever it had found on the riverbank. A small bit of bright yellow came into view on the river side of the large rock, and she slowed her progress, apprehension and horror rising in her chest. When she was close enough to see around the stone, she stopped dead, mouth open, eyes wide, staring in disbelief at what lay on the ground beyond.

The body of a woman with long blond hair covering her face was spread-eagled, facedown in the sand, her left arm extended as if she were reaching for the water that rushed by a few yards away. Her hair was matted and damp, sand clinging to its strands as if she had rolled on the ground. One strap of the yellow tank top that fit her torso tightly was off the shoulder, partway down her right arm. That hand was hidden under the body, but her arm was covered in blood, dried brown, from a dark bullet hole in her shoulder. The back of the tank top was widely stained the same color from another bullet wound, this one to the torso, just below her shoulder blade.

The dead woman wore tight black pants and a pair of high-heeled strap-sandals, one of which had twisted off her foot, for it lay as if it had dangled from the ankle strap as she tried to run. The bottom of that foot was caked with clotted sand and blood. She had evidently stepped on something sharp after the shoe came off.

For a horrified, untenable few seconds, Bonnie Russell's

mind all but stopped working. She was consumed with the idea that she had found the sister she had searched for so long. Then, slowly, reason took over. It couldn't be so. Brenda had been dead for twenty years; this woman, a matter of hours, possibly days.

Slowly she became aware of a scent on the breeze coming toward her from the direction of the woman who lay in the sand. It was a sickening, sweet smell that combined with the already decaying odor of the body itself, filling Bonnie's nostrils and making her stomach lurch—the scent of roses.

In shock, she stood without moving, staring down at what the fox had found on the riverbank. She saw that it, or some other animal, had been at the right arm, for it was chewed, a chunk of flesh torn away to the bone.

Stumbling away, a few unstable steps toward the trees, she fell to her knees and vomited onto the edge of the sandbar. Tears poured unchecked down her face, and the paroxysms continued long after her stomach was empty. When they finally stopped, she wiped her face on the sleeve of her coat and got to her feet, white and trembling. Without looking again at the body, refusing to think, she staggered back the way she had come, her balance improving as she went until she was capable of climbing the hill to the place where she had left her car.

Leaving it where it was parked, she crossed the road and went up the long drive to the house on the hill above.

"Please," she said in a thin anguished voice to the man who answered her pounding on the kitchen door. "Call the troopers. There's a woman's body down there on the riverbank."

Chapter 12

 "Hi. I'm done for the day," Jessie told Lynn Ehlers on the phone at seven-thirty that evening. "Even took a shower."

"Well, thank God for that," he teased. "I'll be right along."

While she waited for him to show up in his truck, Jessie stepped outside to take a look at what had been accomplished that afternoon.

All the forms had been removed and lay once again in piles in the yard, ready to be picked up by one of the contractor's trucks. The outside of the bare concrete walls was painted with sealer and had blue foam insulation in place, ready for Hank Peterson to move the dirt back in the morning with his Bobcat. Tomorrow the floor would go on before they could start raising logs.

COLD COMPANY · 103

Crossing to Tank's box, she let her lead dog off his tether, then crouched, careful not to muddy the knees of her clean jeans, to give his ears and shoulders an affectionate rubbing.

"Hey, good dog. We're gonna have logs late tomorrow—big, heavy logs that will make strong walls. There's gonna be a house for me, and for you to visit sometimes this winter, when it gets cold. How's that sound?"

He grinned a doggy grin at the sound of her voice, closed his eyes in ecstasy, and leaned harder against the knowing fingers that had found a sweet spot between his shoulder blades.

Jessie patted him a last time and stood up again. The basement was now looking like part of a real house. Anxious to see the log walls go up, she could, for the first time, begin to picture how the rooms would be. She badly missed the cabin that had burned. This one, however, would be even better, with more room and light.

I've been camping out all spring, she thought. First in a tent, then in a borrowed motor home. Like an old bear, I need my own cave.

She seldom noticed how much she defined herself in terms of her living space. Anyone who wanted to know could figure out a lot about people by paying attention to where and how they lived, what they kept and valued, what they got rid of, and the things they chose to decorate their lives and houses. She recalled how adrift and anchorless she had felt when everything she owned had gone up in smoke, wanting, consciously and unconsciously, to go home to a place and things that no longer existed. Now it was all beginning to exist again, and she found herself more settled and confident.

But it didn't necessarily have to be a house, she decided, remembering times when she had felt perfectly at home out on the trail with her dogs, living out of a sled bag full of only the essentials that would feed and protect them. There were also people who spent most of their lives never owning any of the places in which they lived. Others lived out of suitcases and traveled the world, making wherever they landed home for the moment.

I couldn't do that, she thought, walking across the yard toward the new basement, Tank padding along beside her. I need a place to come home to.

It had been sunny all afternoon, and all the puddles were gone from the yard. The forecast called for good weather for the next few days, but who knew what witchcraft meteorologists used in their predictions. She hoped they wouldn't decide to be angry with anyone along Knik Road in the near future. For now it was still pleasantly warm. She lifted her face and took a deep breath of the breeze that blew in from the surrounding trees, bringing a hint of evergreen fragrance with it.

The sound of a vehicle behind her in the drive drew her attention to Lynn Ehlers, pulling his pickup into the yard. As she fastened Tank back onto his tether, Ehlers stepped out and walked across to the new foundation.

"Looks good." He turned to Jessie, with a smile. "So do you."

"Thanks." She felt herself flush at his words and turned away toward the Winnebago. "I'll get a jacket in case it gets chilly later."

•   •   •

The evening went well.

Lynn and Jessie went first to Antonio's in Wasilla, where they shared a pizza and an hour's conversation about dogs and the training they planned for the summer and fall. Then they drifted on to Oscar's Place, the current haunt of many of the people involved with sled dogs, who now congregated there while they waited for the owner, Oscar Levant, to finish rebuilding Oscar's Other Place beyond Jessie's yard on Knik Road. That favorite watering hole of most mushers and dog handlers had also been torched by an arsonist, a few days before Jessie's cabin was burned, and they were all anxious to have it back.

It was taking shape more quickly, for rebuilding the pub was less labor intensive, as it was not being built of logs that required special techniques. For now, Oscar's customers were willing to wait, but they kept close track of the progress of the Other Place, some often stopping by to lend a hand, hoping to speed things up. Oscar had promised to throw an opening celebration, plans for which were already in the works.

At what was the original Oscar's Place in Wasilla, Jessie and Lynn perched on tall stools at the bar while they waited for a turn at one of the pool tables in the back. Oscar, who was working hard to keep up with the demand for liquid refreshment from the crowd of people who filled the place, greeted Jessie with a grin.

"Hear you're about to put up logs."

"Yup, day after tomorrow. How's your place coming along?"

"Good for you. Mine's doing okay. Another couple of weeks and I can open, I think. Leave some of the finish work for later. This bunch is beginning to growl that it's taking too long."

Jessie grinned and took a sip of the Killian's he handed her without asking, already knowing her preference. "You ought to do a Tom Sawyer on the paint and finishing—get some of them working something besides their mouths."

"Good idea, but there's more hands than I can use already. Who's this?" Oscar asked, nodding at Lynn.

"I'm sorry." Jessie apologized for her oversight. "Oscar Levant meet Lynn Ehlers from Minnesota. Did the Quest with me this year."

Oscar wiped a damp palm on the towel he had slung over one shoulder and reached across the bar to shake hands with Lynn. "Welcome to my place. What can I get you?"

"Hey, thanks." Lynn looked beyond Oscar to assess the assortment of beer labels behind the glass door of the cooler. "That's quite a variety you stock. I'll have a Budweiser, please."

The pub was, as usual, noisy with conversation and the crack of pool balls, combined with country-western music from a jukebox in one corner that was almost impossible to hear, let alone recognize. The smell of hot popcorn, slightly scorched, hung in the air. The requests for drinks were almost nonstop, but the grin on Oscar's face revealed that he was thoroughly enjoying the press and the relaxed good humor of the crowd, half of whom Jessie recognized as regulars from the Knik Road area. She was therefore not surprised when Hank Peterson appeared between her and Lynn.

"Hey, Jessie. Running away from home?"

She introduced him to Ehlers and glanced back toward the pool tables, while the men shook hands.

"Looking for a game?" Peterson asked.

Jessie nodded.

"Thought we might," Lynn told him.

"Ah." Peterson grinned wolfishly. "Fresh blood. You any good?"

"Well . . ."

In a few minutes, Lynn was skillfully knocking balls around one of the tables with Peterson.

While Jessie waited to play the winner, she looked around the crowded room, but no one she knew was close enough for conversation, so she sat quietly, enjoying her surroundings. Across the room, Dell and Stevie from the construction crew were sitting at a table with several other people. Seeing Jessie, Stevie raised a beer bottle in salute.

A dart game was in progress in a nearby corner, a short long-faced man attempting to teach a taller woman in a red-and-white striped shirt how to throw the sharply pointed missiles so they would stick into the board. Jessie grinned as his efforts produced little result. The darts kept flying wide of the target, the woman clearly more interested in having his arm around her than in hitting the circle on the wall.

With a sudden odd sensation of being watched, she looked beyond the game to see J.B. sitting alone at a table, staring at her across the room with a questioning sort of expression. He didn't move when he saw that she was aware of him, but when she smiled and waved before turning away, he grinned and gave her a two-finger salute. Somehow, however, she had a feeling that the grin hadn't quite reached his eyes.

As she swung back toward the sudden grinding of ice in the blender Oscar was using to whip up a margarita, she noticed the face of someone else she recognized coming through the front door: the reporter who had portrayed her with such venom in the paper several days before. As he glanced around the room, their eyes met and held for a second. Jessie returned her attention to Oscar, hoping the reporter would sit somewhere else, but he crossed the room and, without invitation, hiked a hip onto the edge of the stool beside her, knocking the jacket Lynn Ehlers had left hanging on its back onto the floor.

Grinning, he stooped to pick it up.

"Hi, there, Jessie. Buy you a beer?"

The confident assumption in his voice that she would welcome his presence ignited a flame of resentment that stiffened the tone of her brief response.

"I have one, thank you."

"But you'll soon need another. Hey, bartender!"

Jessie noted the quick response of Oscar's head turning and the narrowing of his eyes at the reporter's imperious demand for attention, knowing he did not like to be yelled at, treated his customers with courtesy and expected the same. Catching his eye, she raised a palm in his direction, indicating that she did not want the drink the uninvited man beside her was trying to order. Oscar came quickly along the bar to halt in front of her unwelcome benefactor.

"You bothering this lady, son?"

His abrupt question startled the cocky reporter into a defensive denial.

"Hey, just trying to be friendly. I'll have a Heineken's."

Oscar, well aware of Jessie's frown of discomfort and rejection, nodded slowly, then issued a warning. "I'll serve you, but I'd suggest you drink it somewhere else."

Reaching into the cooler, he retrieved a beer, removed the cap, and rapped it down on the bar.

"That'll be three-fifty."

As Oscar rang up the sale and deposited the money in the till, the no-longer-smiling reporter took a long swallow and turned again to Jessie.

"I assume you didn't like my article."

Jessie held her temper and answered without looking at him. "No, I didn't."

"Well, hell. You should have talked to me. I had to go with what I had. If it wasn't your side, that's not my fault. I'm sorry, okay?"

Still not looking at him, Jessie gritted her teeth and took a deep breath.

"Sorry about what? That it wasn't *my side*, or that you wrote it the way you did?"

"That you wouldn't talk to me, obviously. It would have been a much better story if you'd . . ."

That was enough. Jessie interrupted his refusal to take responsibility by swinging around to confront him directly.

"And since I didn't want your television crew trampling all over what had taken a lot of work to build, you decided to get even."

"Whoa!" He threw up both hands as if warding her off. "It wasn't *my* crew. I just rode out with them to get the story for the paper. I've tried to apologize several ways. . . ."

As she gave up, decided to pretend he didn't exist, and turned back to her beer, Lynn Ehlers's strong voice broke into the reporter's defensive monologue.

"Who are you anyway, fella? You're in my seat—next to *my* date."

Wide-eyed, the reporter slid off the stool, grabbed his beer, and held out a hand to the strong-shouldered man who confronted him.

"Sorry. I'm Gary—ah, Huddleston, *Anchorage Daily News*." His half smirk was suddenly a bit nervous.

"Well, Gary, *huddle* somewhere else," Ehlers told him, glancing down at the hand without taking it. "I think it's clear that Jessie would be more comfortable with you gone."

When the irritating reporter had vanished into the crowd, Jessie was still giggling.

"*Huddle* somewhere else?" She grinned at Ehlers, as he climbed back up on his bar stool. "Lots of sled-time improve your one-liners, Lynn?"

"Not so you'd notice," he returned. "Come on. Let's have another beer and play pool. I whipped Hank—barely—so it's your turn now."

Chapter 13

It was nearing midnight when Lynn and Jessie returned to her place on Knik Road. The sky was still lighter in the west than in the east, and a few stars glittered overhead in the openings between the tops of the tall birch trees that lined her drive. The radio in Lynn's truck was tuned to KLEF, the local classical FM station, and the soft notes of Debussy that filled the cab were very much to Jessie's liking. She leaned back against the seat, relaxed and a little tired, thinking that except for the appearance of Gary Huddleston it had been a great evening. Lynn Ehlers was good company, with or without his dogs.

She yawned as he pulled into the space next to the Winnebago.

"Sleepy?"

"Yeah. I got plenty of exercise today. A run with the mutts early this morning, then we worked hard all afternoon."

It was just dark enough for the motion sensor to switch on the yard light, flooding the area brightly enough for Jessie to see that some of her dogs were moving around and a few were barking. They aren't used to Lynn's truck yet, she thought. But as she shoved her arms into the sleeves of the jacket she had been wearing around her shoulders, a hint of motion on the far side of the lot, where it shouldn't have been, made her sit up straight. A dark form had swiftly disappeared into the trees behind her shed.

"What?" Lynn asked, turning his attention in the direction in which she was looking, startled by her reflexive motion.

"Did you see that?"

"See what?"

She hesitated. Had she really seen something? Yes, she had.

"Someone just walked out of my yard into the trees."

"Who?"

"I don't know," Jessie said, wide awake now, concern drawing her brows together. "He was walking away."

"I didn't see anyone."

"He was only there for a second, at the edge of the light."

She stared at the place where the figure had vanished, troubled and confused. Opening the door of the pickup, she slid out onto the ground and started across the lot toward the shed.

"Hey, Jessie, wait," Lynn called, climbing out after her. "I've got a flashlight."

They walked together to the point where Jessie thought she had seen someone disappear but saw nothing.

"Maybe I imagined it."

In the grass and weeds that carpeted the ground near the trees there were no footprints or marks of anyone passing, but some of the new blades had been crushed underfoot and Jessie noticed the droop of a twig that could have been snapped by someone in enough of a hurry to be careless.

"There. See that?"

He crouched to examine the twig.

"It's fresh, all right. Let's take a look around the rest of the yard."

For half an hour they searched: the basement excavation, the storage shed with its new hinges, all her equipment, the dog yard. Remembering a former intruder who had left traps for her dogs, Jessie was particularly careful in inspecting their boxes, using a rake to thoroughly toss the straw bedding, but she found nothing suspicious. She had checked the motor home door first of all and found it locked, as she left it.

When they had gone over everything she could think of, Jessie stood, once again staring into the trees behind the shed.

"Nothing's missing or seems to have been touched. Who could it have been?" she wondered in frustration. "I *did* see someone, Lynn. Didn't I?"

"I think you probably did," he assured her. "You're familiar with your own yard and would notice. I'd trust your judgment."

"Well—*hell!*" Jessie gave up and began to walk toward the Winnebago. "I'll look again in the morning. Want some coffee before you go?"

He hesitated before answering, as he kept pace beside her.

"No, I think not. You've got a lot on your plate for tomorrow, and it's late."

She nodded, feeling relieved but a little disappointed to have the evening end—and on a bad note. Thinking how much it bothered her to have someone trespassing in her yard without identifying himself, she did not notice for a minute that Ehlers was no longer beside her. Swinging around, she found he had stopped, and in the glow from the yard light she could see he was looking after her with a thoughtful expression.

"See something?"

She waited till he moved to catch up.

"No," he said, as they faced each other. "I just—look, Jessie. I asked around about that trooper you were seeing during the Quest and found out that he's gone. Right?"

"Yes." Her response was almost a question, but her attention was now focused on him, intruder forgotten for the moment.

"Well, does that mean . . ."

She took a deep breath and interrupted, knowing what he was asking.

"It means we're no longer an item, Lynn. We decided to let it go."

It was the first time Jessie had said that out loud, defined what she knew for someone else. There was still pain involved, but less than she had expected. It must not have been such a big deal after all, she thought at first, but knew immediately that wasn't true. For her, Alex Jensen had been a *very* big deal.

"Do you mind if I ask why you let it go?"

Why? She could tell him the basic reason.

"He took a job in Idaho and I wasn't willing to give up what I do here to go with him."

Lynn nodded slowly. "I see."

But she knew that wasn't all. There were other things that had to do with her independence and compromises she was unwilling to make. It was too soon in what she thought might be some kind of relationship with Lynn Ehlers to try to define those things. If something developed, it would deserve that kind of honesty, but not yet.

"It was complicated, Lynn. But it's over."

He tilted his head and gave her a questioning look. "Sure?"

"Yes."

A pleased grin spread across his face, emphasizing the smile lines around his mouth and eyes.

"So—you want to get together again sometime soon?"

"I'd like that."

"We'll do it then."

She thought he would kiss her, but instead he laid an affectionate arm across her shoulders as she walked him to his truck. "If you hear or see anyone you don't recognize in the yard, call me. No. Call the law, *then* call me. Do you have a handgun?"

"Under my mattress."

"Good."

She smiled at him, realizing that they were matched in height and she didn't have to look up. It was comfortable.

"Thanks, Lynn. It was a lot of fun."

"Except for that idiot reporter and your winning both games of pool."

"Well, yes. But he's not worth considering, and I got lucky."

"Sure you did." He grinned. "I'll call you."

Climbing into the pickup, he was gone with a wave.

*   *   *

She considered Lynn Ehlers as she untethered Tank from his box and walked with him toward the Winnebago, wanting company for the night in lieu of the intruder she had seen. Most of the dogs had been awake during the search of the yard but had now quieted down again, though a couple of them raised their heads to see if anything interesting was happening. They relaxed and lay down again at the sound of her voice.

"It's okay. Go back to sleep, guys."

Lynn was an appealing person for several reasons besides his easygoing nature. He understood her love of sled dog racing because he was involved in the sport himself. He knew the dedication and hard work required to make it work, as well as the joy of running teams through wild country. There was nothing about him that made her feel pressured to be anything but herself. He seemed content to get to know her gradually, demanding little more than her company and attention.

Besides, she thought with a smile, he shoots a wicked game of pool.

Unlocking the door, she stepped in and closed it behind her. She made it to the galley before she was overwhelmed by her sense of smell. In the dark interior of the motor home, the scent of roses hung strongly in the air, filling the space as if there were dozens of them. But it was not quite right. It smelled sticky and sweet, like cheap perfume or soap, the kind of scent that clings to your hands and clothes, cloying, nauseating: headache country. Slowly, Jessie reached, found, and turned on the light over the stove and turned cautiously to face the table.

In the pale beam of the galley light, the roses in their vases glowed a rich red against the dark shadows of the window behind them. Arranged with exact spacing between, they stood together in line: the petals of one about to fall, one fully open—and one a tight bud in a vase just like the others.

There were now *three* roses—*three!* Jessie knew there had been only *two* when she left the motor home and locked the door.

Three?

Without moving a muscle, she glanced hurriedly around what she could see of the space in which she stood, then turned slowly to look behind her.

There was no sound or hint of motion. But someone had obviously been inside the Winnebago while she was gone—and it couldn't have been Lynn Ehlers, who had been with her all evening.

What the hell was going on?

Swiftly, she went through the motor home, turning on all the lights, searching for anything out of the ordinary. There was nothing. All the doors and windows were closed and locked, except for the one over her bed. It was open a crack, but could only be opened from the inside.

Returning to the table, she stood looking down in disbelief at the roses that had so quickly assumed an entirely different significance. Instead of playful gifts from some anonymous well-wisher, they now represented some kind of threat. Their very beauty gave them the power to intimidate—reinforced by their terrible smell. Leaning forward, she sniffed at one of them and almost gagged. It was not the roses themselves, she realized. Someone had sprayed them all with artificial scent, practically drowned them in it, for drops of the pervasive stuff lay on the table beneath each one.

Going quickly, Jessie took a soapy sponge to wipe the table, turned on all the vent fans, opened all the windows as wide as they would go, and found a can of neutral air spray, which she used heavily throughout the interior. She rinsed the spray from the flowers under cool water in the sink, and slowly the smell began to dissipate.

Her immediate thought had been to toss them outside, but she thought better of it. Though she couldn't stand to sleep in the same space with the smell, she would keep them to show to Becker tomorrow. Enough would remain to give him an idea of how the place had smelled—like a whorehouse, she thought—and probably for Timmons to test and find out what it was.

Dropping to a seat on the sofa behind the driver's seat, she sat waiting for the reek to be gone, angry and upset. It was one thing to have roses left on her doorstep, quite another to find someone had delivered one *inside* her living space, along with such a sensory menace.

Who was responsible for these strange gifts? Why? And what, if anything, could she do about it?

Chapter 14

Everyone arrived almost at once the following morning. Vic Prentice and crew came early to bolt floor joists into the notches provided for them in the tops of the concrete basement walls and to lay down a wood floor. They were hard at it when Hank Peterson rolled in a few minutes later. He was soon skillfully wheeling his Bobcat around the yard, hauling dirt to backfill against the concrete walls. Before any of them had been busy for more than half an hour, John Timmons showed up, with Phil Becker and the crime lab assistants in tow.

"Gotta finish what we started the other day," Timmons growled. "Phil and I need to talk to you, Jessie." He rolled off in his wheelchair to get his technicians started at their work, instructing them to stay out of the way of the construction crew as much as possible.

Jessie, with visions of anthills, stood for a moment, watching ten people, all occupied in what was usually an empty yard, except for her dogs. At the far end of the basement, Dell and Stevie were working on opposite ends of a joist they had just set into place. At the other, Bill and J.B. were engaged in a similar activity. As she watched, J.B. called a question to Vic, who was counting the joists that were left to make sure they had the required number. He answered and J.B. went back to work, but, beyond him, Jessie saw that Dell had hesitated in what he was doing to watch and listen to the exchange. He was staring fixedly at J.B., an odd frown of assessment on his face. When he noticed Jessie was watching, his scowl instantly vanished. He directed a single nod of recognition in her direction and turned his attention to the work he was supposed to be doing. But there had been something in his fleeting expression that made Jessie wonder what his attentive consideration of J.B. was all about.

Dell was a quiet man, slow to speak and react, though he seemed to listen a lot, she realized. If anyone knew the details of what went on within the work crew, it was probably Dell. She liked him, but she knew less about him than about the others who were working in her yard. On a lunch break he was most often to be found resting full length on a pile of lumber, billed cap pulled low to shade his eyes, with every appearance of napping. But she had noticed that from beneath that concealing brim he watched and was aware of everything that went on around him, and this was not the first time she had seen his attention focused on J.B.

Dell glanced up again and found her still watching him,

which made her feel a little embarrassed. She hoped he wouldn't mistake her attention for personal interest, like his working partner.

Turning away quickly, she scooted into the motor home to make a third pot of coffee that somebody was sure to want, intending to go help with the construction of the floor as soon as she finished and forgetting about Dell for the moment.

Becker, parking his patrol car just outside, where it was out of the drive, walked around the Winnebago and rapped on the screen door.

"Come on in, Phil," Jessie called, in answer to his knock.

As he stepped in, she glanced out the window to see a huge truck pull into the yard with the first load of logs and Vic Prentice trot over to meet it.

"That's not supposed to be here till later this afternoon."

Giving Becker a distracted grin, she shoved the pot she had just rinsed back in place to catch the coffee that was beginning to drain through a filter.

"Everyone else is here. You might as well be, too."

He stood by the table, looking down at the three roses that Jessie had put back where she had found them the night before.

"These what you called me about this morning?"

Leaving the coffee to brew itself, she slid onto one of the benches at the table and looked up at him with an anxious frown.

"Yes. Somebody put the third one there last night and the smell was not to be believed."

"You mean it was delivered last night?"

"No." She shook her head emphatically. "I mean it was right

there on the table with the other two. The door was locked, but someone got in, left it there like you see it, sprayed all three with some horrible rose perfume, and went out, locking the door again. I walked in late and almost threw up." She shivered, recalling the smell.

Becker frowned. "Who has keys to this place?"

"Vic Prentice has the only other key. But I asked him this morning and he showed it to me, on his key ring. I had mine with me. So how the hell could anyone get in?"

While he thought about that, Becker removed his western hat, leaned forward, and smelled the flowers Jessie had rinsed off the night before. He made a face and stepped back, rubbing the mark his hatband had made on his forehead.

"Nasty. Anything else different or missing?"

"No," she assured him. "And I looked through everything."

"You're sure you locked up?"

"Yes, because I tried the door just after we came back and it was locked."

Becker's head came up like a hound on a scent. "We?"

"A friend, okay? A musher I ran the Quest with last February. Lynn Ehlers."

And why, Jessie suddenly wondered, did she feel defensive about telling Phil Becker she'd been out with someone besides his friend Jensen? Considering the circumstances, it was ridiculous, but she felt it.

"I can't get in there, so you'll have to come out here," Timmons' gravelly voice announced from the other side of the screen door, where he was peering at the roses on the table beyond Becker. "And bring me a mug of that coffee I smell, please, Jessie."

Pulling a bench she kept near the door to a position near his wheelchair, Jessie sat down and repeated what she had told Becker, who had gone to examine the doors on the cab of the motor home and consider how someone could get into the locked vehicle.

"I think the passenger door was jimmied," he said, coming back to stand next to Timmons. "There's some fresh scratches on it. Probably never even touched this one, just locked the cab door before shutting it again on the way out."

"That simple?" Jessie said, disgust in her tone.

" 'Fraid so. Car thieves do it all the time in a few seconds."

"And he *wanted* me to know he could get in," she added. "The other roses were left outside."

"How do you know it was a he?" Timmons asked.

"I guess I really don't," she said. "But I saw someone who moved like a man leaving the yard as we drove up." She indicated the place in the trees where the dark figure had disappeared at the back of the yard the night before. "That must have been whoever left the rose."

"Tell us about the roses," Becker requested, an odd, intent expression on his face.

Jessie complied, telling both of them everything she remembered, beginning with the first to arrive. "You remember, Phil. You were here when I found it." She reiterated her confrontation with the stubborn woman at the shop and her refusal to reveal the sender of the flowers, and then finding the second rose on her doorstep when she returned from driving Bonnie Russell to Palmer.

"Now this one. I was a little uneasy after the second one

showed up, but I thought it was just someone being nice in an odd way. Now I'm worried, Phil. More than that—I'm scared. This is too similar to last year's stalker for my taste. It isn't the least bit appealing or friendly anymore. There was something threatening about that appalling smell. Who the hell is sending these things—and why?"

Becker and Timmons exchanged a concerned and knowing glance, which did not go unnoticed by Jessie.

"You know something," she said. "What's going on? Tell me."

"Bear with me for a minute," Timmons suggested, leaning forward in his chair. "You must have wondered who sent the first two. Who did you put on your mental list?"

"Well—" Jessie hesitated, once again feeling defensive and reluctant. "Of course I thought of Alex, but that doesn't really work. I haven't heard from him since he left, but that's the way we left it. I wondered about Lynn Ehlers, but I was with him last night. It could be a shy racing fan. There's a whole list of people I know who could have sent flowers, I guess, but none of them leap off my mental list as having any kind of a reason I can think of. I figured I'd just wait and see, until this third one showed up. Things have a way of solving themselves, if you give them time. I just don't know, really."

"The solutions aren't always pleasant," Timmons said, running a hand through his fuzzy hair in an aggravated gesture that made it stand out from the top of his head. "On the surface this seems like a harmless, thoughtful thing to do—send you flowers. Only to some sick son of a bitch, it could be just the opposite, as you well know from last year—and last night. Right?"

She nodded, concern widening her eyes.

"What is it?" she asked again, hands held palm up toward him in pleading frustration. "Tell me what's going on, dammit."

"Okay. Okay. Take it easy. Becker?"

The trooper hunkered down in front of Jessie and pushed the brim of his hat back so he could more closely watch her reaction to what he was about to tell her.

"Look," he said. "This may have nothing at all to do with you, but the bodies of two women have been found in or near the Knik River in the last couple of days. Some kids and a fisherman found one three days ago under the bridge. It had floated down from somewhere upriver and we sent a team to try to find out where it came from, but that spot must be under water now, because they haven't found anything. Then, yesterday afternoon late, Bonnie Russell stumbled across another body."

"But what . . ."

"Let me finish."

At Becker's interruption, Jessie swallowed what she had been about to ask.

"We know who the first woman is: Kay Kendal, an exotic dancer who's been on a missing persons list for three weeks. She left a club in Anchorage one night after work and disappeared. Her roommate reported her missing a week later.

"We don't know the identity of the woman Bonnie Russell found yesterday, but from the way she was dressed, we think she was another working girl. The Anchorage police are on it—checking all the clubs, especially one called Bottoms Up, where the first woman worked. There are a couple of others who went missing early this spring. From the way they've disappeared, and where these two have been found, we think it might be . . ."

"*Hansen!*" Jessie breathed, recognizing the pattern Becker was describing as that of Alaska's most notorious serial killer.

"No! Not Hansen." Timmons was emphatic. "Robert Hansen is still safely and soundly incarcerated in Seward at Spring Creek and will *never* get out. He tried to escape once in Juneau, so now they keep a close watch on him. It's not Hansen, Jessie."

"Then . . ."

"A copycat." Becker picked up the story. "Someone making it look like Hansen's work. But two things stand out in all this. One thing is that not all these women are prostitutes. The first of last spring's missing women was a secretary at an insurance company. The second was a divorced woman with two kids."

"But what can all this have to do with me and whoever broke into the Winnebago last night?" Jessie asked in frustration.

He grimaced at the tight, controlled tone of her voice and hesitated a moment to glance again at Timmons before answering.

"The other thing—the thing that ties them all together—is this: Except for the woman Bonnie Russell found on the riverbank yesterday afternoon—and we won't know about her until we find out who she is—the others were all sent flowers by some anonymous person before they disappeared."

"Oh, God!" Jessie breathed. "Roses?"

"Yes. Single red roses." He nodded toward the inside of the

motor home and the three vases that stood on the table. "Like those.

"And though we can't tell about Kendal, because the river had washed her body clean, the clothes of the woman yesterday were saturated with the same smell as your roses."

Chapter 15

In the sunlight, clearly visible beyond the early-afternoon shadows cast by the peaks of the Chugach Mountains into the valley's west side, a small red and silver plane soared low over the Knik River. Its shadow flowed swiftly across the ground below, following the contours of the riverbanks and the rushing waters they contained. The plane caught the attention of an eagle perched in the top of a tall spruce, waiting for an incautious rabbit on the bank, or a salmon resting in the shallows along the shore. For a moment or two the large raptor watched the plane closely but soon decided it was not worth investigating.

High on the hill above the end of the road, a woman raised her head at the whine of an engine, rose from the chair she had been sitting in to read the morning paper while she ate her late lunch, and stepped to the window. She watched the plane pass below her, heading upriver. It gleamed brightly in the sunlight as it flashed in and out of her sight beyond the trees and disappeared around the shoulder of a hill. Thoughtfully, she sat back down, but her concentration was broken, and she leaned back and considered what she had seen. Though she waited a long time, listening carefully, she did not hear the plane return. It had either gone over the mountains to Turnagain Arm or had landed somewhere beyond the road along the river.

She thought it was the same plane she had seen before, within the last week, late in the evening, when there was just enough light left to be able to see that part of it was red. There had evidently been enough light for it to land somewhere up there, for she had not seen it come back; but sometime after midnight, she had wakened to the sound of its engine before rolling over and going back to sleep.

Remembering the woman's body the police had retrieved from the riverbank the day before, she frowned.

Some of the people who lived on the road that ran along the west side of the Knik River had been there when Robert Hansen had brought his victims into their front yard—as most of them considered this side of the river. She and her husband had not; they had bought the house and property only ten years earlier. But though their neighbors did not often speak of it, she had heard enough to be glad that that particular horror had taken place before they had moved in, and she resented the idea that something similar could be happening again. This current nastiness had to be the work of someone else, for Hansen was and would remain incarcerated. But the thought—*someone else*—sparked a note of fear in the back of her mind.

After another few minutes of deliberation, she got up again and went to the telephone. Laying a hand on the instrument, she hesitated, for those who lived along the road were independent sorts that tended to take care of their own problems, and she was not inclined to contact law enforcement as a general rule. Knowing the troopers had already had men and dogs search the area where the body had been found, she almost let it go. But uneasiness and concern overrode her predisposition, so before she could change her mind she quickly dialed the number on the card the officer had given her.

*   *   *

For the first time since they had started building her new cabin, Jessie hardly noticed what was happening in terms of her cabin building. Prentice was negotiating with the crane operator, who had arrived shortly after the truckload of logs, as to when they would be ready to start raising them into place. The crew was fully occupied in putting down a floor as fast as possible over the joists they had wrestled into place and bolted down. The sound of hammers filled the clearing, along with terse directives from foreman Bill. But Jessie's attention was focused on Timmons and Becker, her interest in construction overwhelmed by what she had just been told about the roses.

"Why me?" she asked. "What does any of this have to do with me?"

"We don't know," Timmons told her. "But there's got to be some reason. It may be that he thinks you know something because you live here. Maybe he's trying to scare you off. There may be someone else—Bonnie Russell's sister, maybe. What if she *is* buried on this lot? Maybe this is the guy you bought the property from, someone named . . ."

Jessie broke in. "Daryl O'Dell Mitchell."

He gave her an astonished look. "I thought you didn't remember his name."

"Called about the deed and found out."

"Oh. Well, turns out he was the nephew of the owner, and the property was transferred to him back in 1978. But there's no record of the old man's death."

"James O'Dell," Jessie supplied.

"Right again."

Timmons frowned in concern at the expression on Jessie's face, which clearly indicated the confusion and apprehension going on in her mind.

"Do you think this Daryl Mitchell killed the old man?" she asked.

"Someone did," Becker said. "Right, John?"

"Unfortunately, yes, someone did. But Jessie, take it easy. You've got to . . ."

But Jessie interrupted again, having no truck with advice at the moment.

"Could this guy be back in Alaska and after me just because I found his uncle? Does that make sense?"

The two men frowned at each other in frustration, trying to decide how much to tell her.

"We're doing a search to find out where he moved," Timmons said. "If he took a job in the Lower Forty-eight, he had to use his social security number. Where he worked will show up on his tax records, but it takes time to get into that."

"We don't know enough yet, Jessie," Becker added. "Have a little patience and give us some time. It may not be this Mitchell guy at all."

"Who, then? You've got to have some idea."

"That's what we're working on." He sighed and gave up a few more speculations. "There are another couple of leads. One woman we think is missing worked at another Anchorage bar, but they tend to go back and forth to cities on the West Coast—even to Hawaii. She could be anywhere: Seattle, Portland, San Francisco. We've put out the word on her. But I know one thing for sure. Considering what we know about these roses, it's not a good idea for you to be staying out here alone."

"But I *have* to be here."

As she waved a hand at her dogs and everything that was going on at the building site, his scowl deepened.

"What if *my* roses have nothing to do with this? It actually might be some friend, you know."

"And it might not," he snapped back, finally losing some of his ability to put up with her insistent questions. "That would have to be a pretty big coincidence, and I don't like the odds."

"Okay," she capitulated. "What do you suggest that—"

One of Timmons's assistants came trotting across the yard.

"Call dispatch, Phil. She said it's urgent."

As Becker went off to the patrol car to call in, Timmons tried again to convince Jessie of what he would consider reasonable.

"Phil didn't say you couldn't stay here, Jessie. He said you shouldn't be here *alone*."

"Oh. Right." She hesitated, thinking. "So if I had someone else with me, you think it'd be okay?"

"Well—if you had the right someone, it might be. But it would also be easier if you went somewhere else. Don't you have a friend you could stay with?"

"I've got my forty-four."

"Not good enough," Timmons protested. "A lot of people are killed with the handgun they keep for defense. Just having one doesn't guarantee anything."

As Jessie gave that some solemn thought, Becker came back from his call with a concerned look on his face.

"Someone along the old Knik River Road just called in and said they saw a plane fly up beyond the end of the road, and it hasn't come back. It may have gone farther south over the mountains, but the woman who called thinks it may have landed. I'm going up there and take a look. Maybe we'll get lucky, John."

"And maybe it's just a fisherman. It's a bit soon after this last woman, isn't it?"

"Who knows what this guy's pattern is, or what he'll do next? It can't hurt to check it out. The caller was the wife of the couple Bonnie Russell went to yesterday after she found the body. The woman said she's seen this same plane before. It could be our guy. I'll stop by later, Jessie." He turned to leave, but swung back to give her a stern look and add, "You aren't staying here alone. Got that?"

He was gone in seconds, raising dust in the driveway in a way that reminded Jessie how much the ground had dried out in the last few days. Timmons went back to working with his lab assistants in their examination of the rest of the yard. Jessie sat for a few minutes in the sun, considering what she had been told and wondering what to do about it.

Angry that someone she didn't know could threaten her, she was stubbornly tempted to stay where she was and ignore it, depending on her own defenses to keep herself out of harm's way. But whoever had intruded into her living space the night before could do so again. With care, he could be inside before she was aware and ready for him.

Not with Tank inside with me, she thought. But there were problems with that too. The women Becker and Timmons were telling her about had disappeared without its being noticed until they didn't show up as expected, at home or at work. There was no way of knowing how this had been accomplished and prepare for it.

She scowled and slapped her leather work gloves against the side of the bench in frustration. *You're too damned independent for your own good sometimes, Jessie!* she told herself, and knew it was true. For the moment, she gave up on the problem, but it lay in the back of her mind, a persistent nagging worry. With Alex Jensen living in the same house, she had felt a certain amount of protection and company with which to share the fear of a stalker. Now she had only herself to depend on. But it did no good to be unreasonably stubborn—and, as a voice in her head reminded her, it could get you killed.

Banishing the thought, she got up and walked over to where, under multiple hammer blows and the crack of a nail gun, the floor was rapidly expanding to cover the basement. Prentice came across to tell her what had been decided about the early log delivery.

"They'd already been loaded on the truck, so they brought 'em on out, hoping we'd be able to start today."

"Will we?" Jessie asked expectantly.

"Yeah." He grinned assurance in her direction. "I sent J.B. to get two guys from another job to lend a hand. Give us another couple of hours to finish the floor and put down those half logs, and then the log crew can start up with the rest. Okay?"

She nodded, but didn't answer, still wondering whom she could ask to stay with her that night that would satisfy Timmons and Becker—and herself. With the defining walls of her cabin about to take shape, the idea of going somewhere else appealed to her even less.

Stevie came trudging by them with part of a sheet of plywood subflooring she'd taken to the saw when it didn't quite fit where it belonged.

"Two hours, boss? You must know we're better than that."

"Not if I count your coffee breaks."

"Have I had one this morning? Not!" She grinned and moved on without stopping, but Jessie didn't respond.

"Hey, you okay?" Prentice asked, noticing her frown and lack of response.

"What? Oh, yeah, Vic. I'm okay."

She looked up and gave him a smile, but it was forced and she felt it.

"Look, Jessie. If something's wrong, maybe I can help." He paused to check her reaction. "I can at least listen."

She shook her head. "Thanks, Vic. I just—ah, no. It's just something I have to figure out."

"Well, let me know if there's anything I can do." He laid a friendly hand on her shoulder, went to follow Stevie back up the ladder to the unfinished floor, and was soon pounding nails with the rest of the crew. Refocusing, Jessie went to help.

.   .   .

By one-thirty the floor was laid. Waiting till Vic's people had gone for lunch, Jessie walked through what would soon become her living space. She envisioned the large window that would go into the wall nearest the dog yard and stood in front of that space, imagining a view of all her mutts. Despite all the noise and activity going on nearby, none of them seemed disturbed. Tank lay on top of his box in the sun, muzzle on front paws, keeping track of what was happening in a lazy sort of way. Bliss had rolled to her back and was asleep, half in, half out of her box, on some straw she had dragged out, probably getting tired of the pressure of lying on unborn puppies. Tux, totally unaware of the existence of his progeny, was lapping water from his bowl. He looked up as if he knew he was being observed, walked to the length of his tether, and lay down as close as he could to his best pal, Pete.

Jessie turned around to assess the rest of the space the main floor of the cabin would occupy. It seemed suddenly larger than she had anticipated, but she realized that was an illusion. Walls would make a difference.

Timmons, finding nothing, had packed up his equipment and assistants and departed, shaking his head in resignation.

"You hear me, Jessie," he had said, frowning through the lowered window of the van. "It's *not a good idea* to stay out here alone."

Vic's people, like Jessie's dogs, were relaxed around the yard on piles of building equipment and supplies. Dell, as usual, lay sprawled on a pile of lumber, hat over his eyes, supposedly catching a snooze with Stevie nearby. Vic and Bill had gone into the motor home to take another look at the blueprints. Hank Peterson, who had finished moving and smoothing dirt before joining the flooring effort, was balanced on a sawhorse, munching an apple. He grinned up at her. "It's lookin' good, Jessie."

"Be even better soon," she returned, and climbed down to find something edible for herself. It had been a long time since breakfast.

· · ·

Before lunch was over, the crane had roared to life and its operator was swinging logs into place around the perimeter of the finished floor.

Except for Bill, after a bit of cleanup, Vic's crew had gone.

"You've all done a full day's work in record time." Vic waved them off. "Get outa here. I bet you can think of something to do with a sunny day."

But the work continued, for with the logs had come another crew of experienced builders from the company. Their expertise lay in knowing precisely how to shape logs and fit them together, one on top of the other, until they formed walls in the predetermined configuration. They had already built the cabin once, as it had been designed, in the company yard where the logs were turned and cut. Each one had then been numbered, the structure taken apart, and the logs put on the trucks in reverse order, so that the first to be loaded would be the last to be delivered and raised on site.

They worked rapidly, skillfully, reassembling the cabin like an enormous set of Lincoln Logs. Swinging the heavy logs around carefully in order to miss the trees that grew close on one side, the crane operator lifted each one to where it belonged. Then he lowered it slowly, while two men maneuvered it into place, allowing precut holes in it to settle over the long bolts J.B. had set into the concrete before it hardened.

Hank Peterson stayed for a while to watch and gratefully accepted a beer Jessie retrieved from the motor home. They sat together on the pile of lumber Dell had vacated, enjoying brew and sunshine and watching the logs go up, one by one.

Vic Prentice finally sent Bill home as well and joined them when the logs were two high around the perimeter of the cabin floor.

"So whaddaya think, Jessie? Beginning to look like a house?"

"Yes!" Satisfaction filled her voice, and he was glad to see a smile back on her face.

Chapter 16

 When the logs were five high, the crane was shut down for the night and the building crew departed. Hank Peterson had already gone, but Vic Prentice had stayed to be sure everything went as planned.

After Hank left, Jessie sat watching the work till midafternoon, thinking hard about staying alone that night. She understood her reluctance to ask anyone for help and the stubborn independence that was responsible for her attitude. The motivations behind her inflexibility were unimportant at the moment, so she refused to assess them. She recognized that she was struggling between two fears—one of depending on someone else and the other of some unknown person's possible intrusion. The two seemed to weigh equally in her mind, so there was no easy solution.

What can I do to lessen the odds if this nut with the roses shows up again? What can I do to make myself safe? she asked herself and felt better. Doing something—anything—was superior to worry. What were her assets? Could she improve or add to them?

The roses had possibly been intended to please but confuse her, perhaps to create a benign feeling that would lessen suspicion. If she hadn't caught sight of her floral benefactor disappearing into the trees the night before, it might have worked. But she *had* seen him, though he might not know it. And now, thanks to Timmons and Becker, she knew—or thought she knew—that this was no generous racing fan or secret admirer. That knowledge was an asset, for she was now aware and on guard.

The dogs in her kennel were a help, for some of them barked at every unfamiliar vehicle, person, even animal that entered the yard. She could count on them to warn her of an approach, welcome or not. Bringing Tank inside with her for the night would be a good idea. He would, she knew, be excellent protection, for he wouldn't hesitate to place himself between his mistress and any threat. Maybe she would bring in dependable Pete as well.

In the back of a closet in the Winnebago, Jessie had a reliable Winchester Model 70 Pre 64 given to her by her father. He had taught her to shoot the bolt-action rifle, and she was comfortable with it. It was one of the few things that had not burned in the arson of her cabin, and she kept it mostly for sentimental reasons, her Smith & Wesson .44 being handier to carry on the trail with her dog teams, where she might need to shoot an angry or recalcitrant moose. She thought about getting the rifle out but wasn't satisfied with the idea of so large a weapon in the limited confines of a motor home. It would be too easy to bump the barrel against something, spoil her aim, and miss a target. However, there might be another solution to this problem.

Just after three, she took Tank with her in the pickup and made a quick run into Palmer to a gun dealer's where she had done previous business. Vic kept an eye on her property for the hour she was gone, though he asked no questions, assuming she had gone for supplies—which, in a way, she had.

At five o'clock, he was the last to pull out of the drive, promising to be back early the next morning, all his focus on the work at hand and knowing nothing of what Becker and Timmons had told Jessie about possible danger or the threat of the roses. After she watched him pull out of sight, she went immediately to her pickup and carried a couple of packages into the motor home, where she set about familiarizing herself with what she had purchased and preparing to spend the night alone. When all was as ready as she could make it, she stepped back outside to admire the afternoon's progress on her house, wearing her .44 in its holster around her waist, unwilling to be caught off guard. Though abductions probably took place at night, when darkness made it harder to see, such an assumption could be a serious mistake.

The persistent silence that filled the clearing once the crane was silent gave her back a sense of ownership in her own property. It always seemed more hers when she was alone, with only the familiar kennel and woodland sounds around her. She knew them all and enjoyed them now.

The musical *twee-twee-twee* of tiny warblers combined pleasantly with a siskin's *sweeeeet* and the kinglets' thin *see-see-see* rising from the branches of the spruce, where they were hunting insects and larvae or seeds from the cones. A couple of squirrels chased each other from tree to tree, taking daring leaps of faith through the air and drawing disdainful glances from several of the dogs, who didn't bother to move or bark, knowing from past experience that they were uncatchable.

In an hour, Jessie had fed and watered all her dogs, checked their physical condition, and given each a ration of attention along with their food. It lifted her spirits to spend time with them, for their affection was unconditional and uncomplicated. Though different in looks, temperament, and ability, they were all alike in their absolute trust and respect for her, and she knew she would never be comfortable leaving them alone. The last time something like this had happened, one of them had been badly hurt.

Though she never felt confused or insecure with her dogs, people were different. It was often hard to know how they felt or what they were thinking. Each was a risk, difficult to weigh and, to Jessie, best kept at a safe distance. When she was uncomfortable, as she was now, she was even more aware and cautious of that calculated distance.

And there are old reasons for that too, she told herself, finishing with her jobs in the dog yard and locking up her shed. But once again she refused to think about them, knowing just how much she needed to remain attentive and alert.

Phil Becker showed up, as promised, close to seven, and was not pleased when she told him she intended to stay by herself that night.

"Dammit, Jessie. I told you staying out here alone was a bad idea. Do I have to carry you around in my back pocket?"

His frown was a thundercloud of disapproval.

Ignoring his glower, she answered him with calm confidence. "Better not try. Look, I appreciate your concern, but I've got it figured out and I'll be just fine."

"You *think* you will," he shot back. "What if this guy shows up again?"

His *think* struck a nerve and her response was sharper than she had intended. "Then my guys will let me know and I'll take steps."

"You can't depend on a bunch of dogs to protect you when they're tethered to their boxes," he fumed in frustration.

Regaining her composure, she refused to argue, preferring to convince him with quiet reason, knowing his worry was sincere.

"But I can depend on their warning. They know *you*, but some of them barked anyway, didn't they?" she reminded him. "Anyone comes into the yard, they'll let me know, loud and clear. I'll bring Tank and Pete inside for the night, and I've made other preparations."

"What preparations?" he demanded.

She took him inside the motor home to see.

A sleeping bag on a foam mattress that she used on training runs with the dogs lay in the shelter of the bed on the floor, out of sight from any window, all of which had the blinds and curtains tightly closed over them.

"I'm sleeping there, where I can't be seen from outside, not in the bed."

Becker shook his head. "It's too easy to jimmy either of the cab doors. You might not hear it till it was too late."

"Tank will. And if he knows, I'll know."

"What else?"

"This." From an out-of-sight corner within reach of the

sleeping bag, Jessie brought forth the shotgun she had purchased at the gun shop earlier that afternoon.

"Anyone with any sense at all will be very careful of a frightened woman behind a shotgun at close range."

He couldn't help grinning his approval. "Not a bad idea, but I still think . . ."

"Phil, I'll be fine. I've got the phone and I'll use it if I hear or see anything. Okay?"

"I'll stay." He sat down on a bench at the table and folded his arms stubbornly.

For the first time, Jessie exhibited irritation.

"No, Phil, you *won't*." Hearing annoyance raise her voice, she backed off and offered a compromise. "I wouldn't mind if you sent whoever's on duty around a couple of times tonight, though, just to be sure everything's kosher."

As she watched him consider this option, she wondered just how much of his intractability was due to some request from Jensen to take care of her. It would be like Becker to take that sort of responsibility to heart.

He looked up, still frowning disagreement, and finally gave in. "Timmons won't like it."

"He'll live."

"That's just what I'm worr . . ."

"Bad choice of words. Sorry," she apologized, with a grin. "Don't tell him, okay?"

"Ri–ight. And you think he won't ask first thing in the morning—if not later tonight?"

Jessie changed the subject, knowing Timmons too well to wonder any such thing.

"Find anything upriver today?"

"Nope. Heard a plane taking off, but on foot past the end of the road we couldn't get in far enough to catch up with it. Whoever it was must have flown on over the hill, because the plane didn't come back in our direction."

Becker's forehead wrinkled in concern and disappointment at the near miss.

"What are you going to do about it?"

"Still thinking. Commander Swift's reluctant to put somebody out there for days or weeks without any results. We've been short-handed since Alex left. Tomorrow I may fly up and take a look beyond where we reached today, if I can get hold of Ben Caswell and his plane."

He left, still shaking his head, but looked back to wave as he turned out of the driveway and onto the road, headed toward Wasilla.

*   *   *

As promised, Jessie brought in Tank and Pete, who were both glad to lie down under the table. She ate dinner and settled on her improvised bed on the floor with a pile of pillows behind her against the wall and a historical mystery she'd been saving, knowing a favorite author would claim a large share of her attention and keep her from thinking too much. She took a flashlight, the phone, and a list of numbers she might need, just in case, and put out a hand to pat the shotgun appreciatively, before beginning to read.

At nine, she felt sleepy and took a nap, knowing that as soon as it grew as dark as it was going to get she would want to stay awake for an hour or two. Turning off the reading light she had been using, she left the light on over the stove in the galley and drifted off into uneasy dreams. She woke sometime later to the sound of a dog barking outside. Several other dogs added to the cacophony of yips and barks. Tank and Pete both raised their heads to listen but did not join in.

Slowly, with great care, Jessie rolled forward onto her knees, quietly opened the door, and crawled into the lavatory. In the narrow hallway that led to the bedroom of the motor home, the bathroom was divided, a shower stall on one side and a lavatory with toilet on the side facing the driveway, along which she could now hear the sound of tires approaching. Cautiously, with one finger, she pulled down a single slat in the venetian blind till she could see out—and breathed a sigh of relief. A patrol car was coming slowly up the drive with only its parking lights for illumination.

When the officer knocked softly on the door, she was there to open it.

He was young and stiffly official. "Officer Duncan, Miss Arnold. Everything okay here?"

Assured that it was, he was gone again in minutes, and Jessie went back to her bed. But the incident had shaken her confidence slightly. Turning out the galley light, she lay in the gathering darkness, feeling vulnerable and worried. There would be no more sleep this night.

Still, she dozed a little from time to time, waking to small familiar sounds from outside. It was very still at one o'clock in the morning when Tank, who had curled up on the mattress by Jessie's feet, suddenly stood up and turned to stare toward the front of the Winnebago. His movement startled her from a dream she was having about struggling through deep snow during the Yukon Quest race and feeling she was getting nowhere. Sitting up, she listened with him, and adrenaline flooded through her at the sudden metallic sound of someone quietly trying the door on the passenger side of the cab. The sound stopped, and there was nothing for a moment, before whoever it was tried again on the driver's side.

Heart pounding, Jessie climbed silently to her feet, laying a hand on Tank's muzzle, to warn him not to bark. She had stretched out a hand for the shotgun when she remembered Pete but could not reach him in time. Moving from under the table, where he had been sleeping, he barked sharply. Instantly, the sound at the door stopped. One dog in the yard barked in response to Pete, but the rest were quiet.

From behind the motor home, somewhere close to the edge of the trees, she heard a thump and a muffled expletive, as if someone had tripped over something. Then, for a long minute, there was no other sound. Tank relaxed and turned to let her know that whoever had been trying the doors was not now an immediate threat. Satisfied with himself, Pete sat down and waited to be congratulated.

With a shaking hand, Jessie reached for the flashlight, turned it on, and found her list by the phone.

First, she called the troopers' office, then tried Lynn Ehlers. Call the law, then call me, he had instructed, and she took him up on the offer. To hell with independence.

But his phone rang and rang until she could almost hear it echoing in an empty house, and no one answered.

"Damn."

Selecting her second choice from the list, she dialed again and waited. Hank Peterson answered on the third ring with a groggy, "Hullo. It's fuckin' one-thirty in the morning. Whaddaya want?"

"Hank? It's Jessie." She could hear the slight quiver in her own voice.

There was a hesitation, then, "Jessie? Arnold? Jeez, Jessie, I'm sorry I . . ."

She interrupted his sleepy string of apologies.

"Listen, there's someone in my yard, trying to get into the Winnebago. Can you come?"

He was wide awake now!

"I'm on my way. Call the cops."

His receiver clattered back into the cradle, cutting her off and leaving her "Already did" hanging in air.

She could only hope he would arrive before whoever was out there tried again to get in and she would be forced to defend herself.

Chapter 17

Peterson came roaring up the drive in the flatbed truck he used to haul around his Bobcat, still wearing the T-shirt he slept in, though he'd yanked on a pair of sweats over his underwear shorts. He leaped out, snatching a wrench from under the driver's seat, and came running to pound on Jessie's door, bare feet in a pair of leather slippers.

"It's Hank, Jessie. You okay? Open up."

Young Officer Duncan arrived right behind him, without flashing lights or siren, and was out of the patrol car with his gun in his hand when Jessie opened the door. She called out to let him know that Hank was not the person who had tried to break into the Winnebago, and he holstered it.

"What happened, ma'am?" he asked, such a total contrast in

his neat duty uniform to Peterson in his sleepwear that Jessie's sense of humor was tickled. She giggled and realized that it was a nervous reaction.

"Someone tried to get in through both cab doors," she explained to the men, "but one of the dogs barked and scared him off. I know he ran into the woods, because I heard him trip over something and swear."

"Did you get a look at him?"

"No. There wasn't time, and it might have been too dark anyway."

It was dark, though not totally, for there was still a pale line of light on the western horizon that she could see through the trees across Knik Road.

The young officer nodded. "He picked the darkest couple of hours, all right. I'm going out to take a look around."

"I'm coming with you," Peterson told him. "Lend me a jacket, Jessie?"

"Sure, but if you think I'm staying in here by myself, you're both crazy."

They searched the clearing and the edge of the surrounding woods even more thoroughly than Jessie and Lynn Ehlers had searched it the night before. When he found a footprint next to a stump behind the motor home, Officer Duncan marked it and said he would call in for someone from the crime lab to come the next morning to make a cast. Several branches had been broken, seemingly from a person rushing to leave the scene. One had a gray thread of what looked like wool from a sweater or other knit garment hanging on the sharp broken end of it. Other than that they found nothing, until a second officer arrived from farther out Knik Road.

"There's a green pickup parked off the road in the Settlers Bay parking lot," he informed them. "Whoever it is won't be moving it anytime soon. I took the distributor cap."

Jessie scowled, as a sudden unwelcome idea found its way into her mind.

"Does it have a dog box in the bed?"

"Yes. Do you know whose it is?"

"I might. Let's go take a look and I'll see."

Getting out of the patrol car, she stood looking at the green pickup and shaking her head.

"Whose is it, Jessie?" Peterson asked.

Without a word, she turned, walked across the parking lot, and called across the road toward the trees on the other side.

"Lynn Ehlers? If you're in there, come on out."

There was a rustle of brush and the Minnesota musher, wearing a dark jacket open over a snagged gray sweater, came walking out of the trees toward them, a rifle over one arm, its barrel pointed at the ground.

"Put down your weapon," Officer Duncan snapped immediately, hand on the pistol in his holster.

"It's okay, officer," Jessie hastily assured him "I know this man. He's a friend, aren't you, Lynn?"

It took a few minutes to convince the officers that he should not be placed under arrest and questioned, but they eventually departed, giving him back his distributor cap with dubious looks and a warning not to try anything similar in future.

"This lady may refuse to press charges, but you frightened her half to death," the young officer scolded him sternly. "She would have been justified in shooting you. And I'll be watching you, so don't forget it."

*   *   *

"I'm sorry, Jessie, I didn't mean to scare you," Lynn apologized when he, Jessie, and Hank were all back in the motor home with the two dogs and their arsenal of weapons. "I've been watching your yard for the last two nights—came back last night after you'd gone to bed. I tried the doors to make sure they were locked and you didn't hear a thing. How was I to know you'd take a dog inside tonight—or have company?" he added, giving the sleeping clothes Peterson was wearing a jealous glance.

This was one error too many for Jessie, who sat down abruptly on the forward sofa and laughed until tears ran down her face.

"What?" he demanded, ego obviously smarting. "What's so damned funny?"

Hank was also chuckling, realizing the humor in the situation, and Ehler's defensive question made them both laugh even harder. The scare Jessie'd had, the irony of the situation—thinking she was taking care of herself, when all the while there had been someone else looking out for her—the very fact that she was trying to stop laughing and couldn't: none of it helped.

"You just—don't—understand, Lynn," she attempted to tell him.

"Oh, I think I do," he snapped back.

"No—you—really don't."

"Sit down, Ehlers," Hank told him. "We'll clear it up for you as soon as Jessie gets sane again. Beer, anyone?" He helped himself to a bottle from the refrigerator and handed one to Lynn.

Jessie shook her head at the offer, wiping her eyes with the backs of her hands, but came to the table to join them.

"I called the troopers first," she told Lynn, gaining control of her hilarity. "Then I tried to call you. Nobody answered. Obviously you weren't there; you were here, but I didn't know that. So I called Hank, who came in a hurry, in what you see him wearing. He's a very good friend, nothing more. He wasn't sleeping here, Lynn."

He stared at her as comprehension dawned, along with a shamefaced expression to match his embarrassed blush.

"Boy!" he said finally. "I really screwed that one up, didn't I? Sorry, guys. Tonight was pretty much of a total screwup, I guess. But I know how you like to take care of yourself, Jessie, and I didn't want—"

"I know, Lynn. It's okay," she interrupted, still smiling. "Actually, you'll have to admit it's pretty funny. I thought I was being so self-sufficient, and the minute something goes down what do I do? I call the police and you—and Hank, when you don't answer. You were being considerate of my stupid independence and, in the process, scared me into howling for any help I could get."

"Hey," Hank broke in, "I'm not just *any* help! But it was a lot like the Keystone Kops."

Lynn nodded and, finally, grinned. "Might as well laugh, I guess."

"What I'd like to know," Hank asked, "is why you thought you needed to watch Jessie's yard in the first place."

Startled, Jessie realized that Hank knew nothing about the intruder she had seen, and neither he nor Lynn knew what Becker had told her concerning the roses. She spent the next few minutes explaining the situation to both.

Hank, sensing Ehlers had more to say to Jessie that would not be said with him there, went home to catch a few winks before it was time to come back again for work. Jessie walked him to his truck and thanked him for coming to her rescue, even though, as it turned out, she didn't need rescuing. He became serious after he had climbed into the truck, leaning out the window with concern that was rapidly becoming a familiar litany to her.

"It sounds to me like you'd better think again about all this, Jessie, and maybe stop trying to take care of everything by yourself. I might not be able to get here fast enough if this guy you saw came back again and caught you off guard. That cop didn't get here until *after* I did. Just keep in mind that friends help each other. It's what friends are for."

"I know, Hank. It's hard for me. I've taken care of myself for most of my life. That's all mixed up with some old history, but I'm trying to work it out, okay?"

"Well, don't get stiff-necked. Call if you need me, and I'll try not to swear at you over the phone."

•   •   •

Lynn stayed to keep Jessie company for a while longer as it gradually grew light again outside. When the sun began to come up at three-thirty, he went home to catch up on his sleep, but before that they sat together at the table over the breakfast Jessie made and talked a little.

"Where's your family, Lynn?" she asked, pushing fried potatoes around her plate with a fork. "Do you have any brothers and sisters?"

"Oh, yeah." He grinned. "They're spread all over Minnesota—three brothers and two sisters. My dad says I collect dogs now because I miss the company of all us kids when we were growing up. He could be right."

"Are they older or younger?"

"Both. I was fourth in the litter. You?"

She laid down the fork and picked up a strip of bacon with her fingers.

"My folks sort of had two families. I have a sister nine years older in Ohio."

"That it?"

It was a simple and not unusual question, but Jessie felt her breath catch in her throat, once again confronted with the past. The emotional roller coaster of the last few hours collided with the loss that had been hovering at the back of her mind and derailed her without warning in a sudden flood of tears.

"Dammit!"

Lynn froze in surprise and puzzlement as a sob escaped her. Concern deepened his voice. "Jessie?"

Swiping angrily at her face, she picked up her cup and took a long drink of hot coffee, scalding her mouth. Jumping up from the table, she snatched a glass and gulped water from the galley tap, then grabbed a handful of tissue to dab at her face and blow her nose.

Lynn waited, saying nothing, till she came back and sat down. When she had settled, he gave her a troubled and questioning look.

"Sorry," she told him. "I don't like to talk about this, Lynn. It's old and it's over, but it's still painful, okay? I had two sisters. Jane's, the oldest—the one in Ohio. Then there was Lily, who was three years younger. But she's . . . We lost her."

"You mean she died?" he asked gently.

"No–yes." Tears started again, but she ignored them. "I mean we *lost* her. She disappeared one afternoon, on her way home from school. She was only seven years old, and she was just gone. We've never known—what happened to her."

"Jesus!"

Once started, Jessie couldn't seem to stop. Words tumbled out in a flood of self-recrimination.

"It was my fault. I was supposed to walk her home. But I wanted to talk to a teacher first, so I told her to wait. Instead, she started without me. The police thought someone must have taken her, but there was nothing to find; no one saw anything. It was my fault. My parents just about went crazy looking for her. My dad still looks. Everywhere he goes, he's always looking for Lily."

"It wasn't really your fault, Jessie," Lynn said carefully, quietly. "It was the responsibility of whoever took her."

"I know. I've been told that all my life. But I know my parents didn't think so. It was never the same, for them or for me. That's how I learned to take care of myself—feeling guilty and not wanting to be in the way while they searched for her."

The tears were running down her face as she stared out through the blinds he had opened when they sat down.

Without another word, he stood up and came around to her side of the table, slid in, and reached for her. She let him hold and rock her as she wept, accepting, for the moment, the small hushed sounds of comfort he breathed in her ear.

When she had cried herself out, he put her to bed, covered her warmly with her northern lights quilt, and sat on the edge of the bed until she had fallen into an exhausted sleep. Though Pete kept his place under the table, Tank came and jumped up to curl at Jessie's feet, a thing he did when she was sick.

Ehlers, recognizing the bond between them, knew she would be all right and left her, making sure the doors were securely locked and the blinds once again closed.

But he stood for a long time, watching the shadows lengthen and darken in contrast as the sun came up to splash light across the clearing, appreciating the scent of warming spruce needles, listening to the birds begin their familiar daily chorus, the buzz of a lazy bumblebee, a dog or two stirring in the yard.

"No wonder," he muttered finally, in a low voice. "No wonder."

Then he hiked back along the road to replace the distributor cap under the hood of his green pickup.

Chapter 18

 At close to eleven o'clock on a midweek evening, the side streets of Anchorage were deep with purple shadows. But the tallest buildings on the main streets that ran east from Cook Inlet still retained a hint of the sunset that had set the thin close-clinging bands of cloud on the western horizon afire with brilliant hues of gold and fuchsia that slowly faded into mauve.

Some people and vehicles moved along Fourth Avenue, but it was far less crowded than it would have been on a weekend night. A musical performance at the Performing Arts Center had just let out, and the crowd was dispersing along Fifth and Sixth. Few had parked as far away as Fourth, so only a couple or two and a small group of women strolled toward their cars, parked in a lot below the bright-yellow Sunshine Mall, which seemed to catch more of the late light than the less colorful buildings around it.

Outside the Bottoms Up, two blocks east, it was quiet, the parking lot only half full of cars and trucks. A dark brown pickup swung into the lot from the alley that ran behind it and pulled into a rear space next to the concrete-block building. Its driver shut off the engine, stepped out, and locked the door, pocketing his keys. He then walked past the other vehicles and around to the front door.

Inside, he stopped for a moment to let his vision adjust to darkness not matched outside at this time of year.

Only half the seats in the place were occupied, most of them at tables near the extended runway of a stage. A spotlight illuminated the nearly nude woman who was gyrating to the loud music in nothing but a fabric brief that scarcely covered her crotch and narrowed to a thong in back. Her naked breasts bounced with her suggestive moves, the color of her nipples enhanced with a bit of the same lipstick that stained her mouth.

For a long minute, he watched the woman as she lay down and spread her legs wide apart to exhibit herself to two men at a table next to the runway. Someone at another table whistled as one of them reached to tuck a bill under the thin strap she wore around her hips. But she was not to the taste of the man at the door, not what he had in mind in coming there. Her thighs were too heavy, in his estimation, and her large breasts too obviously silicone. He liked them to quiver more naturally.

Turning, he walked across the room to an empty table in the dark, beyond the bar and away from the stage, where he could see not only the woman who danced but those who watched as well. A scantily clad barmaid was instantly at his elbow to take an order. She stalked away in a pair of high-heeled shoes and returned quickly with his drink. Close behind her came a tall woman, another dancer, who had been sitting with two others on tall stools at the bar. She cocked her head and asked a question, but he frowned without looking at her and waved her away without a word. With a shrug, she went back across the room and sat down, elbow on the bar, chin on her palm, a study in ennui.

The front door opened, letting in outside light that seemed brighter than it was in contrast to the darkness within. Two uniformed policemen walked through it and paused just inside, giving the place and its entertainment a thorough visual inspection. The shorter of the two gestured toward the swiveling hips of the occupant of the stage and made a comment to his partner, who grinned and nodded, attention now focused on the dancer. Crossing to the women at the bar, they asked a question or two, but all three shook their heads and the officers left the way they had come in, with a last look at the woman in the spotlight as they went out the door.

The man in the shadows observed all this without turning his head and relaxed slightly when they had gone. The music ended, and the dancer disappeared behind the curtains. There was a pause before the music started again with a livelier beat and another woman stepped onto the stage. His attention was drawn to her face, figure, and particularly her dark hair, but the brunette did not interest him either. Lifting his glass, he drained it in one long pull and raised it in the direction of the waitress, who quickly brought him another. He sipped it more slowly, casually observing the action on the runway but clearly waiting for something more to his liking.

The third dancer to appear from behind the curtains was a blonde. A glitter of rhinestones caught the light from her pubic area and around her neck as she strutted onto the runway swinging her hips, a little awkwardly but in time to the bump-and-grind music. It was immediately apparent that she was younger—hardly more than a girl—and less skilled than the previous women. Where they had been blasé, seldom exhibiting more expression than a sensual parting of the lips to mask boredom, this one was very aware of her audience and working hard to please. A tight artificial smile gave away an attempt to cover nervousness, and her eyes never quite met those of the men who surrounded the stage. Though her rhythmic thrusts and poses were decidedly amateur, she was energetic in presenting herself for the attention of her audience.

The man at the table in the back straightened slightly in his chair at her appearance. This was what he had come to see, and his eyes never left her as she strutted and writhed through the exotic number.

The preceding dancer, now strolling through the room to solicit table dances, approached and laid a hand on his shoulder in an attempt to distract his attention from the girl on the stage. Without so much as a glance, he jerked his shoulder from under it and shook his head emphatically. She curled a lip, drifted off with a shrug he did not see, and was instantly as absent from his mind as she was from his purview, his interest fully focused on the young woman in the spotlight.

When the music ended and she vanished behind the curtains, he did not linger, knowing she would not dance again this night, at least on this stage. Finishing his drink, he refused another, and handed a few coins to the barmaid, earning the disgusted look she cast at his back as he left.

Unlocking his pickup, he climbed in and sat, waiting silently in the dark, patient and predatory.

When the blond woman came around the corner of the Bottoms Up he watched her head across the parking lot toward a car. Before she could reach it, he had started the engine of the brown truck, backed it up, and pulled forward to cut her off. She stiffened as he addressed her through his open window, but soon relaxed when she recognized him. This man was familiar and, if not a regular, at least an occasional customer she knew by sight. She smiled and turned her head to glance at a car that passed on the street with a whistle from a male passenger.

In the glow of the streetlight, he could see the side of her head, and he grinned.

She wore a red rose in her hair.

Chapter 19

Jessie didn't sleep for long after Ehlers left. She was awake again in just over an hour, finding herself alone except for Tank, who raised his head when she moved, and dependable Pete, whom she could hear shifting position under the table in the galley.

She lay staring at the ceiling for a few minutes, feeling ashamed of her outburst of tears. She didn't cry often and hated it when she did, considering it a sign of weakness. Now, twice in only a few days, she had allowed herself to be defeated by her emotions.

Covering her face with both hands, caught in an ache of humiliation and fatigue, she rolled over toward the window, pulled the quilt over her head, and considered the causes for her uncharacteristic behavior. Tension was the culprit, she decided.

And what exactly was causing so much tension? The threat of the roses, she could identify and understand. But hadn't she done everything possible to protect herself? Except for letting others take charge when they had every right to do so, she knew she had.

An idea she had heard somewhere and taken for her own crept into her thinking: If something bothers or upsets you, one of two things is happening: Either you are taking too much responsibility for someone else, or you are letting someone take too much for you.

That had always made sense, but what specific responsibility was she not taking, or taking when she shouldn't? She had had little control over most of the events of the last few days. Her discovery of the old man's body; the delays in construction that resulted; the confusion caused by Becker, Timmons, and other people, like Bonnie Russell, making demands: all created tension by eroding her ability to be in control. But *was* she letting someone else take too much responsibility for what she should be doing herself? From the reaction of those around her—even Lynn Ehlers and Hank Peterson—it seemed the other way around and she was taking too much on herself. Was that true?

There were other things to add to the equation. She recalled her resistance to more digging when Timmons had showed up to search for another body in her yard. Her reluctance was not simple fear of another interruption, she also disliked having other people intrude on her personal space. Her property, especially that occupied by her kennel and cabin, was personal space. The idea that there could be another body lying beneath the ground somewhere on *her* land was a possibility that had haunted her thoughts like a restless spirit refusing to depart—a ghost demanding attention, unearthing, and remedy. But if the butterfly necklace had been found in her yard, didn't it make sense that the woman who wore it could be there as well? Was she buried out there—somewhere—waiting to be found?

Well, by God, if she is, I'll find her and have the matter over and done, Jessie told herself, and sat up abruptly, causing Tank to jump down from his place at the foot of the bed and stand waiting to see what she intended. She got out of bed still dressed from the evening before and went hunting for her shoes. Finding them on the floor at the foot of the bed where Lynn had neatly aligned them, she jammed them on.

She started to take the shotgun, thought about the awkwardness of carrying it around in the woods, and belted on her dependable Smith & Wesson .44, grabbed a jacket, and went out, taking Tank but leaving Pete to guard the Winnebago. Locking the door behind her, she dropped the keys in her pocket and started across the yard.

"Come on, buddy. We'll do our damnedest."

It was growing light enough to see everything in the yard, but it was still fairly dark under the trees that edged the clearing. Jessie stopped by the half-built cabin and assessed the spot where the old man's bones had been dug from the ground.

If I were going to bury someone, why would I do it so close to my living space? she asked herself, trying to think like someone with a body to hide. Because it was handy and could be done quickly?

That didn't make sense, for it was also where anyone coming to the cabin might notice and question disturbed earth alongside it. Besides, Timmons thought the old man might have frozen to death and been buried later, when the ground thawed. If that was true, wouldn't a second body be buried in or near the same spot—even in the same grave, for that matter? Since the lab crew had carefully searched this area and found nothing, did that mean there wasn't another body or that that person hadn't died to be buried at the same time?

This grave had been dug on the south side of the old cabin, she realized, the side that would thaw first in the spring. Was the answer to the old man's burial as simple as that? It seemed reasonable. But if he had frozen to death, where had his body been kept until winter released the ground from its icy grip?

Where would I keep a body—maybe two bodies—I was waiting to bury?

It would have to be out of sight of the cabin and anyone who happened to visit the claim on which it sat. The woods, of course. Somewhere deep in the woods but close enough to make retrieval quick and easy. Perhaps a second body had been buried there instead of here in the open.

Jessie turned and headed for the trees behind her storage shed, an area Timmons' assistants had not yet searched. As she entered the woods, the shadows of the sheltering branches of the trees blocked off most of the light but left her enough to see. Tank halted next to her and looked up.

"Hey, guy. Got any good ideas?"

If he had, he wasn't sharing. She walked a little deeper into the grove, his presence at her side reminding her that other animals still roamed these woods at times: bears, foxes, wolves. Twenty years ago wolves had not been uncommon, though they were now seldom seen. People back then had built caches on tall stiltlike legs or roped their frozen winter meat up into trees to protect it. Jessie remembered no evidence of a cache, but the old guy might not have bothered to build one with so many convenient trees close to his cabin. A killer who didn't want his human meat to be disturbed, and possibly revealed, by canine predators might have stashed a body overhead in similar fashion.

She walked slowly through the woods looking up into the branches, taking her bearings from the cabin she could glimpse between the trees in the growing light from the clearing. Jessie knew that trunks and lower limbs of trees do not move higher as they grow; growth extends the branches, but the trunk and limbs only grow thicker as rings are added year by year, swelling their dimensions. Any marks, scars, or trauma to the outer bark might scar over but would remain at about the same level as when damage occurred. Pulling weight over a branch with a rope might abrade and scar it in a way that could be visible, so Jessie looked carefully at each one.

Several times she heard noises in the thick underbrush but saw nothing when she whirled to look, hand going instinctively to the gun at her waist. It was just dark enough to make her nervous, but there were all kinds of small natural sounds in an old-growth forest of this kind, and most were familiar and to be expected. Still, she was cautious in her search and glad to have Tank for company.

It soon grew light enough for her to see quite well. The song of birds resounded around her as she searched, and a family of squirrels chided her for intruding upon their territory. In an hour she had examined every tree within fifty yards of where the woods met the clearing behind where the old man's cabin had stood, and found nothing. When it was broad daylight and beams of sunshine filtered through the branches and leaves that surrounded her, she sat down on a fallen log to rest for a minute. Yawning, she reached a hand to pat Tank, who had come to sit on the ground beside her.

"Well, it was a good idea, wasn't it?" she told him, her shoulders slumping in exhaustion and disappointment. With the other hand, she reached up to rub the back of her own neck, weary of holding her head back at an angle to look up into the trees. A robin coasted in to land in the sunlight of a small open spot and cocked its head to listen for underground angleworms.

If she went back to bed now she could get an hour or two of sleep before construction started again and the growl of the crane made it impossible.

"Come on, Tank. Let's give it up and go home."

She stood up and was turning toward the clearing when she stopped suddenly and looked back at the sunny spot. Because of its early angle, the beam of sunshine in which the robin was sitting cast shadows that revealed a depression in the ground, a sunken spot about six feet long and maybe two feet wide. It was slightly deeper in the center; three or four inches lower than the surrounding soil. Grass grew there that did not grow beneath the trees, where the ground was littered with spruce needles and decaying birch leaves, a natural rich loam in the making. Standing there, staring down at the depression, she knew she could easily have walked right over it.

As she moved a few steps closer, the robin hopped up, flew

away in a whir of red-breasted motion, and vanished quickly into the trees. But Jessie wasn't interested in the bird or disturbing its breakfast. She walked a slow circle around the depression, taking care not to step into it or disturb it in any way, and stopped again. If this was what she suspected it might be, she could have moved past and missed it in her search of the trees above her head. If she hadn't been there to see what the light disclosed only at that time of day, the depression could have gone undiscovered. The idea of there being a hidden grave had been valid. She was amazed to have been successful in her search and happy to regain her self-confidence.

She had found, she hoped, the final resting place of Bonnie Russell's sister. It could turn out to be someone or something else, but she doubted it; it was too close to the old man's burial spot where Jo-Jo's butterfly necklace had been found. What would Bonnie feel and do now? It would be a relief for her to finally have closure and be able to account for her sister. But wouldn't all the years of searching and waiting have irrevocably changed her? Would not having to wonder anymore leave a sudden emptiness where there had been focus and determination?

Jessie thought of her own father and remembered what she had told Lynn: My dad still looks. Everywhere he goes, he's always looking for Lily. How would he feel if he were unexpectedly given answers to the agonizing questions that had haunted his life? How would I feel? she wondered. Relieved, or guilty all over again?

Staring down at the promise of the depression in the ground, Jessie knew she had long ago given up hope. She wondered which was the easier to bear, her certainty and acceptance that Lily's disappearance would remain a mystery, or her father's constant never-ending belief that anything was possible. Again, she wondered what her discovery would bring to Bonnie Russell.

Raising her head, she looked intently at the branches of each tree that grew around the depression and finally found the evidence for which she had been searching. In an ancient birch, one twisted lower branch exhibited a scar, healed over and darker than the rest of its pale bark. From where she stood looking up at it, Jessie could just make out a few strands of what looked like hemp barely moving in the small breath of the morning breeze.

· · ·

Jessie's call to John Timmons raised his wife, Gladys, from sleep at five o'clock that morning, but ever polite and used to calls at odd hours, she handed him the phone anyway. His gravelly growl was even more pronounced when he was yanked from dreams.

"Timmons."

"It's Jessie, John. I'm sorry to wake you," she apologized, "but I think I've found the body you've been looking for—well, at least where it may be buried."

His response was guarded. "Where? What did you find?"

She began to tell him about her early-morning search but was interrupted halfway through by his irritated, "You mean you're alone out there? I thought I told you . . ."

"Look, I'm fine," she assured him impatiently, her focus on

what she had found. "There've been people coming and going around here all night. Now listen, please."

There was no hesitation in his response when she finished. "Call Becker and tell him I'll be there in an hour and a half."

"Fine. I'm going back to bed. Wake me up when you get here and I'll show you where it is."

· · ·

Timmons wasted no time. The barking of the dogs in the kennel and Pete from inside the motor home demanded Jessie's attention at a quarter after six. She dragged herself up from where she had crashed on the bed, fully dressed, and went out to lead Timmons and his yawning lab crew to the depression in the woods. Becker, it turned out, was working on another case but would show up when he could.

Getting Timmons to the site in his wheelchair was not easy, as the ground under the trees was anything but level and there was plenty of brush and a log or two to negotiate. But, rocking and rolling, and with a certain amount of assistance, he made it and finally sat beside the depression in the woods, assessing her find with a frown that narrowed his eyes under the beetling brows that were as wild as his fuzzy hair.

Jessie pointed out the scar she had located on the branch of the nearby birch and gave him her theory of how it came to be there.

"Um-hmm." He nodded in agreement. "I think you may have found it all right, Jessie. Get busy, guys. Lots of pictures as you go." He spun himself around toward her, his frown deepening to a scowl of disapproval. "But what the hell were you thinking to be out here alone? You don't listen, just insist on doing things *your* way. What if the guy who left those roses had been out here?"

"I had my fourty-four," Jessie rejoined defensively, "and Tank."

"And what did I tell you about handguns and getting yourself shot with them? Dogs can get shot too, you know. Besides, out here he could kill you without showing himself at all. We'd just find you later, as dead as whoever may be in this grave—if it is a grave."

Huffing in frustration, Timmons glared at her. He'd had fifty miles in his drive from Anchorage to crank up his dissatisfaction with her behavior.

"Aw, hell, go back to bed. We'll be out here most of the morning. I'll let you know what we find—if anything."

Swinging back toward the depression to supervise his lab assistants, he made it obvious that he intended to ignore her and any justification she felt inclined to offer.

"Hey, I found your damn grave for you!" Jessie snapped, and stalked away toward the clearing, smarting from his dressing-down and muttering to herself, leaving Timmons and his crew to the task of digging.

"Relieve tension by doing something constructive?" she asked herself under her breath. *"Hardly!"* If anything, the tension had increased, now that everyone seemed to be angry with her. *"Dammit!"*

And what if her floral benefactor *had* been lurking? What if he was responsible for either or both of the burials on her property and had been searching for this old one, meaning to dig it up and move the remains she expected they would find in its depths? He could have been disoriented by the changes she had made to the clearing and unable to find it in the dark. The roses might have been meant to scare her away, right? It was an idea she hadn't considered.

Tired from too much thinking and lack of rest, she reached the Winnebago and went immediately to bed, as Timmons had suggested. Exhaustion proved better than pills, for she was asleep in minutes, little caring what old secrets they might unearth from the asylum of her woods.

Chapter 20

"Leave her be for now," Hank Peterson told Vic Prentice that morning, when they arrived to find the crime lab van in the yard, the motor home silent, and Jessie not up. "She had a bad night last night and the crane will wake her anyway when it starts." He looked around for the lab workers but, seeing no one, thought no more about it for the moment.

Vic agreed, and they walked off together to talk with the log-raising crew that had just arrived.

J.B., Dell, and Stevie arrived close behind them and went to work to organize the materials for the roof they would build as soon as the other crew had finished. There was lumber to be cut, and Bill had driven in a truck full of insulation and roofing

COLD COMPANY   •   175

paper that needed unloading. They came and went through the yard, attending to a variety of jobs.

The sound of machinery and activity in the yard did wake Jessie, who came yawning to open the door of the Winnebago, a cup of coffee in one hand, a bagel in the other, to see the remaining logs begin to go up. Hank waved but left her alone to make her peace with the new day, going instead to make roofing plans with Prentice.

Jessie was tired and, at first, a little depressed and embarrassed, still remembering her emotional revelation to Ehlers the night before and her anger at Timmons' scolding. But soon she shrugged it off and went about getting dressed for work. "I'm beginning to sound like Scarlett," she said to Tank, who sat by the door, waiting to be let out. "I'll think about it tomorrow."

Letting Tank and Pete out, she tethered the two to their boxes, then fed and watered all her dogs. Though she had refused to spoil the pleasure of watching the new cabin grow by going over the night's events, she was quiet and thoughtful for most of the morning. She did not totally regret what she had told Lynn about her family, but she would have liked him to think her stronger than tears.

Weepy women are boring, she told herself in disgust.

Do you care that much what he thinks—what anybody thinks?

No! Oh, I don't know. Why can't everyone just leave me alone to build this damn cabin?

The amount of anger she was feeling surprised her.

What is it that's making me so angry? she wondered as she sat down on Tank's dog box to think about it. Finished with his breakfast, he jumped up and lay down beside her, and they both watched the crane operator skillfully lower a log into place on the south wall.

She was angry with herself for allowing the stress of outside problems to interrupt her focus on building the cabin. There seemed to be so many of them. But what were those outside problems, really, and what could she do to minimize the disruption? Putting them out of her mind clearly wasn't working, and neither was doing something positive, like searching for another grave.

It started with the skull in the wall of her basement excavation and had escalated from there. Law enforcement—Becker and Timmons—complicated matters with the old Hansen case and its copycat. With Becker had come Bonnie Russell and, by extension, her dead sister, to stir up all the old feelings that Jessie would rather have kept locked away. The depression she had found in the woods and what it might contain was now added to the mix. Lynn Ehlers was not an unwelcome intrusion—or was he? His arrival had inspired a reconsideration of the end of her relationship with Jensen, loaded with disappointment and a sense of failure. Then there were the roses, the awful sweet-sour dichotomy of their alarming beauty and the puzzle of who was sending them, and why. The intruder in her yard and living space, and the women he was evidently killing, seemed another, but it was related to the roses, wasn't it? Anything else? Oh, yes, the small stuff: J.B.'s unwelcome attentions and the harassment of the reporter, Gary Huddleston—who hadn't been back, thank God.

Five major categories of distraction and two small ones. No wonder she was feeling stressed and angry. Getting rid of some of them would lower the tension level, but how was that to be accomplished? She still thought that doing something positive was better than letting the whole related tangle wash over her, snarling her emotions into tears and jeopardizing her judgment. When she was pressured, she tended to stubbornness and frustrated anger, neither of which was useful.

A second truck loaded with logs swung into the drive and replaced the first, which had rumbled off to collect another load. Watching log after log swung into place on the walls was growing repetitious, so, still thinking, she went to clean up the scraps of plywood and materials that had been tossed down in haste as the floor went in the day before. She piled anything burnable neatly beside her storage shed, with a thought toward winter. The rest she began to toss into an industrial-sized Dumpster that Prentice had provided for trash purposes.

Ignoring the comings and goings in her long driveway, she was unaware that someone not on the building crew had driven in until she heard her name and turned to find Bonnie Russell standing nearby with a tentative smile on her face.

"Could you use a hand?"

She was dressed in jeans and a dark red sweatshirt, a pair of hiking boots on her feet. A pair of gloves stuck out of one pocket.

"I thought you might be able to put me to work."

With a sinking feeling, Jessie glanced across the yard at the crime lab van, still parked where Timmons and his minions had left it hours before. She had a hunch they wouldn't care to have Bonnie show up at a site that could possibly be the grave of her sister.

Her concern must have shown on her face, for Bonnie's look

followed hers to the van. She was asking questions before she even looked back.

"Where are they? Have they found something?" The tone of her voice betrayed her tension.

Jessie felt cornered, afraid she might say something Timmons might not want disclosed.

"Maybe," she admitted reluctantly. "But they can't be disturbed right now."

"Where are they?" Bonnie asked again.

Jessie shook her head.

Wheeling, Bonnie walked across to the van and examined the ground around it. The tracks of Timmons' wheelchair on the ground, distinct and unmistakable, headed directly toward the woods at the back of the property. Before Bonnie could follow them, Jessie stepped into her path.

"Don't," she warned. "John doesn't want you there, or anyone else. They'll come back. Wait for him if you want to, but I don't know how long it'll be."

"What've they found?" Bonnie demanded, her face a study in frustrated determination.

So I'm not the only one who wants her own way, Jessie thought.

"I don't know what they've found—if anything. Stay and see," she encouraged. "You *can* help me while you wait, if you like."

The other woman hesitated, staring into the trees as if she could see through them if she focused her concentration. Finally she turned back to Jessie with a resigned sigh. "Okay, I'll wait—for a while. What can I do?"

"Well," Jessie told her, with a grin, "all this stuff is trash and goes in that." She indicated the large Dumpster. "You're a glutton for punishment to offer."

"Not really. Just got tired of my own company."

Knowing she had been working to keep her own thoughts at bay, Jessie sympathized. Remembering what Becker and Timmons had told her of Bonnie's discovery of the woman's body near the river, she didn't think her helper would welcome questions, so she didn't ask. They spent the next half hour working together to collect and dispose of the trash.

"What now?" her assistant asked, when the work area was clear again.

"Now we take a coffee break; then we'll see if Vic has something we can do, though it may not be much till they're finished with the logs."

With another long look toward the woods, Bonnie agreed, unenthusiastically.

They had no more than settled in the sunshine outside the Winnebago with their coffee when Phil Becker came up the drive in his patrol car and got out, his face like a thundercloud.

"It's Grand Central Station around here these days," Jessie said to Bonnie. Then, anticipating the cause of Becker's bad temper, she added, "Hold on to your hat. He's not happy with me, but that's nothing new."

Phil came striding purposefully up to where they were sitting and stood looming over Jessie, where she sat on the step, having offered the bench to Bonnie.

"Where's Timmons? But first, I hear you had company last night and didn't call me. Didn't I warn you . . . ?"

"Hey, Phil, simmer down. It was nothing to do with the roses, okay? Just a friend who was trying to do me a favor by keeping watch but didn't bother to tell me first."

"Well, *somebody* obviously needs to keep a watch on you. You were damned lucky. It could easily have been . . ."

"Roses?" Bonnie questioned. "Jessie, is somebody you don't know sending you roses?"

"Oh, shit!" Becker said, turning to stare at her. "You too?"

"Yesterday, when I was gone, someone left a rose in front of my door."

"Not inside your house?"

"Apartment," she corrected him. "No. It was outside the door, in the hallway."

This piece of news suddenly changed the equation. Becker dropped his annoyance with Jessie along with his questions about Timmons' whereabouts and asked several rapid-fire questions.

"Did you see anyone?"

"No."

"None of your neighbors saw anyone?"

"No, but I only asked three."

"Ask the rest. Did you call the florist?"

"Yes, this morning. But he said he didn't know who ordered it—or told me he didn't."

"You believe him?"

"I had no reason not to. I thought it was just some kind of oversight."

"So did I," said Jessie, frowning in discomfort. "But I don't think so now."

They looked at each other, puzzled and anxious.

"I stopped yesterday and questioned the woman in that shop this side of Palmer," Becker told Jessie. "She evidently really doesn't know anything, though she may have played cute with you. The order came in the mail, cash in the envelope, no return address. It was for three separate deliveries, two days apart, so you won't be getting any more. Unfortunately, she tossed the envelope, and the money is gone, of course. Not that fingerprints were a probability."

She stared at him, relieved that she wouldn't have to anticipate receiving any more roses, but wondering if that was good or bad and what might come next.

"What do I do now, Phil?"

"Nothing," he told her, with a shrug. "But there won't be any more middle-of-the-night antics, right? You're going to stay somewhere else, like it or not."

"Yes, *sir*." Jessie was tempted to salute. "Any suggestions?"

"I don't care where, but—"

"You can stay with me," Bonnie offered.

"Not a chance!" The idea raised Becker's brows in dismay. "You're not going to stay at home either till we catch this person. It crosses my mind that you could be an even more important target to this guy than Jessie, with your connection to the Hansen cases that he seems to be copycatting."

There was a long moment of silence as the two women considered possibilities. Becker took a deep breath and slapped his hat against the side of his leg.

"They could both stay at my place," Hank Peterson suggested. He had walked up quietly and stood listening. Concentrating on the problem at hand, none of them had heard or seen him coming. "If they could put up with a somewhat less than neat bachelor pad, that is."

"Thanks, Hank. I might take you up on that, if Becker agrees. Bonnie?"

The other woman nodded agreement, slowly, still thinking.

"I won't . . ." Jessie began.

"Jess–ie," he warned, and she recalled his words of the night before about trying to take care of everything herself and friends helping each other.

"I hear you, Hank. But I've got a kennel to run and there's all this construction going on. With all these people around it'll be okay for me to be here during the day, right?"

"I don't have a problem with that," Becker told her, "as long as you come and go with Peterson."

He turned to Bonnie.

"I tried to call you an hour ago, so I'm glad you're here. I've got something to ask that may be a little tough for you."

She sat up, seemingly calmn, but anxiety showed in her eyes. "What?"

"You've spent a lot of time along the Knik River, right?"

"You know I have."

"We're going to take a plane up there as far as we can this afternoon and do as thorough a search as possible with the water this high, for—well, anything we can find. Knowing that area so well, would you be willing to go with us—to help?"

There was something he was not telling her. From the expressions on both women's faces, they knew it. Bonnie voiced their suspicion.

"There's another woman missing."

Becker sighed. "I should have known you'd be all over that. Another dancer disappeared last night. Her roommate called the police this morning. Your looking for your sister and finding the one the other day make it hard. Will you go?"

"Yes, of course I'll help. But I'm not leaving here before I know what's going on back there in the woods and what Timmons has found. Then I will, and—if she would—could Jessie come with me?"

"Where *is* John?" Becker asked, remembering his intention to join him.

Turning to point out the direction he should take to join the lab crew, Jessie saw Timmons roll out of the woods and start across the yard toward them. Behind him the lab assistants bore a stretcher that held a plastic body bag. They turned aside, headed in the direction of the van. So, it *had* been a grave and there *had* been someone in it.

"Here he comes now," she said, and was not surprised when Bonnie moved instantly to stop him halfway. She couldn't hear what was said, but saw him shake his head. Clearly dissatisfied, Bonnie accompanied him the rest of the way across the yard to where Jessie and Becker waited.

"Please," she tried again, when he halted the chair. "Is it my sister?"

Timmons looked up at her and frowned but spoke gently. Jessie and Becker listened without a word.

"There's no way of knowing, Bonnie. All we found was bones as old as the old man's—no clothing, no identifying items. We have a lot of testing to do, but I think it'll come down to DNA results, and those take time."

"You have dental records." She was almost begging.

He reached out and took her hand, rubbing the wide pad of his thumb comfortingly across her fingertips, making wordless contact.

Smart, Jessie thought, letting go of her irritation with Timmons and remembering what it was about him that she respected and valued even more than his considerable professional abilities. Under the gruff exterior, he was a warm, sensitive, and compassionate person who dealt in straight truth. Sometimes what he had to say was painful, but you could trust him to say it in the least hurtful way he knew. He had learned many kinds of pain and disappointment on a very personal level, and his ability to empathize and respond to the distress of others was huge.

"Yes, we have those records," he now told Bonnie. "But they may or may not be useful. Hopefully, DNA from this woman will give us a match with yours."

"How long will that take?"

He hesitated, not yet ready to give an estimate.

"It's too soon to say. Why don't I call you tomorrow, or the next day, after I make an initial examination in the lab? I'll have a better idea then."

"Meanwhile," Becker spoke up, "will you go flying up the Knik with us?"

Bonnie turned to Jessie with a question in her eyes.

Jessie had no desire to go trekking in the upper reaches of the Knik River, especially not to help find another body. But she recognized the tangled skein of emotions that held Bonnie captive to this latest element of an old obsession. The woman would go without her, if she had to, but her request for company was not made lightly.

If she's anything like me—and I think she is—Jessie reasoned, it's costing her a lot even to ask.

How could she refuse?

From their expressions, she knew that neither Becker nor Peterson was completely happy with the idea. Hank Peterson was shaking his head in frustration and disagreement but saying nothing. It was Becker's call, but Jessie knew what his answer would be. He needed Bonnie. She was familiar with every twist and turn the river made, or had made, in the last twenty years. No one knew it better.

Chapter 21

Pilot Ben Caswell was waiting at the Wasilla field with his Maule M-4 when Becker, Bonnie, Jessie, and Tank arrived just after noon. He met them with a grin and a huge bear hug for Jessie.

"Hey, stranger. Linda sends her love."

Cas and his wife were friends Jessie had met through Alex Jensen. The two couples had enjoyed one another's company for everything from evenings of bridge to country line dancing, often getting together on weekends for cookouts, until Jensen left Alaska. Cas flew his own plane on contract for the Alaska State Troopers, and he and Jensen had often worked and fished together. The two women had kept in touch over the last four months, but Jessie hadn't seen Cas since Jensen's departure and had missed his cheerful, if thoughtful, company.

"Hey, yourself." Jessie hugged back, then gave a nod to the Maule. "I've never seen this plane on wheels."

"Becker caught me just in time. I was about to change the wheels for its summer floats."

"You have it on skis for the winter?"

"I do. I have all three, and it just depends on what these guys need. Up the Knik, the water's too shallow to land on floats. Flew up this morning to take a look. It'll have to be wheels and a sandy spot."

Jessie introduced Bonnie Russell, who smiled a little hesitantly. Knowing Bonnie was not comfortable with the whole idea of this trip, Jessie was glad of her own decision to come along, though she didn't like the motive behind it.

She glanced at Becker, who stepped forward to shake hands with Cas and thank him for the transportation.

Jessie had kept on the jeans, boots, and T-shirt she had been wearing to work in the yard but had added a sweatshirt, warm jacket, sunglasses, and a floppy denim hat. Around her waist she had fastened the large fanny pack she always carried when she went away from civilization. A mirror, matches in a waterproof case, wire survival saw, penlight, a tightly folded insulated reflective sheet, and some first-aid supplies lay within. There was no room for a water bottle, so she took one that had a shoulder strap. A hunting knife hung from her belt, and at the last minute she had thoughtfully added her Smith & Wesson .44 in its holster.

She knew Becker had noticed the handgun. He had started to say something but changed his mind and let it go with no more than a frown. Many Alaskans are more comfortable sharing the wilderness with moose and bear if they have a gun. Knowing hers was legal—Jessie carried it with her whenever she was on the trail with her dog teams—he ignored it.

The Maule M-4 was sturdy and dependable. But it was also compact, with little cabin space to spare.

"I'll have to take you in two hops," Cas told Becker. "The air's pretty rough up there, coming over the hill from Turnagain and off the glaciers, so I'd like to keep it light."

"That's okay," Becker agreed. "Take the women first. You want Tank to ride with me, Jessie?"

"No, he'll be fine on the floor in back with me. Can't seatbelt a dog anyway. That all right, Cas?"

"Sure. He's been a good passenger in the past, haven't you, fella?" He gave the husky a friendly pat or two and motioned the two women toward the right side of the plane. "Okay, let's do it."

Jessie climbed in, leaving the front passenger seat for Bonnie. Having flown with Cas before, she was comfortable enough with what she could see out the side windows and thought Bonnie would get a better view of the mountains and glaciers from the front. There was plenty of room for Tank on the floor beside her. In one way, she was looking forward to seeing this particular part of the Chugach Range, never having flown over it before. It was reputed to be one of the most beautiful within flight-seeing range of Anchorage, and many commercial pilots flew tourists through the area for a look, often on their way to or from Mount McKinley to the north.

By the time she and Bonnie were settled and had buckled their seat belts securely, Cas had the headphones on and the engine started. He spoke briefly into the microphone and they were on their way, leaving Becker to lean against his patrol car and wave them off.

As Cas tipped the small plane in a wide left-hand turn to the west of Wasilla, Jessie looked down and spotted the construction in her yard next to Knik Road. Tapping Caswell on the shoulder, she grinned and pointed. He took a look and said something she couldn't hear over the roar of the engine, but she understood the thumbs-up and smiling nod of approval he gave her in response.

It was a perfect day to go flying, bright and sunny, with a clear blue sky. A few scattered clouds floated over the Chugach Mountains to the south. In the Aleutian Range to the west, volcanoes Redoubt, Iliamna, even Augustine on its island, were visible in the distance, white with perpetual snow, on the northernmost edge of the Pacific Rim of Fire. They soon disappeared behind Mount Eklutna as Cas flew the Maule across the wide Matanuska Valley and headed up the Knik River drainage.

There were two other small planes in sight, probably tourists catching a look at the Chugach Mountains with their hundreds of glaciers, large and small, including the Knik Glacier, one of the largest.

As Cas swung south around Pioneer Peak, the glacier came into view between the crests, broad and white in the distance, sweeping up in a giant S curve, the source of the river springing from its foot. As they grew closer it became possible to make out gray lines in the surface, gravel and the powder-fine dust created by its tremendous grinding power and weight.

"Oh!" said Bonnie, unheard in the roar of the plane engine.

She turned her head to look back at Jessie. "It's beautiful!" she mouthed. Jessie nodded enthusiastic agreement.

More than beautiful, it was a spectacular river of ice that flowed ceaselessly if imperceptibly, drawn into motion by gravity, slowly carving away the mountains in its path, creating wide valleys out of what, thousands of years before, had been narrow canyons or solid walls of upthrust stone.

Catching Jessie's attention, Cas gestured to a second set of headphones. She leaned forward, put them on, and heard his question: "Want to take a look at the glacier before we land?"

"That would be great. I've never seen it from the air, and there's only one place along the river road where it's visible at all."

"Okay. I'll pick out a landing spot, then we'll make a quick detour over the glacier before I let you out."

Halfway up the valley, they flew past the end of the road that ran along the hillside on the west. Opposite, to the east, Friday Creek ran down out of the hills and spilled into the river. Beyond that the water grew shallow, narrow silver ribbons that braided the small creeks and glacier runoff and divided the sandbars into a jigsaw puzzle. To either side the mountains rose steeply into the sky, and Jessie felt that she and the plane were very small compared to the heights they floated between.

Air currents over glacier country are often strong and turbulent, with opposing currents of cool air flowing down from the snow and ice of the heights to collide with warmer air rising up from the lowlands. In this particular area, prevailing winds also flowed over the Chugach Range from the waters of Turnagain Arm on the other side. As they neared the headwaters of the river, the small plane began to bounce in the unstable air as if shoved around by invisible giants that jerked it not only up and down but from side to side as well. A wing dipped suddenly now and then, as a puff of wind hit from an unexpected angle. Once or twice it felt as if the bottom had fallen out of some huge elevator, dropping the plane and its passengers, who felt they had left their stomachs a floor above. Then, in an instant, they were lifted up again.

"Hold on," Cas cautioned, "so you don't punch holes in the ceiling. This is Mixmaster country but not a real problem. It might have been a smoother ride this morning."

With her headphones on, she could now hear Cas talking to the other air traffic in the area, establishing his position.

"This is Maule nine eight six four Mike, going in southeast over the upper end of the Knik River, low and slow, looking for a landing site."

Under the shoulder of Mount Palmer, Cas dropped down close enough to be able to see the condition of the sand and gravel bars along the riverbanks. Flying slowly, he assessed the tangle of choices carefully until he found one he liked, close to the shore, long and flat and, except for some low brush on the south end, clean and without rocks.

"There," he said to Jessie through the headphones. "We'll set down on that one on the way back."

"Won't that brush be in your way?"

"Not if I can help it. But I've got a metal belly on this bird, so it wouldn't tear my tail feathers off. Now let's go see the glacier."

Punching the button, he spoke again. "This is Maule nine

eight six four Mike, rising southeast to flight-see over Knik Glacier."

When he had finished, Jessie asked a question, interested in the communication system. "Do you always have to do that?"

"In a busy area like this, pilots tune in to the same local frequency—this is one twenty-two point eight. We give each other a heads-up on where we're headed or what we're about to do. Makes a midair collision less likely."

As he finished explaining, the radio crackled with the voice of another pilot, giving identification and the information that he was over the glacier and would be heading northwest down-river to Palmer. Jessie looked and soon located a yellow Piper Cub ahead of them in the sky. It passed to the left, with plenty of airspace between, and vanished behind them.

Tank stirred at her feet, shifting position as the plane rocked a little crossing over the foot of the glacier. She laid a hand on his head. He licked her wrist, but she paid little heed, her attention focused on large chunks of ice that had fallen and were floating in the pond beneath. Some of them, along with parts of the vertical face of the glacier, were such a brilliant blue they looked painted. Every other color of the spectrum was absorbed by the compressed ice and only the profound blue was reflected. Tank settled back, his muzzle propped on one of her boots.

As they flew over the foot and were low over the ice, the Maule shuddered a few times in the turbulence, but Cas kept it low so they could get a good view. To the right lay Lake George, held back by the dam formed by the glacier resting against Mount Palmer, thousands of gallons of blue-green water contrasting sharply against the white of the snow and ice.

Evidence of the glacier's motion was clear to see. It rose away from them toward its genesis, growing lighter in color as it carried less of the gray-brown dust and gravel, for more new snow fell and did not melt on its heights. The lower regions were scored by crevasses of several kinds: marginal crescents along the sides, radial crisscrosses where it expanded as it flowed around a turn, deep parallel longitudinal fissures where it broadened and spread out at the foot.

Over the centuries, snow falling on the upper reaches of a glacier is gradually buried by more snow and, through pressure, compacted into ice. This is not the ice that cools drinks or the surface upon which figure skaters spin. The deeper glacier ice is buried; the more pressure that is applied by succeeding layers above it, the more compact it becomes, until it is up to nine times as dense as snow and impermeable to air or water.

This kind of ice behaves differently than other kinds, which are breakable and tend to shatter. Glacier ice becomes plastic and gravity draws it inexorably downhill. As it creeps imperceptibly along, some unseen parts of a glacier flow faster than others, creating stresses that, rather than stretching or spreading, split the surface ice in crevasses and fissures that can be hundreds of feet deep.

Slightly less than five percent of Alaska, approximately three hundred thousand square miles, is covered by perhaps a hundred thousand glaciers, if even the smallest cirque and valley glacier is counted. The Knik Glacier is medium-sized, close enough to civilization to be easily seen and large enough to be recognized with a name.

Caswell flew the Maule low over the ice but, knowing he still had Becker to bring up, was almost immediately ready to turn around. Looking down into the crevasses over which they were passing, both Jessie and Bonnie were silenced by the magnitude of the glacier and the variety of its conditions. In contrast to the brilliant white of the glacier that glowed in the sunshine, the ice was a thousand different shades in the shadows of its crevasses.

"This is Maule nine eight six four Mike, making a right turn to the west to go down the Knik Glacier. Will be on base leg for landing northwest on a gravel bar at the base of the glacier," Jessie heard Cas say into the microphone, as he dropped the right wing to begin the turn.

As the plane slowly tipped to the west, Jessie suddenly caught a gleam of brightness in motion against the shadows of the mountains, just a flash of silver in the sunlight, coming up from the river flats below to the right of the plane.

"Cas, I think—"

"I see him, Jessie."

Still turning, he spoke sharply into the radio.

"This is Maule nine eight six four Mike, over the Knik Glacier. Identify. Red and silver Super Cub, you are on my heading. Acknowledge."

There was no response.

"Acknowledge! Red and silver Super Cub, *acknowledge!*" He was shouting now. "You are on the heading for my turn! *Acknowledge!*"

The red and silver plane did not respond on the radio but the pilot seemed to see them, for he suddenly began a steep climb so close that Jessie could see scratches on the underbelly of his plane. For an interminably few seconds, she was sure it was going to fly directly into the passenger side of the Maule, but somehow it missed, sliding by just feet above them as it passed over.

Cas clearly was of like mind and assumed they were about to be hit, for he instinctively shoved the stick forward and attempted to drop from under the other plane. The sky fell out from under them with no warning, and before Jessie could speak, they were headed for the broken surface of the glacier beneath them.

Chapter 22

 The right wing, already lowered for the turn, hit first and dug its tip into the sun-softened snowy surface of the glacier. The rest of the right-turning plane continued in a rolling cartwheel that swung the nose in an arc with the crumpling wing tip as fulcrum. The propeller slammed into the snow, abruptly halting the forward motion of the fuselage, except for the tail, which was lifted high in the air, transcribing another arc over the nose. As the tail came down, the plane flopped over sideways to land on its back, very close to the forward edge of the glacier.

Inside, some things continued to follow the original forward impetus of the plane while others did not. Accompanied by the shriek of rending metal and sharp reports of shattering glass, the cabin became a tin can full of hard sharp edges in which everything that was or could come loose became dangerous projectiles hurtling forward to impact whatever lay in their trajectory. A tool kit hit the back of Jessie's seat and the lid popped open to release metal shrapnel in the form of wrenches, nuts and bolts, pliers, electrical wire and tape, and several dozen other items. Two sleeping bags fell forward, then toward the ceiling, as the plane flipped over. A machete in a leather case was suddenly airborne, along with a can of oil that vanished through a broken window, one of many individual items and broken pieces of the plane to be scattered over the glacier along the path of the wreck. The oil can, however, did not come to rest on the surface but rolled and slid until it reached a deep-blue fissure in the ice and fell bounding from side to side against the ice until it was swallowed by the crevasse.

Within the fuselage, there seemed to be no specific direction to the crash. When one motion abruptly halted, another took over. As Jessie was tossed about she caught a glimpse of Caswell thrown forward against the instrument panel, head bouncing off the compass, the throttle and prop-control knobs burying themselves in his belly. She fell toward the front of the plane, then was whiplashed to the left as it rotated sideways and the tail came over. Her head struck the back of the forward passenger seat, then rebounded to hit the right window. She could hear Tank yelp and growl and felt his weight on her feet, trapped between her lower legs and the seat ahead. She stiffened her knees, hoping she could somehow hold him there and keep him from being hurt.

The horrendous sounds of the wreck seemed to go on and on—breaking and ripping, a crash, a bang, thumps and smashes, someone's scream cut off. It all seemed to happen in some weird kind of slow motion but was over in seconds. Though her seat belt held, it suspended her as the plane came to rest on its back. Her head struck the seat again, and for a little while she was unaware that, except for the small tinkle of a few bits of falling glass, something rolling to the rear, and the gurgle of liquid, it was suddenly and completely silent.

The small red and silver Piper Cub did not circle the site but gained altitude quickly and steeply and headed south up the glacier to disappear over the crest to Turnagain Arm.

* * *

Jessie didn't want to wake up, but something wet came and went on her face, her head ached, and her stomach hurt. She decided to ignore it and let everything fade away again.

Tank was whining. Had she forgotten to let him out? Something was holding her down. No, it was holding her up.

She wanted to see what it was but could get only one of her eyes to open. Tank's muzzle came vaguely, fuzzily, into view. He licked her face and whined again. Her arms were hanging over her head. She attempted to raise the right hand to her face, but the effort created a sharp pain in her shoulder, so she raised the left. Finding blood and her right eye swelling shut, she let her hand drop and tried to think. Tank licked her fingers. Her open jacket had fallen to hang behind her and she caught sight of the edge of the zipper and focused her limited vision on it. How odd to see it there, above her head.

Someone groaned and she looked beyond the zipper to find Caswell in his seat, ahead of her and to the left. He moved slightly and groaned again.

What the hell happened? she wondered. She tried again to move and realized that she was hanging upside down from her seat belt, inside an airplane. Tank was looking up at her from where he was sitting—*on the ceiling?* Like a dream, she seemed to remember a lot of noise and falling.

Cas moaned quietly. He was hurt. She wanted to reach him to see how badly but was restricted by the seat belt.

Her head ached and the belt was cutting painfully into her upper thighs and stomach. Reaching with her left hand, she found she could just touch the ceiling that had been overhead and was now the floor. Looking down at it, she could see her own blood dripping in splatters near Tank's feet. Shoving him farther away and bracing herself on her left arm, she tried again to move to the right. Pain stabbed through her shoulder and, turning her head as far as she could, she could see that the sleeve of her jacket was torn and soaked with more of her blood.

We crashed, she suddenly remembered. I must have hit something sharp. Though it was extremely painful to bring it up, the arm moved and didn't seem to be broken, so she used her left hand to unfasten the catch on the seat belt.

Unrestricted, Jessie fell straight down but kept her head from hitting the floor with the remaining strength of her left arm. Crumpled next to her dog, she lay motionless and fled away into dreamland again to escape the resulting agony that had knifed through her body.

"Jessie?" A whisper that was half groan filtered into her returning consciousness. "Jessie. You there—okay?"

"Mm-m-m."

She could hear Tank's toenails click against the metal on

which she lay. If he was moving, he must be all right. She was lying on something that hurt her hip, so she shifted a little to rid herself of the pain inflicted by the handle of a screwdriver.

"Jessie?"

Cas! That was Cas' voice, so he was alive. But what about Bonnie? She couldn't remember anything about Bonnie.

Very slowly, she opened her eye and pushed herself to a sitting position with the uninjured left arm. The part of the world she could see spun and darkened, then gradually settled and grew visible again. On her knees and one hand, she crawled toward the front of the plane, shoving a roll of some kind of wire out of the way, trying to be careful of the fragments of broken glass that littered the surface. The plane rocked slightly as she moved.

Glancing out an inverted window, she was astonished and frightened to see the lip of the glacier under an unbroken wing. Beyond and below it, the braid of streams that formed the upper part of the Knik River was clearly visible. They had come close to falling onto it from the ice on which they now rested. She wondered, briefly, why the impact of the crash had not caused a piece to calve from the face of the glacier, then gave up the thought. There were things to be done.

Reaching up, she took hold of the pilot's seat and pulled herself to her knees so she could look up at Caswell. One arm hung limply down, but he had pulled the other up, tucking one thumb into his belt, as though to ease some pain. Jessie remembered her glimpse of the control knobs punching into his belly. His face was covered with streaks of blood from deep cuts in forehead and chin, and both eyes were swelling shut. Under the mask of

red, he was so pale he looked dead, but he was breathing in shallow rasping gasps.

She reached to lay her fingers on his throat below the jaw, to
see what a pulse could tell her. It was there under the cold
clammy skin, but weak and rapid. He turned his head blindly
toward her touch. "Jessie?" he whispered again, between
breaths.

"I'm here, Cas."

"Okay?"

"Better than you. I'll do."

A pause, as he sucked in air.

"Your—friend?"

"Don't know. I'll look."

She turned cautiously to find Bonnie hanging upside down
from her seat belt as well, limp and silent. Fragments of glass
glittered in the sunshine that poured in through the broken passenger window onto her hair, clothes, and a small amount of
blood that was splattered over them. She was not moving, nor
could Jessie hear her breathe. There was no pulse and nothing
she could think of to do.

Sitting back on her legs, Jessie stared up at her, feeling sick,
wondering if she should try to let her down and attempt CPR
but knowing it would be wasted effort. Better to leave her where
she was. The woman had evidently hit the instrument panel face
first and, judging from the lack of blood, died instantly. Bonnie
would never know if the second set of bones Timmons had retrieved from the woods was her sister or not. A deep sadness
grew in Jessie as she turned back to Caswell.

"She—didn't make it."

His breathing hesitated a moment before rasping on.

"Sor-ry."

"Not your fault."

"Should have seen—sooner."

"No. What can I do? Get you down?"

"Can you?"

"I can try."

He came down heavily, with a thin scream, when she released the belt and did the best she could to support his falling body. They lay tangled together on the inverted ceiling for a few moments, then Jessie struggled to get him on his back and straighten his body. He lay gasping and unable to speak for a few minutes.

Then, "Hard to—breathe."

She knew he was undoubtedly bleeding internally, but there was little she could do except try to keep him from going into shock and monitor his breathing.

Every loose thing in the plane that had not fallen out in the crash was now in a clutter on the floor, making it fairly easy to sort for useful items. Raising his feet on the now-empty toolbox, she spread a sleeping bag over Cas. The arm that had hung down was broken between the elbow and shoulder, for she felt the bones grate as she straightened it. There was nothing to use as a splint, so she had to be satisfied with removing his belt and using it to strap his arm to the side of his body.

When she had done all she could for the moment, and aching with her own pain, she located her water bottle among the things that cluttered the floor and crawled back to raise Caswell's head and shoulders onto her lap. She drank a swallow or two, then used a bit of it on paper towels to clean some of the blood from his face and hers, anxious to examine the cuts they had both sustained. Though two of his and one of hers were deep enough to need closure, the bleeding had slowed and was clotting on its own. She left them alone, but it felt a little better to be cleaner.

She sat with him, keeping a close watch, and assessed her own injuries. Her head and right shoulder seemed to be the worst. The jacket had stuck to her arm as some of the blood dried, so she left it alone. A couple of ribs were painful but didn't feel broken, and she was covered with bruises, abrasions, and small cuts.

Tank, on the other hand, seemed okay, though he favored one front paw. Jessie examined it, found a splinter of glass, removed it, and cleaned the cut.

"Becker." Cas spoke suddenly in a louder voice.

"What?"

"He'll come."

"Oh—yes."

It was what she had been half-consciously counting on, hoping it would be sooner rather than later.

"Helicopter—when I don't—come back. Someone will—report."

It was the longest speech he had made and it took effort, but Jessie was relieved to hear it, to know he was thinking logically.

After that, he lapsed into silence and seemed to doze off every so often. When she spoke or touched him he would groan, but he was breathing, so she concentrated on that.

It seemed a very long time until Jessie knew that Caswell had been correct in his assessment of Becker's response. She was half asleep herself, leaning against the side of the fuselage with Tank beside her, when she heard the distinctive voice of a helicopter in the distance and knew, with relief, that it was speaking her language.

Chapter 23

"Why?"

For the third time, Jessie asked Becker, who drove her home from the hospital early the following afternoon.

She had stayed overnight so the doctor could be sure she was not, like Caswell, suffering from internal injuries. She had stitches in her shoulder and head but had insisted on leaving, though the doctor had not recommended it. He had pointed out that she would continue to be so stiff and sore for a few days that she might need help getting around and wish she were still in her hospital bed. Jessie, however, had wanted to go to the only home she had at the moment, where she could, if not get back to work, at least watch the progress on her new cabin. So he reluctantly let her go, with a prescription for pain medication and an appointment to return in a few days to have the stitches removed.

Caswell, on the other hand, with a ruptured spleen, three broken ribs—one of which had punctured and collapsed a lung—a broken right arm, and head injuries, would remain for several days, and it would be weeks before he flew again.

"Why would anyone . . . ? I don't think it was an accident, Phil. He headed straight at us. I saw him."

"You don't know that, Jessie. You said you only had a glimpse through the window—saw only part of the plane—its underside. You didn't even see the pilot. He could have been pulling up as he tried to avoid you."

"He came up from the river and must have seen us. We were right in front of him, and he didn't answer the radio. I think he tried to force us down without crashing himself!" She had to admit she could be mistaken, that her conviction and her anger could be an after-the-fact reaction, though in her heart she didn't believe it.

"If he didn't intend us to crash, why did he fly off and not report that we had gone down?"

"Maybe his radio was broken. Maybe he panicked. Maybe he's the guy who's responsible for these missing women. Maybe he's an inexperienced pilot. Maybe . . . Oh, hell—who knows? You were lucky that someone else saw you go down."

A pilot flying over the glacier with a couple of tourists had seen the crash and reported it as he circled the wreck, unable to land on the rough broken surface. Someone had come running across the airstrip to inform Becker, who had immediately used the radio in his patrol car to call for the rescue helicopter, then made a siren-screaming run to meet it before it left the hospital. It had taken off and was landing carefully near the accident site in less than an hour, a touchy maneuver on the broken surface of the glacier.

"Okay, maybe! But who was flying that plane, and if it was a serious attempt on us, how could he have known we'd be there?"

"I don't know. If it was the same plane that's been seen up there before, no one's ever got the identification numbers." Becker shook his head in frustration. "He flies up the east side of the valley, where people don't live because there isn't a road. He's too far away for people to read the numbers from the west side, even with binoculars.

"As for how he knew you'd be flying there at that particular time, there are several possibilities. Caswell filed a flight plan that could have been seen by any number of people. Folks at the detachment knew we were going upriver, for all the good that does. They're supposed to be close-mouthed about operations but . . . we talked about flying upriver at your place, so anyone there could have known."

Jessie was quiet for a minute, thinking about what he had said.

"What about this Daryl Mitchell? Have you found out anything more about him?"

"Yes, a little. By tracking his social security number through his tax records, we know he moved to Oregon, where he worked construction and drove a truck for a couple of logging companies in Springfield. Credit card records indicate that he bought a truck and contracted with one logger to haul timber to the mill. That stopped a little over a month ago, when he sold the truck and bought a one-way plane ticket from Portland to Anchorage."

"So he *is* in Alaska."

"Looks that way—and we're working on locating him."

"Did any women disappear while he was in Oregon? Were any killed in similar circumstances? Be straight with me, Phil. Alex always told me what was going on when it concerned me. Can we . . ."

Suddenly, without warning, Becker was angry. Pulling the patrol car into the parking lot of a grocery store they were passing, he stomped on the brake, shoved the gearshift into park, and, with a scowl on his face, turned to address Jessie—not gently.

"Not *we*, Jessie. Alex may have shared some details of his cases, especially last year when that bastard stalker was after you. But I am *not* Alex, and you are *not* involved in this case." He thumped the steering wheel for emphasis and continued. "If you are, it's peripheral. Even if we find out that Mitchell *is* the guy who's abducting these women, it does *not* concern you unless he's threatening you directly. We don't even know if your roses fit in with the others—though I personally think they might. But that's all speculation. Aside from staying safe until we solve the case, you have nothing to do with it. You make assumptions, get mad and stubborn, and involve yourself in things that are none of your business—like that arsonist this spring, when you took off without telling us and came close to getting yourself killed. I'm tired of baby-sitting you. Finding the answers is not your *job*. Understand?"

Astounded at his outburst, Jessie stared at him, eyes wide, speechless. All she could do was nod, white-faced and chastened.

Phil Becker was suddenly someone she didn't recognize. She had never seen him so irritated. As he pulled back onto the highway, however, she remembered how he had been when she first met him—a rookie Alex had taken under his wing, who had potential and a knack for working homicide cases. She realized she had still been thinking of him that way.

But he had changed—a lot. Now that Alex was gone and Becker was on his own, he was more confident and professional about his work. He was still friendly, easygoing, and enthusiastic, but except for the western hat, which he had copied from his mentor, hardly a trace of the rookie sidekick remained. Without Jensen overseeing his work, he was coming into his own, comfortable and secure in his abilities as an investigator. His observations, opinions, and ideas were solid and well thought out—not offered for approval.

Baby-sitting? It had not really occurred to her that by doing things her way and on her own she was actually adding to his problems—taking his attention away from the investigation rather than helping. Was this true for other people around her as well—Hank, Lynn, Timmons? Had it been true with Alex?

The idea startled her into a continued silence.

"Don't sulk," he told her, and managed the hint of a grin. "I'm over my mad now. But I meant every word."

"Not sulking," she responded quietly, if a little stiffly. "Just thinking I owe you an apology, Phil. You're right. I *do* make assumptions. I *am* stubborn and want to do things myself. I've made it harder for you sometimes, haven't I? I'll try not to from now on."

"Deal." The grin was genuine. "And I'll keep you up-to-date, as much as I can. Just don't assume . . ."

"I won't. I promise."

. . .

The cabin's walls were up, the crane and log crew gone, when they reached Jessie's yard. Vic Prentice's crew, including Hank Peterson, was hard at work putting a roof over the rafters and ridgepole. It would extend about a yard beyond the walls, covering and protecting the logs, especially from water, which could rot and eventually destroy them if they were unshielded. The slope of the roof would also extend to cover the front porch. That side already had two dormers in place, one for each of the second-story loft bedrooms.

As Becker pulled into the yard and Jessie got out of his car, the whole crew stopped what they were doing and came down to welcome her home.

"Hey, kid, how you doin'?" Prentice asked, reaching her first.

As he leaned to give her a hug, Jessie shrank from it, taking a step back.

"Oh, please, Vic. There isn't a part of me that doesn't hurt. Can I have a rain check?"

"Sorry, I forgot. You're gonna be okay, though, right?"

"Yeah, the doc says I'll be fine," she assured him. "Just a sorry excuse for a helper for a few days."

"That's okay. You take it easy. We're doing good things here."

"I can see that. It looks great."

She fended off two more welcoming embraces with a palm raised toward Hank and Stevie, and greeted Bill, Dell, and J.B.

COLD COMPANY • 211

Bill, frowning as he saw the ugly bruises on the right hand and arm she had extended and the dressing over the stitches on her head, waved a hand at the bench beside the Winnebago. "Sit down, Jessie. You look whipped."

"Well, whipped is exactly how I feel, but first I want to see what you've done since yesterday. Hank, would you let Tank off his tether?"

"Sure."

He walked across to where her lead dog stood straining toward her and unfastened the restraint. Jessie watched closely as Tank came trotting to stand beside her, but he seemed healthy and uninjured, not even limping from the cut on his paw.

"I took him by the vet's last night like you wanted," Hank told her. "He checked out just fine. No apparent damage except for that cut on his foot and a bruise or two."

"Thanks, Hank."

She leaned to rub the dog's ears and shoulders, then straightened with a wince.

"I'd better get going," Becker told her. "I put your jacket and the other stuff inside. I'm sending out an officer to spend the night in his patrol car." He held up a hand when she automatically started to protest. "No, don't make it harder. You promised. Someone will be here about nine."

"Okay." Jessie gave in without an argument, which raised Peterson's eyebrows, a reaction Jessie noted for later thought.

"I'll check in periodically. Bye." And Becker was gone.

"Now," she said, starting slowly toward the new cabin. "I want a look at the inside before this pain pill wears off."

When they all stood surrounded by log walls, in the center of the space that would become the living room, she couldn't stop grinning, finally able to see exactly how much space there would be and how it would look. The log joists to support the loft, with an interior balcony that would connect the bedrooms, had gone in as the walls were raised, and a preassembled stairway had been moved into place by the crane. The loft still needed a floor, but the space was well defined and she could see that the dormers would allow afternoon sun into the two bedrooms, one of which she planned to use as an office that would double as space for guests.

"Oh, Vic, it's wonderful."

"It's a long way from finished yet, Jessie. But it's a good start. Now, let's get back to work."

· · ·

The visit to the cabin was the best thing she could have done to raise her spirits. But as soon as the crew went back up their ladders to finish the day's work on the tongue-and-groove decking they were nailing solidly to the rafters and ridgepole, she found she was more than ready to go back to the Winnebago. Peterson went along to make sure she was settled. He helped her make a cup of tea and piled up the pillows in her bed. As soon as he had gone, she changed clothes into a more comfortable set of sweats and warm socks and was amazed at the extent of the bruises that seemed to cover her body. She had taken more of a battering than she thought. No wonder I feel so beat up—I am, she thought, taking another pain pill, easing her aching body onto the bed, and trying to get comfortable enough to read. But even a Caribbean mystery could not distract her. Her mind kept turning back to what she could remember of the crash.

She had heard that people in accidents involving head injuries often lose memory of it. But though the doctor had decided she was lightly concussed, she thought she remembered most of it pretty well—from her glimpse of the plane that had forced them down to regaining consciousness in the upside-down plane and hearing Caswell call her name. Now she realized there was a gap in her recollection after the impact. She didn't remember how she had managed to release her seat belt, or the resulting fall, and the rest was more than a little confused.

She definitely remembered finding Bonnie Russell's still form hanging on the passenger side of the plane and the anguish of knowing there was nothing she could do to save her. And she recalled the effort of getting Caswell down and doing what she could for him. There was a huge amount of relief in knowing that he would be okay, but it was mixed with a sad resignation about Bonnie.

As she lay quietly considering, it occurred to her how strange it was that Bonnie had died so close to where she had long believed that her sister might have died as well. But if the remains Timmons had carried away from Jessie's woods turned out to be Jo-Jo's, Bonnie had been looking for years in the wrong place. Now she would never know. That's the saddest of all, she thought.

The pain pill was gradually taking effect, and she suddenly discovered that she hadn't thought about anything at all for . . . she didn't know how long. She had simply been lying there, staring drowsily out the window at the green of the trees against the blue sky.

*   *   *

She woke three hours later, when Prentice and Peterson came in to check on her before leaving late that afternoon.

"I'd stay, but you've already got a nurse and cook," Hank told her.

"Who?"

"Me," said Lynn Ehlers, leaning around the door to the galley with a large spoon in one hand. Jessie suddenly realized that she'd vaguely been hearing food preparation noises. "That okay with you?"

"Oh, Lynn, you don't need to . . . Ooh!" She started to sit up and found that most of her body protested painfully.

"I think maybe I do," he said. "Don't worry about it. Phil Becker said it was a good idea, when I called him."

"Uncle!" Jessie conceded. "I give. If I feel this bad, I can imagine how Cas must feel."

"Thought you'd want to know how he's doing, so I asked Becker. He said Caswell is resting comfortably and will be fine. *He* was asking about *you*. His wife said she'd be out to see you in a day or two."

How like Linda Caswell to be so considerate, Jessie thought.

"We're off," Vic Prentice told her, heading for the door. "Rest and get better and don't worry about the work. We're saving lots for you to do, believe me."

He vanished with Peterson, and the rest of the evening was a blend of taking naps and waking to talk to Lynn, who eventually went to bed on the sofa in a sleeping bag he'd brought along. From where she lay she could see him reading one of her new books on sports medicine.

"Call me if you need anything," he told her. But she found she could let him sleep. She woke a couple of times—once to take another pain pill—but the night was easier than she had anticipated and it was comforting to know Lynn was within the sound of her voice, if she needed him.

Chapter 24

The cheerful music of a warbler somewhere in the nearby trees slowly woke Jessie from a sound sleep. *Sweet, sweet, sweet,* it called. *Sitta, sitta—sweet, sweet, sweet.* She opened her eyes and saw sunshine falling between the slats of the venetian blinds onto her bed. Without moving, she closed them again and listened drowsily. The covers, the mattress beneath her, and the pillow were all deliciously warm and snug, the same temperature as her body, discouraging any thought of moving, let alone leaving such a desirable cocoon.

Chip—chip—chip. Somewhere beyond the bird's song, one squirrel scolded another. She could hear the tiny sound of their paws on the rough spruce bark as they chased each other up around the trunk. She imagined them leaping from tree to tree, seldom venturing to the dangerous ground in their never-ending search for food. New growth had extended the spruce branches with brilliant green tips, but it would be months before the cones grew fat and ripened and the squirrels began their race with early snow to stash them away for the winter.

The hum of tires on pavement told her a vehicle was passing, headed out Knik Road, perhaps to Oscar's new place, where she suddenly remembered that a work party was scheduled. No, that was on Saturday, and today was . . . She couldn't remember, but knew it was a weekday and the crew would soon be showing up to continue work on her cabin.

Ought to get up, she thought, and started to roll over. Coffee to make and . . .

"O-o-oh!" Sharp and immediate pain reminded her of the accident with a vengeance.

"Jessie?" Lynn Ehlers raised a head from his bed on the sofa, hair standing up comically on one side. "You okay?"

"No, dammit! I'm not," she growled, slowly pushing herself to a sitting position on the bed. "I forgot and tried to move, and there isn't a part of me that doesn't hurt."

"Hold on. I'll bring you another pill."

"No, let me move a little and see exactly how bad this is. Those things make me fuzzy-headed, which I hate. Maybe if I take a hot shower I'll feel better. Did the officer Becker threatened to send show up last night?"

"A couple of them did. They took turns, slept in the car—if they slept at all, which I doubt. They both checked in a couple of times and took off about five this morning."

While Lynn made coffee and breakfast for them both,

Jessie stood under the hot water of the shower until it ran out. She emerged feeling somewhat better, though still sore and lame. When she allowed him to replace the dressing over the stitches on her shoulder, she was unhappy to find a rainbow of bruises all the way to the elbow, which also hurt when she moved it.

"You hit something pretty hard with this arm. The seat in front of you?"

"I don't know. There was a lot of noise, stuff breaking and falling. I remember getting thrown around as we went down and coming to on the floor—I mean, the ceiling that was the floor, because we were upside down. That's all I know. The part in between is gone."

"Makes sense. You hit your head a couple of times, from the look of it."

"Rattled my brain loose. That's why I can't remember."

"Well, sort of, yes," Lynn joked.

She glanced up at him from where she was sitting at the table, dressed once again in sweats—the easiest thing to put on—and then looked back at the floor.

"I keep thinking that if I hadn't been out for the count I might have done something for Bonnie Russell." Her eyes flooded with tears.

"Jessie. Look at me." He waited until she did.

"Becker said she died the instant her head hit the front of the plane—broke her neck. You couldn't have done a thing for her. And you saved Caswell's life by somehow getting him out of his seat belt. If he'd stayed hanging there, in a short time he wouldn't have been able to breathe at all."

She thought about it as he brought her a plate of bacon, scrambled eggs, and toast to go with her coffee.

"Here. This'll give you some energy. You want that pill now?"

"No, it's better now. I think I'll see if I can do without it—at least for a while. This looks great. I'm starving."

"That's good news."

Glancing up, Jessie suddenly noticed an absence at the table. "The roses are gone."

"Yeah. Becker took them."

"Fine. They gave me the creeps."

*   *   *

When the crew showed up to go back to work on the roof, Jessie went outside and walked slowly through the dog yard, having a look at her mutts, while her helper, Billy Steward, fed and watered them. She went across to meet Prentice, who grinned at finding her up and around.

"Aside from a black eye and the rest of you looking like you'd gone ten rounds with Muhammad Ali, you don't seem half bad, Jessie. How do you feel?"

"Thanks *so much*, Vic. You really know how to flatter a girl! I feel—oh, not as bad as I did when I tried to get up this morning. Maybe I can work out a few of the kinks, if you find me something to do that doesn't involve climbing ladders or swinging a hammer."

"I don't *think* so! Today you watch and rest. I'm not gonna be responsible for putting you back in the hospital."

"Oh, well." But she didn't disagree and was soon sitting in the sunshine, letting it warm her battered bones.

After cleaning the galley, Ehlers took off to care for his own dogs but promised to be back that evening with dinner.

"Until they solve this thing, you're putting up with me. Becker and I agreed, so don't give me an argument."

Jeez, she thought, as she watched his truck turn onto Knik Road. Does everyone expect me to put up a fight? Evidently they did. Have I really been that insistent on doing everything my way? Evidently she had.

When all the tongue-and-groove decking was solidly nailed down, the workers laid down a polyethylene vapor barrier and began to cover it with a second framework of two-by-twelve rafters. Between them would go ten-inch fiberglass insulation to be covered with plywood sheeting. Finally, steel roofing would go on, making a roof that would keep heat in and allow snow to slide off easily, without building up the ice dams that result along the edges of roofs with poor insulating properties. Jessie had chosen green for the roof, an optimistic color for winter, but which would blend in with the natural environment in the summer. It arrived on a building-supply truck early that afternoon.

Becker drove in shortly thereafter. "Hey, Jessie. How're you doing?"

"Not too bad, Phil. Cas?"

"Wailing over the loss of his plane when I left. Getting grumpy, which means he's better."

"I can't imagine him grumpy."

"Well, he is. Ask Linda. Threatened to throw a bowl of Jell-O at me. Listen, Jessie. I apologize for yelling at you yesterday, though I meant most of it. I need to ask for your help now."

"With what?"

He removed his hat, rubbed his head, and frowned, narrowing his eyes. "It still could have been just a coincidence when that other plane came up under you out of nowhere."

Jessie frowned and started to disagree.

"No, wait a minute. It's also possible that it was a purposeful thing, as you've speculated. If it was—well, I've been thinking about what you asked yesterday—you remember—about how that pilot could have known you guys would be flying upriver?"

"Yeah?"

"I checked with our people, and no one mentioned it to anyone outside the office. That leaves anyone Caswell might have told or who could have read his flight plan. He says he only told Linda, and she didn't tell anyone. No one asked to read the flight plan, so I think we can count that out. The only people left are the ones here, where we talked about it, or whomever you might have told. Right?"

She thought about it and tentatively agreed. "Okay."

"So. Got any ideas?"

The possibility that the plane crash might involve one of the building crew was daunting. Jessie turned her head to look across the yard at all five—no, six, counting Hank Peterson—busy one way or another, putting the two-by-twelves into place. But one, or all, might have heard the flight up the Knik River being planned the day before.

Without hesitation, she mentally crossed Peterson and Prentice off the list, knowing both of them too well to imagine them as bad guys. Unless . . . Could they have said something to someone else? Bill, J.B., Dell, and Stevie she only knew from their work on the cabin. Who they were otherwise, she had no idea. Now, looking at them though new eyes, she found she could be suspicious of any one of them. It was frightening and unsettling that distrust could creep in so easily.

She turned back to Becker, who had pulled the bench over next to the deck chair Lynn had brought for her to sit outside in, plunked himself down, and waited for an answer.

"Honestly, Phil, I haven't a clue. It just couldn't be Vic or Hank, unless one of them said something inadvertently to someone else—which is possible, of course. The rest are all new to me. I don't really know any of them, but none of them strikes me as—ah—malicious?"

"But you wouldn't rule them out?"

"I couldn't. But I wouldn't even begin to make guesses unless I knew a lot more about each of them."

"Do you remember anyone in particular listening to our conversation?"

"It was a busy day. They were all back and forth, using the equipment and materials, just like always. I wasn't paying any attention."

He nodded. "Well, I hoped maybe—but I wasn't paying attention either, so why would *you?* What I'd like you to do is think about each of them carefully and keep an eye out for anything— well, interesting, shall we say? I'm going to see what I can dig up on them individually."

"Why don't you ask Vic? He hired them. He must know something about them."

"True," Becker replied. "I'll do just that."

Jessie frowned as she watched him walk across the yard and call up to Prentice, who was on the roof. The idea of watching and assessing other people this way set her teeth on edge. Previously, she had felt comfortable and safe with the working crew. Now she couldn't help wondering about each of them. It was depressing—like being a snitch of some kind. She remembered the obnoxious newspaper reporter and how she had felt about his demands. This felt vaguely similar, though she couldn't quite catch hold of how they fit together. Prying into other people's business, she supposed.

Prentice climbed down and the two men walked away from the job, where they could talk without being overheard. As Jessie watched, everyone but Dell paused to see them go before they went back to work. J.B. shrugged at something Stevie said, then began to warble songs from *Showboat*. Hank climbed down and went for more lumber. Nothing seemed out of the ordinary.

Her head and shoulder were aching again, but she knew that not all of it had to do with the injuries she had sustained. Getting up, she went inside to take the first pain pill of the day and find something to take her mind off the chore Becker had set for her. Later. She would think about it later. First she would take the nap the pill would probably induce, then she would pay attention when the crew came off the roof. There was always some friendly banter when they were ready to quit for the day.

She woke to find that they had all gone home and she had missed them. Ehlers was making spaghetti for dinner. Her headache was gone and she was ravenous.

"Here," he said, handing her a bowl of salad. "Start on this. The rest will take ten minutes."

"I *love* you!" she told him, all but snatching it out of his hand.

"Wow! And I got to be this old without realizing that

spaghetti is all it takes? You'd better wait and see if the finished product lives up to your expectations."

She had been about to tell him of Becker's speculations, but they fled her mind as she concentrated on food—and the warm feeling that his smile and sense of humor gave her.

It could wait, after all. Couldn't it?

Chapter 25

 Late in the day, when the sun had dropped behind the western mountains and cast the valley into evening, far up the Knik River, almost under the glacier, an all but invisible man slipped warily through the edge of the trees. Dressed in dark clothing, he carried a day pack over one shoulder containing a bottle of water and a couple of sandwiches to last a few hours, should another wait be necessary. A holstered handgun hung on his belt, hidden under his black jacket. Slowly, cautiously assessing what lay ahead of him, he moved upriver, staying off the sandy banks and bars to make no tracks, crossing streams with extreme care not to leave evidence of his passing, following a route familiar from several trips here in previous weeks.

Remembering a female duck he had startled into flight on

another such evening, and the flock of ducklings that had scattered in panic, he made a wide circle into a grove of birch to avoid the nest, which was hidden in the tall grass beside a stream. A hundred and fifty yards from its delta at the river's edge, the stream cut into the soil and ran more than a foot below the ground surface through roots and loam. This forced him to leap across two feet of water stained the color of tea from the fallen leaves and decaying plant matter through which it had passed on its way to the river. Landing with a soft thump, he crouched and listened attentively for any response that might tell him he had attracted attention.

He was especially vigilant for, though past explorations had been unrewarding, soon after leaving his vehicle in the brush beside a little-used track at the end of the road this night, he had heard the sound of a plane engine. Shielded in the trees, he had seen the aircraft pass overhead and angle down toward a landing somewhere farther upriver. Now he intended to find it and its pilot—to see if what he suspected was fact and, if possible, to right an old wrong.

When nothing gave him reason to think his leap across the stream had been heard, he moved on a few yards, a mere shadow in the darkest part of the woods, then returned to the edge of the trees where he had a better view of the riverbank. It would have been easier to disguise the sound of his travel through this wild area during the day, when the trees were full of birdsongs and the hum of bees in the wildflowers. Chartered planes brought tourists to gaze upon the grandeur of the Chugach Mountains and the sweeping curves of the glacier, and the sound of their engines would have covered the footfalls of a dozen hikers.

Except for the continual music of water running, falling, trickling, it was very still in the half-light of extended twilight. Every dry leaf crushed underfoot, every snap of twig or scratch of thorn against fabric, every pebble that rolled was amplified in the evening silence.

A few steps farther some nocturnal animal fled ahead of him, rustling the grass—a mouse, maybe, or something larger, possibly a squirrel foraging late. No, not a squirrel, for the small rustle moved away into the trees but did not climb. Judging by the swiftness of its retreat, it was probably a fox. He had seen foxes twice on these evening trips up the river; dainty, smart, and neat of foot—smart buggers, foxes. They knew their territory, were quick and agile, and gone in a flash of burnished bronze. Once, when he was a boy, he had seen one dancing on hind legs in playful pursuit of insects drifting in a ray of sunlight that shone into a clearing. On a winter snowshoe trip, he had watched a fox hunting—listening carefully to locate a mouse that moved beneath the crust of the snow, then leaping high to pounce with all four feet together and snap it up for lunch. Foxes had an appealing sense of humor. He grinned at the memory.

When the rustling stopped, the dark figure moved again, circling a tangle of brush that forced him back into the woods for perhaps twenty yards near a rocky point, where another stream flowed down the steep slope of Mount Palmer. Careful not to roll any loose rocks down the hill, he negotiated the stones of the point and for the first time caught sight of a flashlight beam moving intermittently at the other end of a thin curve of riverbank.

It had grown too dark to see who was holding the light. He

would have to go closer. As he left the security of the rocks and stepped into the darkness under another stand of trees, he mistook a flat stone for solid ground. It tipped and made a sharp sound as it shifted against another stone, and a skittering pebble made several small ticks in falling. On the riverbank, the motion abruptly stopped and the light disappeared—switched off, quickly covered, or thrust into a pocket. There was a long moment of listening silence before the light reappeared, wavered, and stopped, as if whoever held it had laid it down to have the use of both hands. A silhouette passed in front of the narrow beam of light and vanished.

The man in the trees waited without moving for perhaps ten minutes, watching, blending with the rest of the darkness. Then, cautiously, he started on, feeling with every step to be sure of his footing before shifting his weight from one foot to the other, moving so slowly he was hardly distinguishable, a shade among the shadows though which he passed.

When he was halfway between the point and the now stationary light, he could make out the shape of the plane he had seen earlier against the evening light reflected from the river. It was parked on a long sandbar, separated from the curve of the bank by a ribbon of water, perhaps three feet wide. Part of the foot of the glacier had now come into view, glowing eerily pale beyond and above the plane and dark water. The peaks of the mountains to the east had begun to glow as the moon, about to rise behind them, revealing their shape against the sky. A handful of stars glittered overhead, two reflected in the quiet strip of water that lay between the plane and the curve of the shore.

Without warning, the next step dropped his foot into a

swampy hole and threw him forward, off balance, groping for support. When he was forced to take another step to keep from falling, his boot hit the unseen water with a splash, and he wound up clinging to a birch sapling. Hundreds of new leaves rustled against each other with a sigh that in the still air would divulge his presence and location to anyone who cared to listen.

Someone did care. Having left the flashlight as a decoy, someone had crept silently to wait and watch from a motionless and undetectable position behind the shelter of a tree. The first rifle shot came out of the dark and struck the man in the water just below the left shoulder, spinning him around to face the shooter and driving him to his knees. Against the reflected light of the river and glacier he was a clear silhouette—an easy target.

It was impossible to see where the second shot hit him, but the shooter was satisfied to see the body crumple into the swampy pool.

The last thing the man in the water saw was the flash of the rifle. The last thing he heard was its report. By the time its echoes stopped resounding from the hills, he was already beginning to grow as cold as the water in which he lay.

Chapter 26

One member of the crew arrived early the next morning and gave the door of the Winnebago a sharp rap just as the coffeemaker inside was gurgling its last.

Jessie, who had once again drained the hot water tank for a shower that loosened her stiffness and eased the aches of her bruises while Lynn made breakfast, opened it to find Stevie, grinning up at her like a supplicant urchin, thermal cup in hand.

"Got coffee?"

"Sure. Come on in."

Cup filled, Stevie perched on the edge of the sofa, inhaled the steam from the fragrant brew, sighed, and sipped with evident satisfaction.

"I bring the bagels and Dell usually makes coffee for us both. I get my heart started when I swing by to pick him up. But he wasn't there this morning, so I'm brain dead. Thanks."

"Where was he?"

"Don't know. He didn't leave a note. It's not the first time, but I haven't asked questions. Maybe he's got a girlfriend." Though her voice was matter-of-fact, she looked a little bleak and Jessie wondered, not for the first time, if Stevie might be interested in Dell.

"You want some breakfast?"

"No, thanks. Coffee's fine. I'll just take this outside and leave you guys to . . ."

"Oh, sit down and have some bacon, eggs, and hash browns," Jessie told her, hastily filling a plate and shoving it in her direction, much to Lynn's consternation—he had cooked for two, not three. "There's plenty. And there'll be toast in a minute, won't there, Lynn?"

"Uh—sure." He reached for two more eggs to fry, wondering why Jessie was being so insistent.

"Well, okay," Stevie agreed cheerfully. "If there's enough. A real breakfast! Wow! Can't tell you how sick and tired I am of instant cereal and stuff you shove in a toaster oven."

Jessie's invitation had to do with Becker's request that she learn what she could about the members of the crew. Seeing this as an opportunity for a conversation she wouldn't have to instigate, she slid in beside Stevie at the table, effectively pinning her against the wall, and accepted the plate Lynn handed her with the rest of the first batch of eggs.

"How're you feeling?" Stevie asked, sprinkling hot sauce on her eggs.

"A lot better, thanks," Jessie said.

She tried to think of how to swing the conversation in the direction she wanted it to go, decided to meet the challenge head-on, and, since Stevie was already on the subject, simply asked what she wanted to know.

"You knew we were going up the river, didn't you?"

"Yeah. Bill mentioned it before you guys took off. Bet you never expected to have to make a hard landing on the glacier, though. That must have been a shocker. You were lucky to be sitting in back, from what I hear."

"I sure was."

Lynn, having fried two more eggs, sat down across the table from them with his own plate, giving Jessie a questioning look.

She ignored him and continued her exchange with Stevie. "How'd you guys find out we'd crashed?"

"Oh, we heard from everybody. J.B. told us when he came back from a dentist appointment in town, and Hank brought the news from that bar they're building down the road. Then Bill went after a load of plywood and saw the rescue helicopter pick up that trooper."

"Becker. So you, Dell, and Vic were the only ones here when it happened?"

"Not Vic. He'd gone to one of his other projects—in Palmer. He's got a crew replacing a roof off Evergreen, near the airport. People sort of came and went all afternoon. We didn't get much done."

So four out of six had been away from the building site when the other plane forced Caswell down on the glacier, leaving only Stevie and Dell to vouch for each other. And how valid was that, with Stevie sweet on Dell? But two of those absent, Hank and Vic, were people she had crossed off her mental list already. Jessie decided it was time to change the subject.

"So how'd you get into the construction game, Stevie? Is it hard for a woman?"

"My dad was a carpenter, and he taught me and my two brothers a lot. They gave up on it early, but I liked it, so I went ahead and got my working papers through an apprenticeship program. The work isn't as hard for a woman to get into as it used to be. I'm as good as most guys, so they can't complain much, but you run into a chauvinist good ole boy now and then. I just ignore 'em. Working 'em into the ground is the best revenge." She grinned at the thought.

"Bet you can do that, too," Lynn commented, smiling back at her as he considered the wiry strength and knowledge of building technique she had exhibited in her work on Jessie's cabin.

"Yeah," she told him confidently, "I usually can."

"Where're you from?" Jessie asked.

"Oregon. Oswego, just outside Portland."

Oregon? Interesting, Jessie thought. Daryl Mitchell had also been in Oregon.

"How'd you get to Alaska?"

"Hired on to build a new lodge at Denali last summer. Then Vic offered to put me on permanent, so I stayed. I like it here. More opportunity and higher pay."

"Lot colder than Oregon," Lynn observed.

"Lot drier, too. Besides, only an idiot stays outside in the middle of the winter. You two mushers excepted, of course."

"Sometimes I think we *are* idiots," he admitted.

Jessie nodded. "A lot of people think so."

As Stevie wiped the last egg yolk from her plate with a piece of toast, Vic Prentice knocked on the door for a coffee refill, which Jessie rose to pour for him. Snatching up her hat and safety glasses from the sofa, Stevie escaped from her place at the table and followed him out the door, calling a thank-you over her shoulder as she went.

"Let me know if you decide to cater out, Lynn. I'd be in the market."

Ehlers spread jam on a second piece of toast, took a bite, and chewed thoughtfully until Jessie had refilled her own coffee mug and come back to the table.

"What the hell was all that about?" he asked.

She hesitated, mug halfway to her mouth, and gave him a look that was on the embarrassed side.

"Becker wants to know anything he can about the crew," she told him. "So I'm finding out what I can."

"Set you to snitch, has he?"

Stung, Jessie scowled at him. "Dammit, Lynn, I don't like it. The whole business upsets me. But somebody knew we were going up there and flew the plane that forced us down, killed Bonnie Russell, and almost did for Cas and me. Somebody left those roses. Somebody is killing women and following Hansen's pattern of taking them up the Knik to get rid of the bodies. I don't like being suspicious of everybody, but— snitch?"

"Hey." Ehlers raised a defensive hand. "Sorry, wrong word. I didn't mean . . ."

Another knock on the door interrupted him and Prentice stuck his head in.

"Did Dell call in, Jessie? He hasn't showed."

·   ·   ·

He didn't show. Phone calls to his number roused only the answering machine, and the crew labored a man short that morning. By lunchtime, Vic was growling.

"Dammit, we need him. He go out partying last night, Stevie?"

Jessie, who was feeling well enough to do more cleanup in the yard, stopped to listen to the answer.

Stevie swallowed the bite of apple she was chewing and affected a casual disregard that Jessie found a bit counterfeit.

"I don't think so. He doesn't hang out or drink much. Might have gone hiking, though. He does a lot of outdoor stuff and goes a couple of times a week—I *think*."

As if she doesn't keep a close eye on him, Jessie thought.

"Where does he go?" she asked, startling Vic, who hadn't noticed her presence.

Stevie shrugged. "How should I know? The trails up Pioneer Peak, maybe—he mentioned it once. Up the river?"

"Did he mention going upriver?"

"Maybe. I don't remember exactly. He goes different places, I think. Why?"

Prentice frowned.

"It's not like Dell to miss work without letting me know. Never done it before."

It seemed to Jessie that Stevie was telling the truth about what she knew—and that Dell had evidently succeeded in keeping his female working partner at arm's length. She remembered seeing them together at Oscar's in Wasilla and wondered why the relationship didn't take. Stevie was an attractive woman—dark hair worn short, friendly gamine grin, something soft and gentle about her that escaped around the edges of the image of toughness she projected for obvious reasons. It seemed odd that he hadn't responded to her apparent interest, but she could be right and he might have another girlfriend. Stevie was clearly trying to keep her business to herself, but Jessie felt certain that if *she* had detected the young woman's interest in Dell, the rest of the crew was aware of it as well.

"You know, Stevie," Prentice mused in a thoughtful voice, still frowning in concern, "if he went hiking and didn't come home last night—wasn't there this morning and isn't here now—there has to be a reason. It's just possible he's still out there somewhere—hurt, maybe. If you have any idea where he went, now might be a good time to say so."

Indifference shifted to disquiet on Stevie's face as she considered that idea. Jessie could identify with her struggle between uneasiness and the revelation of her private feelings. It was difficult to be the interested one, especially when that attraction was not returned—embarrassing, humiliating even. Prentice was Stevie's boss, and the last thing she wanted was to appear weak or ridiculous in front of him. Unrequited crushes could look juvenile.

"We-ell," she said slowly, a flush spreading over her cheeks, "on my way back from the grocery store last night I drove past his place, okay?"

Jessie doubted that Dell's place was actually on the route between Stevie's—wherever that was—and the grocery, but kept her mouth shut.

"He was putting stuff in his car, and he had a fishing pole."

"A fishing pole?" Vic questioned attentively.

"Yes." Stevie scowled. "And that's all I know."

She slid off the lumber on which she was perched and walked away toward the half-built cabin, pulling on her leather gloves, going back to work a few minutes early.

Prentice turned to Jessie.

"So he probably went upriver."

"Maybe, but there's other fishing places and a hundred places he could have gone if he wasn't fishing. This area's a hiker's paradise."

Still frowning, Prentice pulled off his cap and ran a hand through his thinning hair. She knew he was more anxious than he appeared, for when he was stressed the soft sound of his southern upbringing thickened his voice slightly and his grammar went to hell.

"It's only been a coupla hours. If he don't show up by tomorrow mornin'—or call—well, we'll see about it."

Jessie nodded agreement but turned toward the Winnebago and its telephone. It was, she thought, something Becker should be made aware of *before* tomorrow.

As she walked across the yard, she glanced at the roof where the rest of the crew, not to be outdone, had followed Stevie and was now back at work. J.B. was sitting back on his heels, hammer in hand, watching Jessie with a speculative look on his face.

Oh, not again, she thought.

But the minute he saw that she was aware of his scrutiny, he looked away quickly and went back to pounding nails.

Chapter 27

Becker showed up sooner than Jessie thought possible, considering that it took two phone calls to track him down. He had been at the crime lab, working on identifications for the construction crew and going over back histories of the women whose murders had been attributed to Robert Hansen. Hearing of Dell's disappearance, he made the trip from Anchorage to Knik Road in just over half an hour, without his siren. He came with another trooper and a warrant to search the current residence of Daryl O'Dell Mitchell.

"I already had the warrant," he told Jessie. "Dell *is* Mitchell—the nephew of the old man whose body you found. I should have figured that out at least a week ago."

Jessie stared at him, confounded. "Dell. *O'Dell.* I didn't recognize him at all," she said finally.

"Well, he didn't have a beard or long hair when you saw him, did he? And you only saw him once."

"Right."

"He's also a heftier man than he was when you saw him—muscled up from working construction and driving a truck. Who would have expected him to show up on Prentice's crew? And why?"

"He came asking for work. He was qualified. I needed a man, so I hired him." Vic answered the question simply. "He'd asked before about this specific job. Guess he heard about it from someone in the community. He wanted to work a log cabin for the experience, was how he put it. It's the only one I'm building this summer, so I put him on."

"Now he's missing?"

"Yeah, well—he didn't show up this morning, which is unusual. He's a good, dependable worker. Stevie says he may have gone up the river last night. I'd sure like to know he's not hurt somewhere out there."

"I'd like to know why he went," Becker said, all business. "I want to borrow Stevie for an hour, so she can show us exactly where she saw him last."

Stevie came down from the unfinished roof, removed her tool belt and agreed to go along, but she asked, as had Bonnie Russell, if Jessie could go too.

Why does everybody want me to hold their hand? Jessie wondered, not particularly enthused about joining the investigation but slightly curious, now that she knew who he was, to see where Dell lived. She agreed to go, hoping it wouldn't take long.

"Tell Lynn I'll be back soon, if I'm not here when he comes

at five," she told Hank Peterson, who had climbed down after Stevie and stood listening.

"No problem. You'll be safe with the cops anyway. You okay with this, Stevie?"

"What?" She swung around to face him. "Oh, yeah. I'm okay."

"You're sure?"

"Yeah." The look she gave him was a kind of thank-you for his friendly concern.

Everybody likes Hank, Jessie thought, as they walked to the patrol car. He's like an older brother—or younger, depending on who's counting. Then the penny dropped and she suddenly realized what was behind his concern for Stevie. He was attracted to her. She was hung up on Dell, but Hank, who had to know it, was interested in Stevie anyway. What a tangle. Somebody's bound to get hurt here, she thought, shaking her head and hoping it wouldn't be Hank. Oh, hell, she decided, it's their business, not mine, and climbed into the back of the car.

.   .   .

Though Jessie knew Becker had Dell Mitchell's address, he asked Stevie for directions and followed them. She wondered why but didn't ask, assuming he had his reasons.

They pulled up outside a small house on the outskirts of Palmer, which from the style and overgrown shrubbery in the yard had been built sometime in the fifties. Becker sat for a moment, looking it over.

"That where he parks his car?" He indicated a patch of oil-stained gravel next to a carport half filled with firewood, evidently stacked there to keep it dry but leaving no space to park a vehicle.

"Yeah. That's where I saw him putting stuff in the car." Stevie glanced at Jessie and flushed again. The street was not a dead end, but part of a circle that began and ended in another. There was no way she would have passed this house unless she had done it purposely.

Jessie held her tongue and didn't smile; though she couldn't resist a wink, which made Stevie's lips twitch as she held back a giveaway grin.

"What's he drive?"

"Old Mustang—blue," she answered. "Except for one tan front fender."

There was mail in the box by the road and the morning's newspaper on the front step. Clearly, Dell had not been there to collect them.

Armed with his warrant, Becker tried the door. It was unlocked, so they walked in, Becker calling out Dell's name.

"Stay here by the door," he cautioned the two women, and the two troopers searched the house room by room to be sure there was no one home.

The house had an empty feel. Jessie looked around the living room in which she stood, as they waited. The main window that faced the street was covered with faded drapes. They were lined with light-blocking material that plunged the space into gloom, making it too dark to see what appeared to be books and papers of some kind on a small table. By the table was a folding chair, positioned as if someone—probably Dell—had been working there. The rest of the room was sparsely furnished—two chairs with a coffee table between them stood near a woodstove with a pipe that vanished up the chimney of a fireplace. A shelf unit against the wall opposite the window was half full of paperbacks, videotapes, and CDs for a new-looking entertainment center on an adjoining wall. There were no pictures or decorations. An empty glass and a beer bottle had been left on the coffee table, along with a newspaper folded to the television guide.

As she was wishing for more light to see what was on the table by the window, Becker returned, walked directly across the room, and opened the curtains. Glancing down, he stopped dead and grunted in surprise.

"What is it?" Jessie asked.

"Come here, carefully. Don't touch anything."

She walked across to the table, followed by Stevie, and looked down.

On the table was a map that Jessie knew was from the assessor's office, because she had one like it. Next to the map was a small pile of newspaper articles, which Becker flipped over one by one with the eraser of a pencil taken from his pocket. Every one of them had something to do with the latest string of murders and bodies that had been found, including the old man Jessie had found in her basement. She recognized the headline, DEAD BODY DISCOVERED IN LOCAL MUSHER'S BASEMENT, and her resentment flared again at the reporter responsible.

An enlarged copy of a map that included the Knik River drainage lay in the middle of the table. On the original had been drawn several concentric circles, with Anchorage in the center. In the upper right quarter were numbers, one to twenty-three,

244 • SUE HENRY

with circles drawn around them. A line from each indicated a specific location along the river.

"Phil?" Jessie questioned, recognition dawning, "is this what I think it is?"

The map had been creased in half horizontally, the lower half folded under. Becker used the pencil to unfold it, and the rest lay open to view, with several more numbered circles around Seward on the Kenai Peninsula.

"It's a copy of the re-creation of Hansen's map from the Gilmour and Hale book," he said.

"What book?"

"*Butcher, Baker,*" he answered, through tight lips. "There've been two books published about the Hansen case. This was the first—came out in 1991. It included the police re-creation of a map Hansen drew of where he buried the women he killed. This is an enlarged copy. He admitted burying women in sites one through seventeen. The rest he denied, though they were marked on his map."

"What are these, then?"

She pointed out but did not touch three new circles that had been drawn with a red pencil. Inside each was a number: twenty-four, twenty-five, and twenty-six. All three indicated sites on the upper reaches of the Knik River.

"I would have to assume they indicate new burials, or at least new victims, buried or not. I know this is the one Bonnie Russell stumbled across, and it wasn't underground." He indicated number twenty-five. "He must be following Hansen's lead—adding to his list."

The idea that Dell was the person responsible for the abducted and murdered women—that he had been working in her yard and was probably also responsible for the roses that had been delivered to her—made Jessie feel cold. It could have been Dell she saw in the yard the night she and Lynn Ehlers came back from Oscar's. She had not had a good look at that retreating figure. That he could have been so close, watching her—watching everything that went on, including the excavation of his own uncle—seemed unbelievable. Where was he now? Why hadn't he covered his tracks by coming to work that morning? What was he doing that was so important he would risk exposure?

Clearly, she decided, I am no better at judging people than I am at not having my own way. It was frightening that she could have been so mistaken.

"What are you . . ." she started.

"Jesus!" Stevie said suddenly.

Both Becker and Jessie had forgotten she was there, looking over his shoulder.

"If you think Dell did those murders, you're wrong," she told them, white-faced and adamant. "I don't believe it for a minute."

They stared at her, startled.

If he did, Jessie thought—remembering that Prentice also liked Dell and was concerned about him—it's going to be tough on the crew.

"Phil," the second trooper called from the kitchen. "You'd better see this."

The drawer he had opened in his search was the second of four in a vertical set beside the back door. In it lay two boxes of cartridges and a cleaning kit for a handgun. Though the box for the gun was there, the weapon itself was missing.

On the counter sat a loaf of bread, a few crumbs, and a knife that appeared to have been used to apply mayonnaise and mustard. Opening the refrigerator, he showed Becker the remains of a block of cheese. In the garbage was the empty package from some sandwich ham.

"Looks like he made himself a lunch. From the dirty dishes in the sink, I'd guess he had fried chicken and coleslaw for dinner. This may mean that wherever he went he meant to be gone long enough to get hungry."

"Agreed," Becker told him. "Good work, Pat." He stood looking into the drawer, with its evidence that Dell had also taken a gun with him, and glowered. "Guess we'd better get going upriver and find him."

Becker called the crime lab for a team to go over Dell's house and left everything that was on the table by the front window except the map, which he carefully stowed in a plastic evidence bag as Stevie watched and glared at him. He closed the house, and they all went back to the patrol car in silence.

"We'll drop you off . . ." he had started to tell Jessie as they climbed in, when Stevie once again interrupted.

"*No!*"

He twisted in the driver's seat to give her an irate look. "What do you mean, no? You can't just . . ."

"I mean you're not going without me, that's what I mean."

"Oh, no. You're going back to Jessie's. That's what *I* mean."

"You can't stop me from driving up there myself—and I will," she countered, angry and stubborn, frowning from under the purple bandanna she had chosen for work that morning.

"Watch me. I can arrest you."

"For *what?*"

"For obstruction of—oh, hell. For getting in the way," Becker barked. "I haven't got time for any more of this shit."

He jerked the car into gear and stomped on the gas, throwing the others back in their seats as he took off, scattering gravel.

"Well, either I go with you or I go alone, but I'm going, so live with it," Stevie told him in a determined voice. "Dell's out there somewhere and he's no killer. He may need help. I'm going to find him if I can."

Becker, concentrating now on pausing for a stop sign, did not answer. Jessie, wisely keeping out of the argument, like the second trooper, saw his shoulders slump in a sigh of defeat and guessed she would also be going along—to help him keep tabs on Stevie, if nothing else.

She glanced at the woman, who was now staring out the window, arms folded, teeth clenched, and wondered suddenly how often she had looked the same way to people around her.

"Phil," she said calmly, "would you mind stopping by my place for just a minute, so I can pick up my survival gear?"

His answer was a sharp nod and a disgusted sigh of resigned agreement.

To that gear, Jessie firmly meant to add her Smith & Wesson .44 and a jacket that didn't have a shoulder soaked in her own blood.

Chapter 28

"What the hell is going on?" Prentice demanded, trotting up to meet them as the patrol car stopped next to the motor home and Jessie got out. Stevie, not about to let Becker take advantage of an empty backseat to leave without her, didn't budge.

"We've got a suspect on the loose," Becker told him shortly. "We're going up the Knik to see if he can be found."

"You mean Dell?" The contractor's face tightened into an astonished frown of disbelief and disagreement. "I don't think that's possible."

"It's possible," Becker snapped. "More than that, it's probable. There's other evidence besides the fact that he isn't here. Where's the rest of your crew? I want to ask them a few questions before we go."

"You can see they're not here," Prentice stated flatly, waving a hand at the cabin.

The roof was empty except for Bill, climbing its slope with a piece of insulation to put between the two-by-twelves. J.B. and Hank were nowhere to be seen.

"Where are they?"

"Who knows? J.B. said he was having trouble with the tooth he had fixed and went back to the dentist. As soon as he left, Peterson took off too. He didn't even bother to say where he was going. I can't get anything done this way. Stevie, come out of there and get back to work."

She shook her head in stubborn refusal. "Dell's in trouble and I'm going to help."

"Goddammit!"

As Prentice fumed and Becker called dispatch from the car to report his intended activity, Jessie came out of the Winnebago zipping her jacket. She crossed the yard, unfastened Tank from his tether, and brought him across to the patrol car, where they both got in back with Stevie.

"Tell Lynn Ehlers I'm with Becker, will you, Vic?"

Through an open window she could still hear him swearing as they pulled back onto Knik Road and headed for the river.

.   .   .

They found Dell's locked Mustang concealed in some brush at the end of the road, where a track used by fishermen led down to the Knik.

Becker walked slowly around the vehicle, examining the ground with care.

"This isn't the first time he's been here," he said, giving his partner a significant look. "There're several overlapping tracks of the same tires. Here. See?"

There were also a few boot prints that showed where the driver had stepped out into some mud. They led away from the Mustang but soon disappeared into the trees, headed south toward the glacial source of the river.

"Now, here's how it's going to be," Becker told Jessie and Stevie, as he took a shotgun out of the trunk of the patrol car. "You two are going to stay here, while we go up the river a ways. I want you to search this area while we're gone, but I don't want anybody taking off on her own for any reason, understand? You stay here—together. I don't want to worry about who's in the way if I have to use this."

They both nodded, Stevie hesitating for an instant before agreeing.

"I mean it, Stevie. Jessie, keep an eye on her. If she starts to take off, you holler—loud."

Stevie gave the three of them an angry look, clearly aligning Jessie with Becker and his partner and deciding they were all against her.

"I'm telling you, he didn't do any of this," she said. "Why won't you listen?"

"I can't afford to," Becker told her in a tired voice. "If you've got it wrong, it's too dangerous to assume he's innocent. There's so much that says he probably isn't. Can't you see that? We'll worry about who did what after we see if we can find him. But you won't be any help if you keep me from doing my job. If you give me any more trouble, I swear I'll have Pat take you back to town."

"I'll come back on my own."

"No, you won't! I'll make sure of that, if I have to lock you up. Stay with Jessie, and see if you can find anything helpful to tell us where Dell's gone."

The two troopers walked away into the trees, following the trail Dell had left sometime before. There was just enough to aid their search—a broken twig, a scuffed root, a footprint now and then—for he had evidently been more concerned with staying away from where he would leave tracks on the riverbank than with anyone following him through the woods. They lost the track periodically but managed to find it again for the first half mile or so. Then, where he had jumped a stream, it petered out, covered with hundreds of duck tracks, large and small. As they jumped the stream, the mother duck paddled her brood away from them toward the river, protesting loudly as she went. Though they made ever-widening circles around the place where the track came to an end, they couldn't pick it up again.

"Where the hell did he go?" Becker's partner, Pat, asked in frustration.

"Let's go out along the river. Maybe we can find him farther on."

Once out of the woods and on the bank, they could move faster, though their two sets of tracks were clearly visible in the sand, gravel, and mud. Becker could see that the river was running higher than normal for this time of year—noisier, too. He turned and looked back toward the place where he had left the two women, but a stand of birch hid that part of the bank. Since he hadn't heard Jessie shout, he assumed they were still together, doing what they'd been told, but he was worried anyway. He didn't trust Stevie at all, and Jessie had been known to follow her own plan of action more than once in the past. Damned uppity women! He knew he shouldn't have brought them along, but he also knew Stevie meant what she said about coming back alone.

He let it go for the time being and continued carefully south along the river, looking for any sign of Dell Mitchell, convinced he was on the trail of a killer.

.   .   .

Jessie and Stevie watched the troopers move through the trees until they were out of sight before they turned without much enthusiasm to what they had been instructed to do. For perhaps ten minutes they searched the area around Dell's parked car, finding several items of trash, which they collected and piled by the patrol car—a candy bar wrapper, a flattened 7-Up can, a twisted empty Marlboro pack, two tattered grocery bags, and a child's blue plastic bucket, faded almost to gray on the side that had not been buried in the sand. Tank stayed with Jessie, sniffed around where she was searching, and came up with a Ziploc that had probably held a sandwich at some time in the past.

"Trust you to find anything that hints of food," she told him, earning a doggy grin as she plucked his treasure out of a bush, examined it, and found it too old to have contained the sandwich Dell had put together in his kitchen.

"Nothing," Stevie grumbled, tossing the bucket onto the pile. "This is busywork. He just wants to keep us out of his hair! Well, I'm not staying here!"

"That's not very smart, Stevie," Jessie responded.

"Look, I didn't come out here to wring my hands, waiting for the men to come back and let us know what they found."

Her attitude didn't surprise Jessie. She had expected Stevie's take-charge attitude to resurface and had wondered what she would do when challenged by it.

"They aren't just men, they're law enforcement. Phil Becker's had about all he'll take from civilians—meaning you and me. I've given him enough grief in the last couple of weeks. But he meant what he said. He'll send you back."

"Not if he can't find me."

"Aw, Stevie . . ."

"There's a trail at the end of the road that goes up to where you can look down on the river. I'm taking it to look for Dell. You can stay here if you want to."

She whirled and started up to the road that lay above, leaving Jessie and Tank to watch her go.

What am I supposed to do now, Jessie wondered, hold her at gunpoint?

She hesitated. Should she let her go alone and wait, as Becker had instructed? But what if Stevie was wrong about Dell? What if he were involved in the recent murders, as everything they had seen at his house indicated?

Though she had gotten to know the rest of the work crew at least casually, she knew Dell hardly at all. Though he watched everyone, he kept to himself, was usually quiet, and focused on his work, speaking when spoken to but volunteering little of a personal nature. Had that isolation been purposeful? Had he stayed out of her way, hoping she wouldn't recognize him as the man from whom she had bought the property? She had never

254 • SUE HENRY

asked his last name and couldn't remember ever hearing it. Had he used "Dell" as a cover, rather than Daryl, which she might have recalled from the paperwork?

It was possible. But it was also possible that all this was circumstantial. She thought back to the red numbered circles on the map Becker had confiscated. Would anyone but the killer have known where to draw those circles? Though she couldn't think how, she supposed that was also possible.

While I stand here procrastinating, Stevie may be walking into trouble, she thought, and was suddenly angry at the whole situation and her place in it. If Stevie hadn't insisted on coming, she wouldn't be out here at all. In past circumstances would she have hesitated to do what she felt like doing, which was go after the woman?

"Dammit, no," she said out loud, causing Tank, who had sat down at her feet, to perk up his ears.

I'm being so cautious about being independent that I'm waiting around for other people to tell me what to do. There's got to be a balance. Sometimes waiting is dumb.

By now Stevie was a good five minutes ahead and moving fast, not wanting to be stopped. If she wanted to catch up with her, she would have to go now, and quickly. There was no time to leave Becker a note and nothing on which to write one. Reaching down, Jessie grabbed up a handful of sand and gravel and stepped to the hood of the patrol car. Letting it trail from her fist, she drew an arrow that pointed in the direction Stevie had disappeared, southwest, toward the trail she had said started at the end of the road.

Jessie and Tank started after Stevie at a trot. She did not notice that, behind her, the breeze was already blowing grains of sand from her arrow.

*   *   *

There was the barest hint of a trail, more of a path really, which was not officially maintained. It snaked through brush and trees, rising and falling to follow the terrain. The first section was fairly easy to follow, but it soon grew narrow and rough, full of roots to stumble over and sharp rocks that made haste difficult.

Tank had less trouble following it than did Jessie, who was soon thirsty and panting with the effort despite her conditioning. Though she trained and raced her sled dogs over all kinds of country, in a variety of conditions, this was a different kind of exercise than driving a sled behind a team of dogs, with its opportunities to ride the runners and rest while continuing along a trail. Climbing uphill over uneven ground strained muscles she seldom used. When the track dropped, it pounded her feet into the toes of her boots and punished her shins and calves as she strove to slow the descent that gravity encouraged.

The battering she had suffered in the crash of the plane also took its toll. Her bruised ribs were soon protesting each breath she took. The pain in her shoulder renewed itself as she tried holding her arm close to her body to ease the ache of the ribs, but the effort cost more in balance than it bought in relief.

Acknowledging that chasing Stevie might have been a mistake, she continued until she reached a fairly flat space, beyond which the track disappeared around a shoulder of the mountain. There, for a few steps, she slowed, attempting to gather strength and get her breath back as she took a drink from her water bottle. Pausing, she listened to see if she could hear Stevie moving ahead of her, but the air was full of birdcalls and the rush of water falling somewhere close at hand, muffling any other sound. Between two trees, she could see an eagle describing circles high in the air over the river hidden below, riding thermals. How lovely it would be to coast so easily and effortlessly on the wings of the wind.

Glancing down at a damp spot in the trail ahead of her, she noticed the tracks of an animal. Neat and evenly placed, they led straight along the track toward the curve to the right. Apparently a fox had taken the high road to wherever it was going. Jessie smiled and started on again, feeling a bit better. The fox was right. Even if it was uncomfortable for her at the moment, it was easier to travel the rough track than to leave it for the brush and trees below.

She reached the curve, turned, with Tank following close behind, and stopped so abruptly that she felt him bump into the back of her tired legs.

A man was standing in the center of the track, head cocked to one side, with an expectant and mocking look that narrowed his lips but was not quite a smile. He held a rifle casually at his side—pointed directly at her. Beyond him, sitting on a rock, wrists fastened behind her with a pair of handcuffs, was Stevie, a piece of duct tape over her mouth, distress and anger written in tears on her face.

Chapter 29

Phil Becker and his partner had walked a long way along the riverbank without finding any indication of the man for whom they searched. When they came to a place where the brush grew thick right up to where the flow of the river was carving out a new curve in the bank, they went around the obstacle, rather than wade. The trees thinned, then ended, and the ground turned into rock on a point beyond the brush. One of the many streams that scoured the face of Mount Palmer ran tumbling and splashing over the stones in a small waterfall.

"Look here."

Becker stepped over to see what his partner had found, and there on a flat stone was the print of a boot, its tread defined in the dried mud it had left behind after stepping in a pool created by the waterfall.

"That's it, matches the others we saw," Becker said, kneeling to look at it closely. "He came through here."

"Yes, at least someone did, but it had to be long enough ago for the mud to dry—last night or early this morning."

They were clambering over the rocks when somewhere higher on the mountain the sound of a shot stopped them. Listening, they could hear someone shouting angrily far above, though it was impossible to distinguish what was being said.

"Want to bet Jessie and Stevie did not stay where we left them?" Becker asked. "Let's get up there." He turned and started to climb the rocky slope in the direction of the shot. Longer-legged, he had soon outdistanced his shorter partner, then suddenly lost his footing and fell to hands and knees on a stone slippery with moss.

"This is impossible," he complained. "Let's get into the trees. It'll be easier there."

It was, but not by much. The ground was steep and covered with years of nature's compost, fallen branches and decaying leaves. The two troopers scrambled and slid, making headway, but not as fast as they would have liked. There was no more yelling from above, but halfway up they heard something or someone crashing downhill through the brush, out of sight on the glacier side of the rocky slope they had abandoned. As they continued to climb, the trees thinned, but the brush grew thicker in their absence.

"Damn this to hell," Becker panted, struggling with the shotgun he was carrying, as it caught on a bush and all but brought him to a halt. Yanking it free, he lunged on up the hill, swearing mentally when he could no longer afford the breath. He could hear Pat's ragged gasps behind him as his partner managed to keep up only because he had nothing to carry.

They broke out onto the trace of a trail so unexpectedly that Pat stumbled to his hands and knees. He scrambled to his feet and both men stood for a moment, huffing, starved for air. The track ahead made a turn around the same rocky slope they had experienced below and Becker headed for that curve at a lope. On the other side the track lay empty, but in the depression of a footprint lay a clean shell that had been ejected from a rifle.

"The shot we heard," Pat panted, removing an evidence bag from his pocket to retrieve it.

Around the shell were the boot prints of two people—one larger, one smaller—that headed along the trail but disappeared where it headed downhill and wound away into the brush.

Taking the time to go back to the curve they had passed, Becker searched the ground and found another set of boot prints. These stopped on the south side of the curve, except for one that angled toward the river and had broken the lip of the track, causing a small amount of earth to slide downhill.

"Someone went over the edge at this point," he observed with a worried look. "There's no blood, but they were probably hit by that shot we heard and fell into the brush." Who was it, he wondered, Jessie or Stevie?—having no doubt it had been one of them. Wasting no more words, he swung around to follow the two sets of prints that continued along the track.

"We split up?" Pat suggested.

"No. This'll be faster if it goes on down to the river."

They trotted on, watching cautiously for any sign of motion on the track ahead of them, but saw and heard no one.

•   •   •

Far below, Jessie's tumbling body finally rolled to a stop against the trunk of a birch and lay still. For several minutes she did not move but merely hung against the thing that had abruptly halted her plummet down the steep, rocky, brush-covered side of Mount Palmer. Tank caught up and came to stand next to her, waiting.

When she continued to lie without moving, he whined and licked her face.

One small gasp escaped her lips as she tried for the air that had been knocked out of her by the fall. One hand reached out to claw at the ground, and she slowly dragged her upper body uphill enough to relieve the pressure of the tree that was impeding her breathing. Then she gasped again, drawing much-needed air into her lungs, twisted so she could pull the other hand out from under her, and raised herself on both arms. After several deep breaths, as the color began to return to her face, she leaned forward and threw up.

Rolling over to sit facing downhill, she leaned against the birch trunk and rested from the resulting pain. Tank came to stand on the other side of her, and she lifted an arm over his back to hug him close and pat him wordlessly. The motion hurt her injured shoulder, but knowing her lead dog was alive and seemed all right was worth it. Glancing at it, she saw her shoulder was once again bleeding through the sleeve of her jacket over the stitched cut she had suffered in the plane crash. So much for no more blood-soaked jackets.

Lifting the other hand, she explored the cut on her head, found the dressing in place, and was relieved that throwing her arms over her head as she cast herself off the trail had helped to protect it from further injury. Her hands, however, were bleeding from any number of scratches and cuts, and one fingernail hung loose, where something had caught it on her way down the hillside.

The rest of her body hurt so much she couldn't tell which of the two batterings had caused it. Nothing seemed broken, but one knee throbbed so suspiciously that she hesitated to stand and put weight on it. So she sat where she was and thought about what to do next.

It was very quiet. Her fall had disturbed the accumulation of old leaves and spruce needles on which she rested and the clean earthy scent of it rose around her, familiar and comforting. Somewhere in the brush a squirrel chattered. Jessie looked down and saw that one of her feet was lying in a trickle of water that flowed downhill. She moved it and realized that she was hearing the tiny gurgle the stream made over a root of the birch, having washed away enough soil to expose it.

Tank whined again and she moved her hand to hold his muzzle in a warning to be still. She listened to a distant crashing through brush to the north of her position, hidden from sight by the rocky ridge. Was she being pursued? She sat still and waited. The sound grew louder, and she realized it was going uphill. How long had she lain against the tree? How long had she sat here, for that matter? Could the rifleman have already gone down and be coming back up, determined to find her and make sure she did not escape? The crashing continued up the slope. She listened until it disappeared and sighed in relief.

Whatever was wrong with her knee—or the rest of her, for that matter—it was time to move. Sitting there waiting to be found was not smart, but where should she go? As the crashing had gone up, she decided to go down—easier anyway. If she could find a place to hide closer to the river, she could wait for Becker to discover that she and Stevie had not followed his instructions to the letter and come hunting for her, as she was sure he would. If necessary, she had the .44 and knew how to use it.

But what about Stevie? Where and how was she?

There was nothing Jessie could think of to do about Stevie at this point that would not result in putting both of them in jeopardy. She had saved herself from the shot she had heard as, instinctively and without hesitation, she had thrown herself over the edge of the trail and into the brush, initiating her terrible tumble and hoping Tank would follow, as he had.

"Good boy," she told him in a whisper. "Quiet now."

Slowly, using the birch for support, she labored to pull herself to a standing position, feeling every bruised part of her protest the action. The knee was the agony she had anticipated, but for the time being it held her weight. Gritting her teeth, she stood swaying until the resulting dizziness cleared. Then, quietly, one careful painful step at a time, she started to follow the trickling stream down the hill toward the river below.

·   ·   ·

Back on the hillside, Becker and his partner still hurried along the track, which now headed decidedly downhill, toward a thin curve of riverbank.

"Look," Pat said, stopping at a place where he could see the river between the trees and brush.

A red and silver plane sat on the upper end of a sandbar, separated from the bank by a branch of the river's headwaters. The Knik widened at this point, dividing into many ribbons of water. These were running full, all but submerging several of the bars they had separated and that until now had stood high and dry. The rear wheel of the plane was almost in the water that rushed around the bar on which it sat. If the pilot didn't return quickly to fly out, leaving would soon be difficult if not impossible. Looking down at the river, Becker checked carefully for any movement that would indicate that the people they were following had reached it and might be headed for the plane, but saw no one.

The face of the Knik Glacier was in full view, and just in sight atop it Becker could see the remains of Caswell's Maule M-4 lying upside down on the surface. Remembering times he had flown with Cas in that plane and how much his friend had loved and been proud of it, he felt his anger rising at its demise and at the fact that Cas was still in the hospital.

"Come on," he snapped. "I want to catch up with this guy."

Of the two sets of tracks they had followed, the smaller had exhibited an unevenness in depth, as if the person who made them was having trouble negotiating the rough trail. On a switchback that required a step down and over a large stone, the damp surface was disturbed where the person who made the smaller tracks had evidently fallen. Something purple lay next to it on a rock.

"Stevie," Becker said, grabbing it up and unfolding the bandanna she had been wearing when he last saw her. "This is Stevie's. It must have been Jessie who was shot and went over the edge of the trail back there. We've got to find her—soon. But first we'll have to tackle Mitchell. He's got Stevie, and he's going to be between us and Jessie."

They went on down the trail, running now, leaping over obstacles, taking more chances. Becker was ready with the shotgun, should they find themselves in sudden close proximity to the person they sought.

. . .

From where she had stopped falling, two-thirds of the way down from the track above, Jessie moved slowly but steadily toward the river. The bed of the stream was almost a trail, so she walked in it, hoping it would also disguise her tracks from anyone following, should Stevie's captor decide to search for her. Most trails to glaciers she had experienced divided, taking hikers both to the top, where they could walk onto the surface, and to the bottom, where huge pieces of ice calved off. These pieces fell into a pond that formed at the foot and became icebergs that floated or drifted aground as they melted. If the trail went down to the river below the glacier, he would follow it down, she thought, so she kept a careful watch for any sign of him below.

Because the stream ran down the hill in a series of waterfalls that splashed and small pools that were deep enough to run over the tops of her boots, Jessie's feet were soon soaked and cold. At one spot, she paused to let the icy water run over her hands, which were beginning to stiffen and ache. It numbed the sting of the cuts and scratches and deadened the throb of the torn fingernail a little as it rinsed away some of the blood and dirt.

As the ground began to flatten slightly, the going grew easier and the stream widened, so she stepped from the water and walked through the grass and weeds that grew beside it. She was nearing the river, still in the shelter of a small stand of birch, when she saw something dark in the stream ahead of her. At first she thought it was a large rock that sometime in the past had bounced down and landed a long way from its source, but she changed her mind as she came closer. It moved.

She stopped and laid a hand on Tank's head, cautioning him to stillness and silence, and watched carefully. The dark form moved again and made a groaning sound. It was a man, and he was trying to pull himself from the icy water. Carefully, she took another step, but a rustle of grass betrayed her. The man who was lying half in and half out of the stream jerked his head and one defensive hand in her direction. In it was a handgun.

Between herself and the river, Jessie had found Dell Mitchell.

Chapter 30

"Jessie?"

She froze, fingers curled under Tank's collar, for he was growling at this apparent threat.

She and Dell stared at each other.

"Please," he said, and his hand began to shake. The gun dropped from it to the bank of the stream and, with another groan, he closed his eyes and collapsed onto his side, slipping a little farther into the swampy pool the stream had become as it flowed onto ground that flattened, then sloped to the river.

As she stepped cautiously toward him, Jessie could see that there was blood—a lot of blood—on his shirt and jacket. Some of it was bright and fresh, but the rest, staining the fabric a rusty brown, was older and had already dried.

Dropping to her knees beside him, she moved the handgun out of his reach, still alert for trouble, not trusting him even in this condition.

"Dell?" she said quietly. *"Dell!"*

He opened his eyes again. "Thought you were . . . please, Jessie—I—can't . . ."

Suddenly summoning strength and anger from somewhere, he clutched weakly at her arm and spoke clearly.

"Please, get me out of this damn cold water."

This is the halt leading the blind, thought Jessie, as she used some of her remaining energy to tug Dell's inert lower body from the pool and onto the bank. He groaned and tried to help her but wasn't much assistance. Her knee screamed pain, which she ignored, but when his legs and feet lay with the rest of him, on his back on solid ground, she collapsed on her back beside him, in the shelter of the birch saplings that surrounded them. A breath of breeze stirred the leaves, and as she rested she watched their shadows play over Dell's pale face.

"Thanks," he said after a moment, opening his eyes. "Thought I was gonna freeze—if I didn't die first."

He looked up at her with the hint of a smile that faded into a concerned frown as he observed the condition of her clothes and body. "What the hell happened—to you?"

She hadn't considered what she must look like after the fall had compounded her already battered appearance and didn't care now. Looks were, after all, not of primary importance.

"I fell," she said shortly. "A long way. What the hell happened to *you?*"

"Shot me—twice—last night."

"Who?" But she knew the name before he spoke it.

"J.B."

"Why?"

"He knows *I* know. Must've thought he killed me—like those women—but he didn't, quite."

It was enough. Jessie didn't ask any more questions, knowing she had been mistaken about Dell, but all of it could be sorted out later—if there was a later. Where were J.B. and his rifle now—and Stevie? Was there anything she could do for Dell before trying to find out?

"Where are you hit and how bad? I'll have to get help."

"Shoulder and—below the ribs. Went clear through—I think. Is he—gone?"

"Shit, no. His plane's out there on a sandbar, and he's got Stevie. Did you see Becker? He's around here somewhere with another trooper."

As Dell shook his head there was a sudden shout from somewhere farther along the riverbank toward the glacier. Jessie began to get to her feet, favoring her strained knee.

"What?" Dell questioned. "Hey, don't go. He's got—a rifle."

"*Don't I know it?* He tried to shoot me. That's why I came down the mountain in such a hurry."

•　　•　　•

Becker and his partner had fairly galloped down the last of the trail to the river and burst out onto the bank to see two figures struggling to cross the knee-deep water that lay between them and the plane that rested on the sandbar.

Carroty-red hair identified Stevie, and Becker assumed the taller male figure yanking her along was Dell.

"Hey!" he shouted, out of range for the shotgun but not his service revolver. He drew it, as did Pat. "Stop where you are! Drop the rifle, put your hands on your head, and walk back here, Mitchell."

The answer was immediate and negative. The man in the water halted, turned to face them, and swung Stevie around in front of him. Raising his rifle waist high, he fired a shot in their direction, forcing them to leap for cover behind a log that lay at the edge of the trees. He then began to back up, dragging the woman with him.

"That's not Mitchell," Becker said, frowning and raising his head enough to peer over the top of the log. "It's that other guy on Vic Prentice's crew. J.B."

"Whoever it is," Pat returned, finding a semiprotected point of view from one end of the log, "he's using that woman as a shield."

"You can't get away, you know!" Becker shouted to the figure still moving toward the plane. "Let the woman go and give up!"

Another shot thumped the covering log, but after firing it, J.B. took another step backward. His foot, instead of the firm ground he anticipated, sank into a deeper part of the channel that the increasing flood of water had cut into the riverbed. He flailed for a second or two, trying desperately to regain his balance, but vanished, rifle and all, into the flow, dragging Stevie with him.

Astonished, leaving the shotgun, Becker rose from his position behind the log and watched them disappear. A little way downstream, he saw Stevie's red hair temporarily break the surface and sink again.

"Dammit. She can't swim with those cuffs on," he said, taking several rapid steps toward the water. "She's gonna drown."

"Wait," his partner warned. Turning back toward the isolated sandbar, Becker saw why.

Incredibly, J.B. had managed somehow to keep from being swept after Stevie. By letting her and the rifle go he had regained his footing and was now climbing out on the bar near the plane.

"Go," Becker instructed Pat. "Get her out, if you can. I'll take care of this one." He sprinted toward the water, yelling at J.B. as he went.

* * *

From her location behind the sheltering trees at the other end of the slim curve of riverbank, Jessie had seen J.B.'s loss of balance and knew Stevie was in danger of drowning. She saw Becker start toward the river as J.B. climbed out on the sandbar and moved toward his plane to attempt an escape. The other trooper was coming toward her at a run, but the sand of the riverbank made running difficult and the river was moving fast. As Stevie was rolled to the surface again, closer to Jessie than to the trooper, it was obvious that he was not going to catch up in time to rescue her.

Without thinking, Jessie stepped out of the cover of the trees and attempted to run for the water, intending to try to save Stevie herself. She took only three hobbling steps before her knee collapsed, hurling her to the ground in the gravel of the stream that crossed the sand and emptied into the torrent the river had become. Sharp stones, swept bare by the stream, cut painfully into her already lacerated palms and knees, but she ignored them and tried unsuccessfully to regain her footing. Her injured knee hurt like hell and simply wouldn't hold her.

As she looked toward the river, desperate, frustrated, and dizzy with pain, she caught sight of someone in motion farther down the bank. Hank Peterson came out of the woods at a dead run, reached the river's edge, cast himself into the roiling water, and, as it swept him along, swam out to a position in line with the place where Stevie had last been seen and disappeared beneath the water. He was lucky. On a second dive he came up with her limp form and made it to a place where he could stagger out and lay her on the bank. Immediately, he went to work to get her breathing again. As Jessie watched helplessly from where she now sat, he had her gasping after a minute or two and vomiting water onto the sand.

Grinning from down the bank, he gave Jessie and the trooper, who had stopped beside her, a thumbs-up, raised Stevie, and began to carry her toward them.

"You okay, Jessie?" Pat asked, starting toward Becker.

"No," she told him, "but I can wait. Dell Mitchell's hurt pretty bad." She pointed to where he lay on the grass beside the stream. "Can you or Becker call for that hospital helicopter again?"

"Yes, and I'll be back," he said, and took off at a lope to where Becker, handgun leveled, was still shouting across at J.B., who had climbed into his plane and started the engine, clearly intending to try to take off.

It took Becker two shots to hit a front tire, deflating it and making it impossible for the plane to go anywhere. Still, J.B. made an attempt, giving the engine power, which only pulled the other tire in an arc around the deflated one and into the rushing water. Now facing the bank, the plane tipped slowly over to bury its nose in the flood between. The engine died.

"Now, you crawl out of there and get back . . ."

Becker's shout was drowned in a steadily increasing roar from the direction of the glacier that startled everyone. The ground trembled, the glacier growled, and a great flood of water began to pour into the river. It took Jessie a few seconds to realize what was happening.

Where the Knik Glacier met Mount Palmer each winter, forming a dam of ice that closed off Lake George above it, the melt had finally widened the passage between until the ice that contained it became unstable. The weight of thousands of gallons of water had become too much for the weakening dam and was breaking it apart, pouring out in its annual flood.

As she watched, a tower of dense blue ice calved off the face of the glacier with a grinding roar and fell in what seemed like slow motion into the lake at its foot. Its thunderous crash resounded through the valley.

But it was not the ice tower alone that captured Jessie's attention. Riding it down was Caswell's Maule M-4, which had been perched on the edge. For the last time it flew, with assistance from the falling ice and from the resulting wave and rush of meltwater that poured through from Lake George and filled the river from bank to bank with roiling turbulence. The iceberg and the plane it bore were lifted and thrown forward, coming to rest squarely atop J.B.'s red and silver plane, crumpling it and him into the riverbed like a piece of aluminum foil.

The iceberg stayed where it landed, impaled in the sand and silt, but Caswell's plane slid into the flood, where it was tumbled and rolled down the valley, parts of it rising and sinking in the muddy water till it finally disappeared altogether.

The water rose until it reached Jessie and pooled around her, tugging gently at the sand around her legs, but was no immediate threat. It was cold and numbed some of the pain of her knee, so she simply sat and waited till Hank came splashing up with Stevie, ankle-deep in water. Becker and Pat also waded over to where she sat and moved to see what they could do for Dell Mitchell, whom the water had not reached.

When the helicopter flew in, there was just enough room for it to land. The paramedics collected Jessie, Stevie, and Dell, leaving the other three to walk back to where they had left their vehicles. Everything else, explanations included, could wait until later—or until the water went down.

Chapter 31

On a sunny morning in August, Jessie Arnold stood in her yard and, with appreciation and relief, assessed the finished log cabin that stood before her. She had just turned from watching Vic Prentice steer the Winnebago motor home down the drive and onto Knik Road, on his way to another building site, leaving her alone on her property for the first time in months.

The new cabin rose in the footprint of the old, chinked and sealed against the weather, windows and doors installed, front porch protected beneath its overhanging roof, broad steps leading up from the ground. On the porch sat a bench, a small table, and three outdoor chairs, including a rocker that had been a gift from Oscar at a surprise housewarming party the previous evening. The symmetry of the green metal roof with its pair of dormers pleased her, as did the color of the new logs that formed the walls, strong and stable, above the basement.

Now that she had examined the exterior of her new residence, it was time to go inside, for there were still finishing touches to be added and decisions to be made, though not as many as Jessie had anticipated. The construction had seemed endless and, at the same time, quickly over. Winter would soon be on the way and she was glad to know that, once again, she would be secure and warm.

As she crossed to where Tank stood at the end of his tether, she limped a little, favoring the knee in which she had torn a tendon in her fall down Mount Palmer in June. The injury had required surgery and had taken her out of the construction game for several long weeks when she was unable to do much more than let it heal and watch the work go on without her. Now, even though she wore a brace, she remained cautious, knowing it would be months until the tendon healed completely and the surgeon declared her fit. There would be no sled dog racing this winter, no training runs, no heavy kennel work.

As she released Tank to come indoors with her, she looked out over her empty dog yard and missed the rest of her mutts. Except for a few old-timers, they had been trucked away to join those of Lynn Ehlers, who had offered to care for them with the help of the friend whose kennel he shared.

Lynn had spent a lot of time with Jessie during the summer. At first, when she came home from three days in the hospital, he had showed up every evening to take care of her, making as casual an assumption as the one he had made after the plane crash.

When she began to be able to do more for herself, his visits dropped off to three or four evenings a week—his days full of kennel chores for more dogs than he had anticipated. He was easygoing about their relationship, never demanding, never pushy. She had no idea where their friendship would lead, if it led anywhere, and they had not discussed it, which was fine with her, and comfortable.

It's going to be a quiet winter, Jessie thought, as she moved to the steps and cautiously climbed them, slowed by the brace. What am I going to do with myself? But refusing to allow her thinking to drift in that direction, she turned it back to her new house.

The door was painted green to match the roof, and on it hung a shiny brass knocker in the shape of another log cabin, ARNOLD engraved over its tiny door. The knocker had arrived shortly after her old cabin burned, sent from Minnesota by a family friend, Janet Korpi, when she learned that Jessie planned to rebuild. *Here's a little cabin, while you wait for the bigger new one,* she had written. *Hope you'll soon be able to put it on the door where it belongs.* Jessie loved it and had kept it as a promise, not only of an eventual completion of her building project but of the generous spirit of friends in distant places. She smiled as she opened the door, first giving it a single rap with the knocker that echoed slightly in the large room into which she stepped.

Inside, the evidence of friends was overwhelming. Dozens of people had come the night before, bringing a party with them: food, drink, and gifts of all kinds, knowing how much Jessie had lost in the fire.

Hank and Stevie had showed up with a huge sofa similar to

the one that had burned. He had found it in some secondhand furniture shop and successfully refinished its wooden frame and retied the springs, while Stevie applied new upholstery and made a whole herd of colorful pillows. They had lugged it in with much assistance and laughter and deposited it in front of the potbellied woodstove—one of the few things Jessie had been able to rescue from the ashes and refurbish.

From where she stood by the door, Jessie could see that atop that stove sat another salvaged item, a cast-iron dragon— repainted bright green during her period of enforced inactivity. Returned to its rightful place, its base filled with water, it would huff and puff humidifying steam from its nostrils through the freeze-dried winter months.

Ben and Linda Caswell had greeted her with hugs and a whole new set of pots and pans. "You'll need them for these," Linda told her, depositing a box of vegetables from her garden in the kitchen.

Cas was doing well, his injuries from the crash healed, and Linda said he was driving her crazy with proposals for a new plane. "He's like a kid in a candy store," she said, grinning. "Everything he looks at is bigger and shinier. He can't make up his mind."

Oscar arrived with several things besides the rocker: a keg of beer, a huge kettle of his famous chili, and a bright red sweatshirt with OSCAR'S OTHER PLACE lettered across the front. His new pub had been open for almost a month, thanks to the help of his many patrons, who had splashed paint, built shelves, moved in a new pool table and bar stools, and generally got in each other's way to get it done in record time. Winter was coming, and there was unanimous determination that their favorite watering hole be open before the snow fell.

When it was, they had celebrated appropriately, then turned their attention to Jessie's place, arriving in droves to hang lighting fixtures, splash more paint, install kitchen cupboards and countertops, and lay carpeting. Whatever needed doing, they did, leaving Jessie to direct their efforts from a recliner, provided by Vic Prentice, to support her injured knee. The volunteer work crew finished in days what would have taken her all winter to accomplish.

With part of the insurance money from her old house, Jessie had picked out a big brass bed to replace the one destroyed in the fire. Across it she had spread her favorite quilt, snatched in her escape from the burning cabin. With both hands she smoothed it—bright with silver stars scattered across a representation of the northern lights that swept diagonally across—and felt at home.

There were many other gifts, serious and humorous, that had not been there the day before, and most of the evening full of friends and fun had given Jessie a great deal of pleasure. It had also included two surprises: one a shocker of questionable taste and the other supremely welcome. Both had included flowers.

·   ·   ·

The first had come with reporter Gary Huddleston, who arrived when the housewarming party was well under way. Jessie, busy talking to Linda Caswell in the kitchen, didn't see him come in. He walked directly across the room and, when she turned in response to his greeting, handed her a vase containing a single red rose.

She stood staring at it, appalled, color draining from her face, unable to say a word. Then she simply opened her hand and let it fall to shatter into fragments on the floor.

"What the hell!" Lynn Ehlers had seen and attempted to intercept the tasteless gift but arrived too late. He grabbed Huddleston by the arm and swung him around. "Are you crazy or just totally sleazy?" he demanded.

Jessie's friends and neighbors grew silent, startled and listening.

"I'm just trying to apologize," the reporter said defensively, yanking his arm away.

"Well, of all the stupid—"

"Lynn?" Jessie had recovered her voice and laid a hand on his shoulder. "I think this is a little different than it seems. Isn't it, Mr. Huddleston?"

She paused to stare at him, narrowly evaluating his embarrassed expression. Under her direct assessment, he flushed a deeper shade of red and looked down at the remains of the vase littering the floor between them. She nodded, satisfied that what she had finally figured out was correct. "You sent, or brought, those other three roses, didn't you?"

"I was just trying to apologize," he burst out. "I didn't know . . . I didn't mean—"

"You didn't *mean* to break into the motor home I was living in? You didn't *mean* to scare me half to death?" Jessie asked him, interrupting his stammered attempt to explain.

"I thought—"

"Somehow, I don't really care what you thought," she told him in disgust. "It was unforgivable. Now I'd like you to leave my house."

The reporter wheeled and walked back out the door without another word.

Linda Caswell, with mop and dustpan, removed the floral remains from the floor, conversation resumed, and the party continued.

"Jessie?" Lynn questioned quietly. "You okay?"

"Yes," she assured him. "We'll talk about it later, but it's good to know about the roses, don't you think? He's a worm, but it's still a relief. He brought them—but J.B. broke in to spray them with that evil-smelling stuff."

      •   •   •

The second surprise guest was warmly welcomed by Jessie and everyone who knew him. For the first time since their terrible day on the river, Dell Mitchell came back to Jessie's house. He stepped through the door in the latter stages of the party and presented Jessie with a huge bouquet of bright blooms in a crystal vase.

"Not a rose among 'em," he told her, with a reassuring smile. "Just flowers that smell good naturally."

As soon as the resulting laughter faded, Jessie had to explain the wave of amusement that had followed his pronouncement.

She was glad to know he would be okay, though he still tired easily. They sat together, not saying much, but enjoying the enthusiastic group that moved and talked around them.

She had seen him only once, at a distance, since their mutual helicopter ride to a hospital in Anchorage. The skeletal remains removed from the grave Jessie had found in her woods had indeed turned out to be the sister for whom Bonnie Russell had searched for so long, so she and Jo-Jo were laid to rest in an Anchorage cemetery at the same time. Phil Becker had taken Jessie to the simple ceremony, which no family member had attended. Dell had been there as well, but had disappeared after the service before she had an opportunity to speak to him.

They had been in the hospital at the same time and she knew his condition had been critical for several days, a result of the blood he had lost and the long hours of exposure and cold. When he was safely recovering, he had told Becker what he knew and what he believed about J.B. Between them and the rest of the evidence, they had worked out a theory that Becker had, in turn, shared with Jessie long before Huddleston appeared at her housewarming party.

•   •   •

"We'll never be able to prove that J.B. had anything to do with the old man's death," Becker had told her, one evening in July, leaning on his elbows at the table in the Winnebago, a beer in hand. "But Dell is convinced he was responsible and thinks it has something to do with the women J.B. was killing at the time. Jo-Jo Miller may have been the first."

"But why did he bury her in *these* woods?" Jessie had asked, resettling her injured leg, which was propped on a pillowed stool in front of her. "He never lived here."

"Need help with that?" Becker had asked, nodding toward her leg.

"Nope, I got it, thanks. Why didn't he bury her up the river, like the rest?"

"We wondered about that," Becker had continued. "From

some old records, we found out that he was evidently renting a place across the road from this property. We can't know for sure, but he probably thought James O'Dell's woods would be a good hiding place with no way to trace the body back to him. Dell and I think that somehow the old guy must have found out. Maybe he found Jo-Jo's grave in his woods, maybe he even witnessed the burial. So we guess J.B. killed him to shut him up. From what Timmons learned when he examined the bones you found in the excavation, J.B. wanted it to look like a natural death, with no wounds on the body. He must have taped the old man up and left him out in the woods somewhere to freeze to death in his underwear. Then in the spring he buried the body on the south side of the cabin, where the ground thawed earliest. After that, having developed a taste for it, he went on killing women, copy-catting Hansen's style and hoping his victims would be attributed to Hansen."

"What was the deal with the roses?" Jessie had asked. "He must have had a reason for sending them to his intended victims."

Becker had taken a long sip of his beer, considering.

"Well, we can't ask him now, but serial killing, like rape, is a lot about power and being able to get away with it. Some serial killers take souvenirs, like the butterfly necklace. Some contact the police to take credit for their murders. They like to be recognized as smarter than law enforcement. The roses were probably like that for J.B., a way to say *I'm coming to get you and there's nothing you can do about it*. Who knows?"

"So he *was* coming after me?"

"If he sent you the roses."

Jessie had stared at him, startled. "You think he didn't?"

Becker had shaken his head. "I've given it some thought. It may be a total coincidence. The other roses came from an Anchorage florist."

"But J.B. was working out here and I live out here. Wouldn't a local florist make sense?"

"Maybe, maybe not. You got any other ideas?"

She had given up speculation upon finding out that the unknown killer was sending roses to his victims. Going back to wondering who might have sent them was too much. She could not know she would soon learn that Becker was right and her roses hadn't actually come from J.B.—just their artificial scent.

"Who cares?" She had sighed. "Maybe someday we'll find out for sure."

"Whatever. If you do find out, let me know."

"Sure." She had moved on to a more important question. "What made Dell suspect him back when he killed Bonnie's sister? Was Dell living with his uncle?" Jessie had frowned in confusion. There didn't seem to be a connection between the two men.

"No," Becker had explained. "But the old man told his nephew there was a guy he didn't like who was hanging around before any of this happened. James O'Dell valued his privacy and resented the intrusion. He said this *kid* was bothering him. But Dell never met him, just wondered about it after his uncle disappeared. He went to the trouble of checking up on J.B. and didn't like what he found out. He watched J.B. and there were suspicious things that happened, but nothing that would definitely point to him.

"Then Hansen was arrested and convicted and the killing stopped, so Dell, unable to prove anything, let it go. But when he read in an Oregon paper that women were disappearing again in Anchorage, he came back convinced that J.B. was responsible. When Dell located him, he got himself hired onto Vic Prentice's construction crew and watched, collecting information on his own till he knew he was right, but still couldn't prove it. Your finding the old man's bones was part of what persuaded him. He went upriver after J.B. because he was afraid we'd never catch him or be able to make a case if we did. Dell may have been right about that," Becker had admitted ruefully. "It would have been better if he'd trusted us and told us what he knew, but he wasn't about to let J.B. get away a second time, whatever it cost him."

Jessie had considered it thoughtfully. "He's lucky he didn't get himself killed."

"Yeah. Well—he almost did."

.   .   .

She thought about it again, as she sat next to Dell at the party, glad he had come and was doing well.

"Dell," she said, remembering there was one thing she had meant to ask him at the cemetery in Anchorage. "Have you buried your uncle's remains yet?"

"No." He smiled a little sadly. "I will, though, before I leave Alaska."

"You're leaving?"

"Yes," he told her. "I've got a good year-round job waiting for me in Oregon. But my Uncle Jim loved this state, so I think I'll leave him in Alaska. He was a great old guy—opinionated but fair, always fair."

He grinned, remembering the man he had loved.

"Where will you leave him?"

"I don't know yet, but I'll figure it out."

Jessie considered for a moment, then asked hesitantly, "Would you like to bury him here somewhere, on familiar ground?"

Surprised at the suggestion, Dell turned to see if she was serious.

"Are you sure you'd be okay with that?"

She nodded. "It seems sort of fitting, doesn't it?"

He had agreed, pleased and grateful. Jessie knew that sometime in the next week or two, before the ground froze, they would find a suitable spot in the woods and lay James O'Dell to rest in a place he had known and loved.

She also knew that having his grave on her property wouldn't bother her—not at all.

Chapter 32

 As if to apologize for the lateness of the spring, summer had lingered in the Matanuska Valley. Though each early September day was shorter by a few minutes than the last and the nights were growing cold enough so they would soon leave a crust of ice on standing puddles, the weather was, for the most part, warm and sunny. Above the headwaters of the Knik River, in the stands of birch on the lower slopes of Mount Palmer, here and there a branch was changing to yellow-green. Soon an icy wind would sweep down off early snow on the summit, snatching leaves and scattering them over the ground in a rich mosaic of gold and amber.

The crowd of birds that had filled the woods with their songs were fewer in number, as many fled south, anticipating the frosty breath of winter that could whistle into their summer haunts and habitats, sneak up behind them to rudely ruffle feathers the wrong way. High in a cottonwood, a raven clung to a bare limb, waiting with patient satisfaction as the country emptied and gradually reverted to its solitary keeping. Now and then, it croaked at its temporary companions, encouraging their departure: Get out. Go away. Whatever's left is mine.

The level of the river had fallen dramatically when Lake George emptied itself and drained away, leaving a tangle of braided channels to once again define sandbars in the headwaters of the Knik River, though their pattern was new. Glacier ice still melted and trickled into them, but the music of streams and waterfalls on the steep hillsides had hushed as temperatures began to fall below freezing on the high peaks of the surrounding Chugach Mountains. Soon the last of them would dry up entirely, watery voices silenced until spring.

On the isolated eastern side of the valley, where Friday Creek ran into the river, a brown bear sat on his fat bottom in the bushes, gobbling berries for dessert after a summer of foraging. Though he would remain while the sweetness lasted, lately he had begun to think of wandering back into the hills toward a warm, comfortable den he vaguely remembered was waiting somewhere up there.

Farther downstream, a moose and her calf waded along the swampy shore of Swan Lake, submerging their heads where the sedges grew thick and could be ripped, roots and all, from the mud. Water streaming from their jaws, they chewed placidly—the mother flicking an ear and turning a slow head to investigate the splash of a Canadian goose landing for a rest stop at the beginning of a long migration.

In the trees that lined the western bank, a squad of squirrels was leaping branch to branch, industriously gathering cones from the spruce and stashing them away for snacks between cold-weather naps. Soon, in snug nests, they would curl together for warmth and snooze away the worst of the approaching cold. A few tenuous birch leaves drifted down from branches that quivered as a result of their acrobatic passage along daredevil routes.

A group of foxes could be well designated a conceit, rather than a skulk, for they exhibit a certain arrogance of spirit and a confidence in the superior cunning of their kind. The fox that came trotting from the woods at one end of a narrow curve of riverbank was a prime example, bright as brass in the glow of the afternoon sun, which hung lower in the sky than it had in June. Swift and graceful, assuredly tidy from rigorous grooming, it traversed the sandy space and paused to lap daintily from the swirl of an eddy on the edge of the river.

When something rustled the brush on the hill, the fox raised its head and cocked an ear, alert to the possible need for flight, but the disturbance was not repeated, so it hesitated by the river for a moment to investigate a thing that had attracted its attention. As it had lowered its head to drink, there had been a sudden gleam from something shiny in the dark line the water made to mark its level on the sand.

Cautiously, it sniffed at the half-buried object and sneezed at its cold metallic scent. Here was nothing threatening, it seemed, so the fox extended a forepaw to nudge the curious thing it had discovered. A bit of dry sand slipped and was whisked away in the whirl of the eddy's flow, revealing a small circle of braided silver in a Celtic pattern foreign to the natural setting in which it lay.

Sniffing again, the fox established that the object was not edible, but before losing interest it gently nudged the curiosity in the edge of the water once more. The remaining sand that held it gave way, carrying the silver circle with it. Tumbling down, cleansed of sand that was swept away in fine grains, it came to rest on the bottom of the eddy and vanished, covered by another fall of sand the water greedily teased from the bank.

With no reason to delay, the fox continued its journey along the curve of the river's bank, leaving a trail of neat and regular paw prints in the sand until, with a quick, graceful bound over a fallen log, it disappeared into a yellowing stand of birch.

Author's Note

Though this mystery is a work of fiction, the Robert Hansen case that is mentioned was real. He was Alaska's most horrific serial killer and one of the first to be profiled by the FBI.

Two books were written about Hansen: *Butcher, Baker: A True Account of a Serial Murderer* by Walter Gilmour and Leland E. Hale (Onyx, a division of Penguin Books USA, 1991) and *Fair Game* by Bernard DuClos (St. Martin's Press, 1993).

Cover blurb from *Fair Game*: "The young and beautiful were his prey. Young and naïve, they flocked to boomtown Anchorage chasing dreams of easy riches. They thought they'd hit the jackpot when they met soft-spoken Robert Hansen. A businessman with plenty of money, he baited his trap with the promise of a joyride in his private plane. They landed into a nightmare. The twisted big-game hunter would fly them deep into the remote Alaskan wilderness. There the savage hunter took over. He terrorized his hapless prey, then raped and murdered them.

"After snaring his quarry and gunning them down, Hansen would bury them in shallow graves on the frozen tundra. For ten years, he carried out his depraved sport undetected, until one of his terrified victims managed to run far enough and fast enough to escape.

"Here is the shocking true story of Alaska's most notorious serial killer, and how a group of determined detectives brought him to capture with the assistance of VICAP, the FBI unit made famous in *The Silence of the Lambs*."

Acknowledgments

Many thanks to the folks who have assisted with information, materials, and support for this book, including:

Major Michael Haller, Public Affairs Office, Alaska National Guard, for arranging a terrific flight-seeing trip up the Knik River Valley to the Knik and George Glaciers. Many thanks as well to the crew of the Army National Guard Blackhawk helicopter who provided such an incredible ride.

Karl Borglum, assessor for the Matanuska-Susitna Borough, for maps and directions in helping me track down the early history of the MatSu Valley, specifically Knik Road.

Fran Seager-Boss, archaeologist and cultural resources specialist for the Matanuska-Susitna Borough's Cultural Resources Department, for her valuable time and expertise in providing me with maps and other resources on the early history of Knik Road, its homesteaders, and its residents.

Bruce Merrell, Alaska bibliographer, Anchorage Municipal Libraries, Alaska Collection, for his patience and time in discovering sources of MatSu history, even though I spread them in heaps on the library floor, all but blocking traffic in that particular section.

Lisa Olson and Rebecca De Armoun, information officers for the State of Alaska Department of Fish and Game, Sport Fish Division, for information on fishing regulations for South Central Alaska, specifically the Knik River.

Chuck Foger, Crown West, Inc., authorized dealer for Precision Craft Log Structures and Lodge Logs, for information on acquiring materials and building log structures.

Jamie and Mark Robinson of Statewide Wholesale, for information concerning Design Master "Floral Fragrance" and the particular qualities of artificial scent for roses.

Bobbi Downs, Flowers by June, for retail information on the availability and pricing of artificial scent for roses.

Nancy Sydnam, friend and pilot, for assistance with information on the conditions and the use of flying frequencies in and around the Knik River, Knik Glacier, and George Lake area.

Dick Betts, skillful pilot, who at eighty-one still enjoys the Alaskan wilderness in his Piper Super Cub, for assistance on how a small plane might crash on a glacier, though he has never been so unfortunate.

Gerry Bunker, for information and pictures of his (and Caswell's) Maule M-4.

Barbara Hedges, for once again adding to my knowledge of Alaskan birds.

My son, Eric Henry, Art Forge Unlimited, for creating the map for this book.

The Abbott clan, and all my friends and family, for years of caring support and belief.

And most especially to Leo McCauly, my good neighbor, for answering many questions on matters relating to the building of basements and log cabins—without laughing—much.